THE ONCE AND FUTURE IDIOT

ADAM D. JONES

 Archgate Press

Copyright © 2024 by Adam D. Jones

All rights reserved.

No part of this publication may be reproduced, distributed, or transmitted in any form or by any means, including photocopying, recording, or other electronic or mechanical methods, without the prior written permission of the publisher, except as permitted by U.S. copyright law.

The story, all names, characters, and incidents portrayed in this production are fictitious. (As far as I know.) No identification with actual persons (living or deceased), places, buildings, and products is intended or should be inferred.

Cover lettering by David Stehlík

Art design by Ryan Swindoll

ISBN: 978-1-953820-08-2

Published by Archgate Press

www.AuthorAdamJones.com

for Jeremy

CHAPTER ONE

ON THE DAY MY TROUBLES BEGAN, I strolled confidently into the great hall to convince King Ulder that I, Erlin, had once again kept his kingdom safe from the evils of magic.

"Our royal inquisitor has returned!" bellowed Ulder as I entered through the large doors.

I approached his majesty with a bow and gave a polite smile to the rest of the crowd, noticing that my audience had grown.

The stone-walled chamber, where the sounds of eating rose to the top of the vaulted ceiling, had rarely been so full. King Ulder sat in the center of a wide table placed at the head of the great hall, surrounded by knights who were bred for bravery and not for table manners. Behind him was a raised area that held both thrones, one for him and another for the queen, who had become reclusive of late. Both seats were empty. Instead of ruling from his throne, Ulder preferred to hold court during his meals, which tended to last several hours. The table for lunch would be set up around ten in the morning, and then the king and his knights would loudly graze on pheasants and deer until it was time to bring out dinner.

"Your majesty," I said loudly, interrupting several conversations, "I'm happy to report that my latest mission was a success."

The crowd hushed, looking eager. Eager for a new story. I cursed my creativity.

When I began this job, I always tried to give Ulder a quick report so I could hurry back to my chambers. The less time spent standing in front of a murderous king, the better. But every so often someone would catch a piece of my dramatic tale and come back for the next. Before long, the great hall was brimming with excitement whenever I arrived.

King Ulder lowered his voice. "Tell us what you found in Faralay."

I was thankful for his question, because I'd momentarily forgotten where he'd sent me. "I found dark magic in Faralay, your majesty. Just as you suspected."

Ulder shook his head very seriously and then reached for a bowl of beans.

I had a vague recollection of the assignment. A farming village called Faralay had been enduring a difficult drought, and the locals worried they were under a curse. These rumors tend to grow and fester until they're at Ulder's doorstep, and that's when he calls on me.

So, I bravely ventured to Faralay and spent a week investigating their curse.

At least...that's what the court believed.

Truthfully, I never saw any reason to actually go to these places. This time, I'd simply visited the nearby city of Laier, which held a large library and an even larger pub. After a week of enjoying books and bar-maids, I returned to Tomelac to announce my success.

But as I gazed at my growing audience, I wondered for the first time if I'd taken this little con too far.

The problem of late had been the success of my stories. With every yarn I spun, the audience would grow, little by little, and now there was hardly an empty seat as the crowd waited for me to launch into my next heroic tale. I began to wish I'd been as boring as the rest of the court.

They were still talking about my most recent report, when I had showed them a dark grimoire that magically filled itself with illicit, bawdy poetry. Of course, this was simply one of my journals where I scribbled during Ulder's endless speeches. After someone read a few lines over my shoulder, I needed an explanation for why my journal contained so many anatomical descriptions. I read a few of the more explicit rhymes for the court, always reminding them to take the grimoire very seriously.

"Was it a sorcerer?" someone asked.

Why not.

"A sorcerer with a dark heart," I said, watching a shiver run through the audience.

Ulder stopped his goblet just before it reached his lips. "No one mentioned seeing a sorcerer in Faralay."

"That's because he was invisible," I countered.

The eyes of the court widened.

This was my favorite part of the job. Even though it was dangerous to tell lies in Ulder's court, I took great pride in holding their attention in the palm of my hand and seeing their stunned gaze follow me while I paced the room.

"This sorcerer's evil power infected the air," I explained, "which, naturally, drove away the clouds."

"Naturally," murmured a few nobles in agreement.

Sir Kay, Ulder's favorite knight, pounded a fist on the table. "If he was invisible, how did you find him?"

I was surprised. Kay wasn't known for understanding how his sword fit into its sheath.

"Flour," I said immediately. I watched Kay's face scrunch up, knowing he was imagining the sort of plants that went in a vase. "I spread it on the ground in the dimmest alleys and waited until a footprint appeared."

"And you captured him...by yourself?" someone asked. I noted a bit of skepticism in their voice. Honestly, that wasn't surprising. I had never been mistaken for a soldier or a gladiator. A professor or a librarian, maybe, but I certainly didn't look like the sort of man who could win a fight.

"I wasn't alone!" I spun to face the nobleman who had interrupted me. "The guards had long given up on finding the miscreant, so I gathered the local farmers and we waited in the shadows." I turned to Ulder, who seemed impressed. "At my word, they leaped from their hiding places and trapped the sorcerer under their plowshares. We held him until the

Inquisitors guild sent a carriage for him. They've probably executed him by now."

"And the drought?" inquired Ulder.

"A rainstorm was reported in Faralay only two days ago."

That part was true, but it had nothing to do with me. Just a bit of luck—aided by the fact that I was sent to Faralay near the onset of Spring.

Ulder raised his goblet. "Would that all of Tomelac's servants showed the courage of our inquisitor, Erlin!"

While they applauded, I bowed low to hide my smile, because I was keeping a bigger secret than anyone could have guessed, something that almost no one in the kingdom had figured out.

Magic doesn't exist.

Chapter Two

Why the deception?

It's not easy to find work these days, so you should never let the truth get in the way of an easy job. Inventing fairy tales about my life allowed me to live in the big city rather than scratching out a living from the dirt.

Not to mention, the kingdom was much quieter when Ulder wasn't executing suspected wizards every half hour.

Lies were my trade, but I liked to think my lies were the good kind. Given the choice between violence and subterfuge, I'll always start spinning a new yarn before raising my fists. I like to think there's a certain nobility in that.

Let the knights think I'm a coward; I've outlived dozens of them.

They were still clapping when I left, which is good. Nothing aids my work like an air of mystery. My most common tool in the court is walking away with a raised eyebrow to avoid having to answer questions that could unravel my little con.

I skulked about as I pleased in those days, sometimes sitting quietly in a corner or atop a castle turret where I could be seen and speculated upon. *Surely, he's doing something important and mysterious,* they would whisper. *Best leave him be.*

And thusly, I had built a life of comfort in the king's castle.

After leaving the court that day, I climbed the circular stairs in the northern tower up to the rooms that served as my quarters and laboratory. I opened the door and—with a deep sigh—I set to dusting.

No servant in the castle would clean my quarters, and it was difficult to blame them. According to rumors (which I had carefully placed with the chattiest bartenders) upsetting one of my possessions could unleash a curse or a dreadful spell. I felt like I'd accomplished something important when these rumors spread, but eventually not cleaning my room led to unfortunate consequences. My mother would feel vindicated.

While my possessions were not always tidy, I at least attempted to make my quarters *look* like they belonged to a court inquisitor who tangled with dangerous magic. My shelves were lined with stoppered glass bottles, each filled with a different substance that elicited all manner of questions from my visitors. They would never have guessed I simply filled them with whatever food I didn't eat. Usually peas.

A sharp dagger lay on my desk (for opening mail) next to a small container decorated with skulls (which contained sugar for my tea). At the end of the table sat a black book with a metal lock. I'd lost the key ages ago and was pretty sure the pages were blank, but seeing it always made my guests suitably uncomfortable.

But the armillary sphere had been the source of my trouble. I had no use for it, but it certainly made me look the part. That is until I let dust collect on the apparatus. Like everyone else in Tomelac, the king's steward was jealous of my lofty rooms. While I was away on one of my trips, he noticed dust on my armillary sphere and raised questions about how I could do my job if I obviously wasn't using my tools.

I was, therefore, thankful when the royal guard discovered bat guano in the steward's room, which I assured King Ulder was a vital ingredient in several wicked spells. Lucky for me, none of the guards could tell bat guano from smashed peas.

I won that round, and I'd learned to be vigilant about my cleaning ever since.

Just as I lifted the feather duster, there was a knock at my door.

"...Erlin?"

It was Porridge, the castle page, breathing so loudly I could hear him rasping from outside. I sighed and threw open the door.

His visit was not a surprise. I had seen him about a minute before on my way up the stairs, passed him, in fact, on one of his many stops to rest and catch his breath. I usually had time to brew a pot of tea before he made it all the way up.

"Yes, Porridge."

"It's Uld...Uld..." He held up a finger while catching his breath.

I leaned against the door frame.

He tried again. "Ulder...King..."

"His majesty wants to see me?"

Porridge nodded. His sash, made for the previous boy who was much smaller, bunched up around his neck.

I continued my speculation. "And it's a matter of great importance to the safety of the realm?"

He nodded, heavy bobs that threatened to sag his head completely off.

More work. But another trip wouldn't hurt. This time I could go to one of the islands to the north, or some other place I wouldn't be seen by the people of Tomelac. Yes, the northern isles were warm this time of year, and my expense account would afford me several days of watching the waves while ordering drinks. I was starting to look forward to it, but I needed more information.

"I assume there's a message? A scroll, perhaps? Porridge, surely you brought it with you. It's a long way back down, and I've already taken off one of my shoes."

He shook his head and pointed down, and I finally noticed a youth wandering up the stairs. He kept to the right side, where one false step would send him falling to his death, and I knew everyone in Tomelac would sleep better if he did. My heart nearly stopped as I realized he was headed for my room.

Porridge found his voice. "This time, King Ulder says you have to take his son with you."

Chapter Three

THE KING'S SON WAS ABOUT AS USEFUL AS SYPHILIS. He lacked the practicality and kindness of his mother and doubly lacked his father's brute strength and imposing features to make up for it. His mouth rarely closed, unless he was trying to talk, and he handled matters of state with the delicacy of an elephant learning to throw pottery.

His name was Garth, and, to the king's embarrassment, he always placed last in the tourneys because his skill with the sword was on par with his ability to lactate. He "read" books by holding them in front of his face (sometimes the right way up) and nodding along. At banquets, he carried all the charm of an empty plate of food; the court ladies had nicknamed him "Lance-a-little."

I watched him totter up the stairs until he made it to my door, praying with each step he'd tumble off and rid me of the pending responsibility I could already feel pushing down on my shoulders. There was no escaping it; I was to be his next mentor.

And while being the royal inquisitor might be the best job in the kingdom, everyone knew that apprenticing the prince was the worst.

The armorer had taken him on early, hoping that the simpler parts of his trade, hitting things with hammers and placing warm things in water, would be within the boy's intellectual grasp. But Garth managed to turn his thumb purple with every other swing of the hammer, and he never tired of pressing a red-hot iron against the armorer's behind. After six trips to the infirmary, the armorer reported to the king that he had nothing left to teach Prince Garth.

The Falconer was next. He was clever. He assumed the work of feeding and raising birds would quickly bore the young prince, and he was right. Not only did Garth find the work dull, but he never learned how to dangle mice into the cages without getting bitten, which turned out to be very entertaining for the rest of us. We would line the windows overlooking the courtyard and watch the falcons take turns biting Garth. We rooted for each bird and placed bets on which would hurt him the most. Those had been good times.

The baker was next, and this was the shortest apprenticeship. After a few burned pies, the king sent his son to the farrier, where it turned out that it *is* possible to make a horseshoe backward. The carpenter told Garth that splinters were capable of growing into full trees, which sent the boy running to his nurse. The miller couldn't get him to turn the millstone in the correct direction. The cobbler caught him pressing a new sole on the very top of a shoe. The mason had to chip his entire left leg out of a wall. The hunters gave him a deer call that was nothing but a cup with the bottom hollowed out and didn't bother looking for him when he got lost. The bowyer enjoyed watching Garth twang himself in the face with bowstrings, while the fletcher, in need of feathers, sent the prince back to the falcon cages where we all resumed our pastime of watching the birds peck the skin from his hands.

Among the castle mentors, I alone had escaped the troubles.

By being away for so long, so often, I managed to avoid being chosen as the next mentor. Oh, and my work was so, so dangerous. And complicated. Even Garth's doting mother would not believe he could understand what I did. Few could comprehend the responsibility of an inquisitor, as I often reminded the court.

"Da says I'm s'posed to go with you," Garth said, pushing past me. "Is this your place?"

"No, my prince, this is the latrine. We like to make sure people *really* need to go before they use our plumbing."

We had long ago learned that Garth could not remember much of what was said and rarely listened anyway, making it relatively safe to insult him. Though I did remind myself to use larger words, the sort he never could sound out.

Garth walked in and admired my collection of oddities. "Da says I need to bring you to the big hall."

I bowed. "My prince, I just left the great hall."

"Another message arrived just now," he said, as he tried to give my armillary sphere a spin. Unfortunately, he did so by grabbing the equatorial band, which does not move, and only succeeded in throwing my contraption to the floor, where it shattered into several pieces.

He examined the remains. "I think it's broken."

"Well, now how will I ever use...that?"

He slowly turned to me. "Erlin...what did you use that for, anyway?"

I mentally grasped for the answer, trying to recall what in Avalon an armillary sphere actually did. Then I heard Porridge snicker, and I knew that by nightfall the entire castle would know that Garth had pinned me with a good question.

I straightened up. "I use it to find mages."

"Oh, I see." He tilted his head as he took in the sphere's broken parts and then looked up at me with wide, innocent eyes. "How...*exactly* did you use it to find mages?"

"It...pointed at them. Yes. That's it."

"So, it was magic?"

Porridge snickered again.

"Of course not, Garth."

"I should tell his majesty if you're using magic."

"I'm not using magic." My teeth ground together. "Your highness."

Because magic doesn't exist, you lumbering salt lick, I mentally added.

"So, how's it work?"

I heard Porridge scamper down the stairs, laughing through his hand. He was most of the way down when I heard him stumble. The sound of a metallic crash and a series of soft *thumps* told me he'd slammed into the serving maid and her biscuit tray.

"Tell you what, Garth. Have your father set me up with one of his nice carriages with the velvet seats for my next trip, and when we get back, I'll teach you how to use the armillary sphere."

"Sure." He nodded, eager to help, but then a confused look took over his face. "The what?"

Chapter Four

It wasn't wise to keep Ulder waiting. He tended to get many ideas at once, and if you weren't careful, you'd find yourself at the back of a queue stretching into the courtyard. And with no one to hold your place, you might find yourself sleeping in that queue and then, much later, explaining to the guards that you are not a vagrant but a person who hunts wizards and that you don't look familiar because you spend so much time out of town. And then you'll explain that to the jailor and eventually to your cellmates. After that, you'll resolve to get in line early.

I heaved a great sigh when I saw the line of petitioners snaking out of the great hall—but I'd forgotten about Garth. Specifically, I had forgotten he was not entirely useless. A prince does not wait in lines.

Rather than taking our place at the back of the hopeless queue, we strolled past the envious petitioners. Along the way, I raised a haughty eyebrow at Petunia, the royal gardener, who waited impatiently behind a row of butchers carrying a pig between them.

When I first arrived in Tomelac, I was placed in the lower quarters alongside the other castle workers where we lived two to a room, and I was not pleased to discover I was bunking with a shearer whose prize sheep often nibbled on my pillow. Soon after, the tower room became available, and most of us eagerly applied to move in there. Petunia had nearly won after she convincingly argued that her work required the room at the top, where she could look down and watch the gardens growing. She had a strong case, but I insisted that my equipment preferred higher altitudes for proper testing of magical artifacts, and that placing me in the tower would make the kingdom safer from evil magic. This appealed to Ulder's paranoia, and Petunia remained in the ground level apartment she currently shared with a soprano.

Thus began our rivalry.

Petunia saw me walking with Garth and mumbled something under her breath about drawing the short straw. I was prepared to mutter a retort, but then remembered it was unwise to upset a gardener.

After moving into the tower, it had taken me nearly a year to discover that the moles climbing into my window were drawn there by a certain herb they could smell from across the city, an herb that had *somehow* made its way from Petunia's gardens all the way to the space under my bed. I retaliated by pouring my chamber pot out the window and onto her trestles. She then replaced the trestles under my window with exotic, hardy vines. (I thought this a weak counter until the morning I pushed open my shutters and cut both palms against the hooked thorns that had climbed over my windowsill.) Feeling vengeful, I then told the king that her water mill was a magic contraption that should be outlawed, thus forcing her to grind her ingredients by hand. This seemed like a triumphant victory until I discovered my teas had been replaced by something that creates a sense of urgency in one's bowels. Girding my loins, I explained hastily to Ulder that her water mill was actually quite natural and useful, and in six weeks' time I resumed normal digestion. Though a truce was now in place, Petunia and I remained wary of one another.

Garth shambled toward the great hall, me at his heels. The others parted to make way, and I strolled in their wake, displaying every air of importance I could grasp as we entered the keep through the large doors. We continued strolling through the antechamber, where Ulder's bombastic voice could already be heard.

My presence in the court was rare, and those who did not know me still found it a privilege to glimpse the court inquisitor, to see for themselves the brave man who stood between them and hordes of evil sorcerers. As we approached the entrance, I took a moment to enjoy the feeling of celebrity.

"You've stepped in something," said Garth. He stopped outside the doors to the great hall and pointed toward my feet.

I looked down. Both boots carried remains of something a horse had dropped off. Wealthy visitors never failed to ride their loud horses through the courtyard in an ostentatious display that always left a mess. Behind us, Petunia laughed until she snorted.

"Horse dropping. I'd recognize it anywhere." Garth nodded very seriously. "I've gotten good at noticing those things since my new job."

New job? I saw Garth's face fall, and I remembered he'd recently taken on an apprenticeship with the stable mucker. He clearly wasn't happy about his new occupation, which involved hauling more manure than your average politician.

I saw a glint of pitiful hope in his eyes. Even though King Ulder hadn't announced any change to the prince's job, Garth was obviously hoping (as I was fearing) that this meeting would end with him being named my new apprentice. I had until we reached the front of the line to think of a way out. I remembered Petunia and wondered if I could quickly interest the prince in gardening.

"Garth, give me a moment to clean my shoes."

"Da's already seen us, and he really hates waiting."

"Fine."

I didn't enjoy being seen in such a compromising situation, but arriving in court with poo on my shoes was certainly a lesser offense than making Ulder wait.

The King truly enjoyed the sight of his groveling petitioners. When he wasn't busy eating, he ruled over the court with one boot planted on a table, standing in the exact same pose as old King Pendragon, his beloved predecessor, in the painting that hung behind the throne.

Wanting to wipe off my boots, I looked toward the curtains...and that's when I saw her.

A woman stood in front of the green velvet drapes, wrapped in a scarlet dress and watching me with eyes of distant blue, like the swirling mist surrounding an island. Dark hair tumbled to her waist in large curls. Unlike the other ladies of the court, she wore no jewelry, save for a single pearl earring that dangled from her left ear.

Of course, it's the law of the universe that when you do something embarrassing—like stepping in a horse's breakfast—a beautiful woman will be there to laugh at you.

But she wasn't laughing. She stared at me and Garth like a student taking one last look at their books before an exam.

I stammered for something to say when Garth caught my attention by punching my shoulder. "Da's nearly done yelling at the jugglers. Any second now."

I turned back to the woman but saw nothing. Where she had stood, in front of the green curtain, I only saw an empty floor. But something lay on the ground.

On an impulse, I stepped out of line and walked over to the place where I'd seen her. The pearl earring glinted from the stone floor. I knelt and picked it up, certain it was the same jewelry I'd seen her wearing. I stood and searched around, but the woman and her mist-colored eyes were gone. Were it not for the earring, I would have assumed she was a dream.

Garth tapped my shoulder. "Our turn."

I shoved the earring in my pocket and headed into the great hall, smirking again at everyone who had to wait in line.

Ulder stood in his usual pose, with one boot planted on the table and his fists resting on his hips.

Behind him, I could see the large painting of old King Pendragon standing at the same table in exactly the same pose. Wearing exactly the same outfit. I squinted at the painting and noticed for the first time that King Pendragon stood in front of a small painting. The painting within the painting showed a figure also standing the same pose. I squinted even harder and thought I could briefly glimpse another, tinier picture frame within that one.

I noticed the queen sitting on her throne, quietly watching. I bowed to her, but she didn't respond. The queen's serious eyes were fixed on Garth.

Like his ancestors, Ulder posed for the onlookers in the great hall and bellowed. "Erlin! A message from Hanbury. Dark news."

Excellent. My reputation would grow significantly. The king's preference for the dramatic would work in my favor. Hanbury was a week's ride from Tomelac. I spent a few moments considering which taverns and libraries to visit while pretending to work, but my daydreaming came to a rude stop when I saw Prince Garth losing half his finger in one nostril.

"And..." Ulder looked around the room, his voice now a whisper. Mind you, his whisper was just yelling in a different way, but we all leaned forward to listen. "This time...it's the Restless Ones."

CHAPTER FIVE

OF COURSE IT WAS.

I'm sure that wherever you live, there's someone, or something, that gets blamed for everything.

For example, in Sirap, where wine is sipped at breakfast and the men wear brighter breeches than the women, there was an unpopular princess who is said to have been the cause of a long drought. Or, depending on who you asked, a series of terrible floods. No one could decide, really, but it was generally agreed that if she would leave the royal palace then the countryside would finally be the right amount of wet.

Her hobby of playing beautiful songs on the harp could not dissuade popular opinion. Until she was married off to a neighboring kingdom (in hopes her bad luck would ruin *their* crops) a button couldn't go missing without a chambermaid pointing her finger at the royal tower and blaming Lady Lire.

History doesn't record what happened to her, but there is a popular story about a torch-wielding mob setting her clothes on fire. The scene is still often pictured in effigy; Lady Lire, clutching her lyre, her breeches ablaze.

Another amusing superstition came from a nearby village that had developed a fear of silver. After crying for help about their collected woes—smelly water, invading hordes, loud flies—it was determined that their excess silver goblets were the trouble. The town had absolutely too many. The curved reflection in a silver goblet is not the same as what is found in a flat mirror, and that wicked reflection is well known to be a doorway for bad luck. At least, that's what I told them when I put their silver in my knapsack and headed home. The invading hordes only visited once after that.

But all of these dark tales were dwarfed by rumors of the Restless Ones. They were cursed to walk the earth in a blind stupor, casting magic about like lunatics. Or maybe their small size allowed them to enter your home through tiny holes in the walls and move things around when you weren't looking. Then again, in your neck of the woods, the Restless might transform into the pack of wolves who ate your cattle and picked their teeth with the smaller bones.

They were a very convenient scapegoat the time I fell asleep in Ulder's court. Upon being caught, I explained I was under the lingering effects of a spell cast by one of the Restless Ones. Occupational hazard. Of course, I was truly in the throes of spiced wine. The cloves on my breath were, I assured Ulder, part of a preventative measure meant to keep the curse from spreading. I bravely suffered the effects of the curse for the rest of the week.

"What have they done?" asked Garth.

I could imagine. Bad luck. Bad weather. Bad bards. Surely the Restless were lurking in the shadows and causing whatever problem people enjoyed complaining about. Truthfully, I enjoyed these cases because the bad luck would usually run out around the time I arrived to help, allowing me to conjure up a fancy story and take the credit, but that wouldn't be easy to do with Prince Lump at my side. If he returned to his father explaining that I didn't actually do anything while I was away, my good days would be over.

"We received this letter." King Ulder reached out toward his wife.

The queen, Lady Dina, kept her fingers curled around the rolled-up parchment and gave Ulder a pleading look. The court held still while they exchanged a long glance. Dina looked to her son, then handed the paper to Ulder.

The king cleared his throat. "Two months ago, we received—"

"Two months!" I clamped my mouth shut. "Your highness." I bowed, pointing my frustrated facial expression toward the ground. I'd never been given a missive so late, but telling the king he was doing his job poorly would not end well for my skull.

"Is something wrong, Inquisitor?" Ulder's voice rattled the silverware.

I realized my interruption had sounded impolite. I looked up. "No, sir. I was simply repeating your words."

"Why?"

"Why? Well, ah...you see...I was trying to commit your words to memory, my king. Something the universities have been teaching. If you repeat the words just after you hear them, it allows for easy memorization. Surely the words of a king are worth remembering."

He grunted at me. "As I was saying...we received this letter."

"...received this letter," I mimicked, maintaining my ruse.

"It's from Lord Tark in Hanbury."

"It's from Lord—"

"Would you *stop* that?"

"Would you st...oh. Yes, of course, your majesty. I'll simply mumble from now on."

"Dash it." He shoved the paper into my hands. "Read it for yourself, inquisitor."

There were pictures. Not unusual since so many heralds were unschooled. Someone had even been kind enough to draw an arrow pointing upward to help the non-reading types orient the page properly. This had been common practice ever since an illiterate military commander in Dunlin held his orders upside down and marched his men away from his own city walls. Dumbfounded, the enemy soldiers set themselves up inside and met no resistance until the Dunlin soldiers returned and asked if they could come back in. They were turned away.

The page I held contained the same stories as always, but one of the drawings stood out. Above sketches of dying trees and frightened people, someone had scrawled an open eye with a swirl in the middle of the iris. It was said to accompany the attacks made by the Restless, but I had only seen that in old books. Hardly the sort of detail an average, superstitious citizen would know. Despite my cynicism, the case was actually interesting.

I would have been impressed had they drawn a dead man, a victim of the Restless, hanging on something. The old stories told of important leaders murdered in their homes, a way of showing that the Restless were strong enough to even enter a Lord's castle. Their traditional way of killing was to leave their victim strung up against a wall or a tree trunk.

But this letter, other than the ominous eye, was nothing but the usual superstitions that cropped up around bad luck.

"Well, it *has* been two months." I rolled up the scroll. "In these situations, I often wait for a follow-up message. I recommend we ask Lord Tark for an update. The last time Tark went missing, he was purchasing a new tapestry in Sirap. You know what a rabid collector he is. Much can change in two months, your majesty."

"Much *has* changed." King Ulder held up another scroll. "The Restless Ones have killed him!"

I took the missive from his giant hand. "Of course they have."

Chapter Six

Somehow, my day actually got worse.

Things were bad enough. Lord Tark being dead meant that I would have to actually, you know, work. Like a normal person. Mind you, I'm a keen investigator when the need arises, but I'm also the laziest man in the kingdom. A week of real work, with the king expecting me to capture a murderer, was more effort than I'd put into anything all year.

Garth took the scroll from my hand and eagerly unrolled it. "Doesn't look so bad," he said.

Indeed, the drawing showed a man, crudely drawn, standing next to a tapestry.

"Why is he holding his hands over his head?" Garth asked.

"My prince, you are holding it the wrong way." I pointed at the drawing and made a twirling motion with my finger.

Garth crossed his arms to rotate the page. "Oh."

Now the sketch showed Lord Tark upside down, hanged alongside his precious artwork.

I was immediately haunted by the simplistic frown drawn on Lord Tark's face. His sad expression forced me to acknowledge that this case was actually dangerous. Until then, my work had only put me at risk of a paper cut.

King Ulder was staring at me.

"I'll investigate right away, your majesty." I bowed low. Upon rising, he was still staring.

"Will there be anything else?" I asked.

It was obvious what he wanted, but I intended to drag things out, just in case I was wrong. There was still a chance for me. I thought about leaving in a hurry before Ulder could speak, but he hadn't dismissed me, and the last person who tried to walk out before getting Ulder's permission had spent their last moments considering their own entrails.

The queen looked to me with pleading eyes, hoping I could find a way to avoid taking her son into my line of work. Nothing came to mind. I frowned, politely, and she looked down at her shaking hands.

Ulder's imperious eyes bore down on me. I was pinned, like his boot was crushing me rather than the vegetables on his plate. He stepped off the table and walked to my side, a gesture I hadn't seen him perform, leaving a trail of crushed greens as he made his way around. I felt the weight of my oncoming responsibility growing heavier with each stomp of his boots.

Over the years, I had given the royal couple several excuses for not apprenticing their wayward son. The job was too dangerous. I was gone for too long. The work required counting past ten.

The queen never failed to clutch at her necklace when I described the dark horrors I faced while protecting the realm from magic, and her desperate pleas always kept her husband from insisting that Garth accompany me.

But he wasn't looking at her this time. Standing in front of me, Ulder put his hand on my shoulder and kept his eyes on mine. "Prince Garth's apprenticeship at the stables is nearly done," was all he said.

Silence filled the hall, and I considered how to escape my destiny. My quick tongue had gotten me out of more trouble than I could remember, but it's important to know when you're trapped.

Next to me, Garth pleaded silently, drawing up his face like a hungry puppy. I felt a pang of sympathy as I imagined him returning to the stables with a shovel and a bucket.

"Your majesty," I said, "it would be...my honor to apprentice your son."

The king squeezed my shoulder hard enough to remind me he was only pretending to be nice about it.

The queen slowly crossed her arms while glaring at me.

And the prince nearly knocked me off my feet with a hug.

I hated every second of it.

Chapter Seven

Excited, Garth grabbed my arm and pulled me out of the room. But instead of returning to my quarters, he dragged me around the big table and pushed us through the thick curtain in the back. This corridor, I knew, led to the royal chambers, and a few other places where common folk weren't allowed.

"Wait here," said the queen, shoving past me. I bowed as she took Garth's elbow and gently guided him down the hall toward his quarters, leaving me alone in the private antechamber.

As the curtain fell back into place, I could feel the curious eyes of the court. All of them were quietly leaning over in their seats, trying to steal a quick look into the secret chambers.

There were two reasons for this.

For starters, everyone in the kingdom held a fascination for the personal lives of anyone famous, which meant they couldn't resist glancing into the royal family's private living area, hoping to see a gossip-worthy moment they could use to make conversation for the rest of the year.

But most of them were trying to catch a glimpse of Ulder's vault.

I'd never seen it myself until now. The imposing iron door would make any banker jealous—but this vault wasn't for securing gold.

Ulder was a collector of a different sort. His vault, which only opened with a key he wore on his belt, supposedly contained wondrous items gathered from around the world, items Ulder believed should be secured in his vault where they could not threaten the kingdom.

Since only children (and kings) believed in magic, I never bothered telling Ulder that his collection was pointless. I even brought him "magical" artifacts from time to time, which were actually sticks or stones I'd found on the way to court. As far as his majesty knew, these were sorcerer's staffs or chunks of demonic brimstone. Upon receiving a new artifact, Ulder would silence the court and slowly carry it to his vault with an air of importance, disappearing behind the curtain while the hushed onlookers listened to the iron door squeaking open and then being thrown shut. I initially didn't want to encourage his silly collection, but it turned out to be his least violent hobby.

I paced the small corridor, noticing a statue in the center. It appeared to be made of steel and was shaped like a man reaching for his sword. This was another depiction of King Pendragon, but it lacked the ostentatious presence of the painting in the great hall. This version of Pendragon stood with his mouth open in a warrior's shout, charging toward an enemy as he drew his blade.

A placard at his feet read *Caliburn*. In all my reading, I'd never come across the word.

As I paced the room, I realized there was no hope for me. Garth was a dummy, but it wouldn't take long for him to realize I was a fraud, and when Ulder found out he would send for the executioner.

Of course, if I actually solved the case, I might be able to convince everyone I really was the brave court inquisitor I pretended to be, but that path was just as dangerous. If I walked around Hanbury openly investigating the murder, I'd surely find myself hanging on the wall next to Lord Tark.

I was doomed.

On days like this, I had a hard time remembering why I even took this job. It paid well, I reminded myself, and pretending to hunt mages made Tomelac's citizens feel safe. Furthermore, spinning yarns about my work kept people away from the hangman's noose. Before I came along, Ulder simply killed anyone who was accused of magic. It was risky to let your crops grow a little higher than your neighbor, or to have too much luck with the ladies, because the jealous sort might start mumbling about magic spells and curses, and that meant you'd be the next name on Ulder's list.

But that was before I came along. I began my work by "purging" magic from the streets of Tomelac, and then moved outward, opposing witches and warlocks across the countryside. The citizens were quickly convinced that Tomelac was safe from sorcery, and Ulder's daily executions were now barely a monthly gathering.

I stood tall. My deception had saved dozens of lives. Maybe hundreds. I may not be a hero...but, then again, the courtyard was filled with statues of well-known "heroes" whose heroic work amounted to nothing more than ending people's lives. In fact, some of them had killed fewer people than I had saved.

Despite my circumstances, my mind returned to the woman I had seen outside of the great hall. I pulled her earring from my pocket and turned it over in my hand. The intoxication of a woman's attention was a dangerous distraction, but my mind's eye couldn't stop recalling the shape of her face.

My pacing turned into the lonely steps of a prisoner whose last meal has gone cold.

For a fleeting moment, I realized I had been left alone and could make a mad dash out of the castle, but Garth re-emerged before I could try.

"I'm ready, Erlin!" he shouted.

I couldn't return his smile. "Good for you."

"Da says a carriage is waiting for us."

Before we left, the queen straightened my collar and looked me in the eye. I'm not sure she expected to see her son ever again. Mind you, the stories I told shouldn't have given her *that* much cause for concern, but the look on her face gave me an odd feeling, like I was stepping into something bigger than I realized.

We stopped by my chambers on the way to the stables. Garth didn't leave my side, chattering nonstop about what he would do when he caught one of the Restless. How he would stab them, or burn them, or hang them, all complete with exaggerated, violent gestures.

I finally cleaned my boots, then grabbed a book from my shelf and headed for the stairs, unable to think of a way to escape this mess with my life.

CHAPTER EIGHT

ULDER NEVER UNDERSTOOD why common people needed money, seeing them more on the "supply" side of the "supply and demand" equation.

So, upon his arrival to the throne, he had his tax collectors take the unprecedented step of collecting *every* coin in the kingdom. His suddenly impoverished subjects were forced to swarm Tomelac selling their goods in an attempt to get some of it back.

A visitor might mistake our bustling markets as a healthy economy. And, much to our misfortune, the surrounding land was only good for growing potatoes.

Leaving Tomelac, therefore, required navigating a sea of potato venders. The first had set up breweries and bread shops, which required the rest of Albion's potato farmers to get a little more creative if they were going to unload their crop.

As I purchased a bag of chips for the journey, I was accosted by every manner of potato-based product. Potato soap on a rope. Potato shoes. Potatoes shaped like the king. All of them were waved in our faces in an endless parade of desperation.

"Do you ever get tired of this?" I asked, but Garth was no longer next to me. The first onslaught of merchants had trapped him.

"So...these are for juggling?" I heard him say.

A merchant with dirty fingers nodded and quickly shoved three ordinary potatoes into Garth's waiting hands. "Yes, my Lord. They're special...juggling potatoes."

"I've been wanting to learn that." He removed a gold coin from his pocket and paid the man. "But the fool is never around when I need to find a new teacher."

"And these are for throwing!" came a desperate voice. A woman had pushed her way to Garth carrying a burlap bag. "You'd have a lot of trouble throwing ordinary potatoes."

"That's handy. I'll take a few of those." Garth handed over enough gold to buy a farm. "Is that enough? I never know."

"It'll just do, my lord." She dropped the entire bag and disappeared into the crowd.

By the time I arrived, the prince was purchasing a potato guaranteed to make him taller.

I grabbed his shoulder. "Garth, take a look at what you've bought."

He inspected the bag. "What am I looking for?"

"Just tell me what you see."

"My juggling potatoes on top, and then the throwing potatoes. Wait...maybe one of those underneath is for juggling. I should mark them."

"Are you serious? Those potatoes are obviously..." I felt the crowd shush while every vendor threw a pleading look my way, begging me not to ruin their sales. I relented. "Garth, those potatoes are excellent choices."

The vendors breathed a sigh of relief.

I patted his shoulder. "The stable master is waiting on us. I believe you know the way?"

"Right. Follow me!" He took off for the stables and slung the burlap bag over his shoulder, looking like a man who'd never carried anything in his life. It seemed impossible to imagine him taking the throne one day, and I quietly prayed I would be long dead before his reign.

The stables were well within the city walls. The smell often filled the entire northern quarter of the city, even floating up to my tower window on the worst days.

Garth and I walked past the rows of chewing, snorting horses toward the stable master, who saw Garth and immediately wiped his dirty hands on his equally dirty pants.

"That's Darel," whispered Garth. "I'll have to tell him my apprenticeship here is over. Do you think he'll be disappointed?"

"I think he'll manage."

"Your highness." The stable master approached with a bow, "you'll want to start with the mules today, and then—"

"Oh, I can't do that." Garth proudly clapped me on the back. "I'm Erlin's apprentice now!"

Darel stepped toward me. I flinched when his enormous hands grabbed the shoulders of my clean shirt, but then I saw a tear form in his eye. "How can I ever repay you?" he asked.

I already had an idea about that. "Remember the fancy mahogany carriage, the one with two rooms and those wonderful velvet seats?"

"Comin' right up—"

"Not so fast," said Garth. "Da says to get the cheapest one."

"For the prince?" I asked. The cheapest carriage was uncomfortable and threatened to fall apart when it rolled over a pebble. "Surely you misheard. His majesty would never let his son travel that way."

"He said you used the nice one last time you visited Hanbury, so people will remember it. I'm supposed to travel in secret."

"Your father has an excellent memory."

The stable master and his assistants attached a pair of horses to a rickety carriage and brought it out for us.

"We're supposed to look like two simple men on simple a trip," said Garth. "That's why I didn't wear my finery." He climbed up into the cabin, refusing the help of a stable hand. "We're just normal folk."

I stepped inside and settled next to him. "You're wearing clothes only a royal can afford, my prince. It may be *your* worst outfit, but these stable hands can barely afford to sew patches onto their elbows."

He looked down at his shirt, lifting the delicate fabric closer to his face. "Mother wants me to look like a normal person. What'll I do?"

I sighed. It began in the soles of my feet and escaped darkly out of my mouth. "Take off the tunic, Garth. And hand me a few coins."

One of the stable hands walked past, one who looked to be about Garth's size, and I held out the money. "Can I buy your shirt?"

His eyes widened at the sight of the gold, and his shirt was suddenly in my hands. I dangled it between two fingers and passed it over to Garth.

Something occurred to me, just as the prince brought the garment over his head and got lost inside. "Garth. Why did you take your shirt off just now?" It was absolutely illegal to give orders to any of the royal family. I could have been locked up.

"Because you asked me to." His muffled voice came from somewhere within the fabric.

"But you're a royal. You don't take orders."

"That's usually the case." Garth's head triumphantly emerged. "But just before we left, mother took me aside and told me to do everything you said. *Everything.*"

A mad rush of power went to my head.

He thrust his arms through their respective holes and then straightened out the front of the shirt. "Besides...I trust you. I mean, you wouldn't want to see me get hurt, would you?"

I patted his shoulder, reassuringly. "Of course not."

Chapter Nine

THE CARRIAGE, IF YOU COULD CALL IT THAT, creaked and groaned with every turn, and when I shifted in my seat it would squeal like a giant bat.

The driver was a sturdy woman who looked as rugged as the old wooden beams that made up the carriage. She cracked the reins when the vendors closed in, pushing us through the potato-wielding crowd. Word had spread that the prince was buying produce, and now we were surrounded by vendors banging on the doors while shouting impossible promises about their crops.

"Did you hear that?" Garth pressed his ear to the cabin wall. "Someone just said they've got a potato shaped like the fruit that grows in Avalon."

"That just means it's shaped like an apple." I shook my head. "And they've never been to Avalon."

"Have you?"

"No one's been there. It's not on any maps. Avalon probably never existed, and if it did, it's long lost by now."

He seemed to be choosing his words carefully. "Then...how do you know they grow apples there?"

"Because it's called 'Avalon.' What else would..." I realized the prince was not going to follow this line of thinking. I would have to push him entirely up the hill of knowledge. "The word 'Avalon' means 'Apple tree,' Garth. It's right there in the name. Someone's trying to sell you a potato shaped like an apple. I have to admit, it is a clever way of going about it."

Garth looked down at his bag of potatoes, scrutinizing them for the first time. "So...they're just trying to trick me into buying things? I thought they were being nice."

"If feeding your family required stretching the truth, you might do just that when you saw someone handing out coins for 'throwing potatoes.'"

"You didn't stop me."

"No, I didn't." I saw innocence and a little embarrassment in his eyes. "Garth, that money will go a long way to help several families. Maybe they'll buy new clothes. Then the clothier might buy extra candles. Then the candle makers will buy a new door from the carpenter, and on and on it goes. Seeing you buy potatoes, I knew it would benefit the rabble, so I didn't stop you. In fact, feel free to buy anything you want while we travel. People need it."

Garth, in a shirt too long and too wide, stared down into his bag of coins like he was trying to name each one. I gave him plenty of time. A new idea in Garth's head grows about as well as a seed thrown into a fireplace.

As the cabin grew quiet, I opened the book I'd brought from my quarters, a well-worn tome with green binding and a wide, open eye on its cover. It was a book about the Restless Ones. And even though they were as real as sea monsters and fairies, I decided to learn what I could. A murderer in Hanbury was hiding behind their legend, so understanding those legends might help me guess the killer's next move.

"Is that a book about the Restless?" Garth asked.

"Yes. Of course, it's mostly just folk tales...ah, which tend to be true in my line of work. Of course."

"Can I read it?"

"Um...*can* you?"

He snatched the book from my hands. "I'm not stupid."

"Lots of people can't read. There's nothing wrong with that."

"Well, there is something wrong with a *noble* who can't read! Who has to sound out the words and get help sometimes!"

I wanted to remind him that reading was not easy and that it was perfectly normal to struggle, but Garth wasn't finished. It was the first time I'd ever seen him get angry.

He went on. "How 'bout someone who only carries books when he's headed for the latrine?"

Not good. That part sounded familiar.

Garth frowned at me. "Someone who scares everyone by being a heartbeat away from the throne, but at least he's only a brain cell away from being declared dead!"

I could only stare back.

Those were *my* words.

I had said them to different people over the years, probably all over the country. And probably in the capital. And apparently sometimes in earshot of Prince Garth.

I tried to speak, but nothing came.

Garth turned away and studied the first page. His mouth quietly formed words while he concentrated on each line, one syllable at a time.

I found myself fascinated by his slow, devoted method. Reading doesn't come easily to everyone. While I could hop through an entire page in moments, Garth had to trudge through like he was navigating a blizzard. The prince courageously pushed on, line after line, working harder at reading than I'd ever worked at...anything. I was truly impressed and wanted to tell him so, but I could tell he was still upset with me.

Bereft of my book and unable to make conversation, I turned my mind to the logistics of our journey and wondered how much progress we had already made. I slid open the small panel in the front of the cabin and shouted to the driver. "How far have we gone?"

"We're almost out of the city!" she said.

CHAPTER TEN

I SAW THE WOMAN AGAIN at the crossroads, and that's when my trouble *really* began.

After three days of silently eating potatoes, avoiding eye contact, and sharing the same book, we stopped at the crossroads of Pyle, a traveler's rest known for its spacious pine outhouses. This may sound like an unnecessary luxury, but after a few days of bouncing around in a carriage it becomes important to, just once, let your food could take its natural course while squatting in the privacy of a tall wooden box rather than over a grove of suspicious leaves.

Until then, Garth and I had often passed the time juggling. I had initially protested, pointing out the shaking cart would make it a useless endeavor, but eventually the boredom wore me down and I began showing Garth what I'd learned in my previous life.

His bitterness toward me meant he wasn't in the mood to ask questions about where I learned to juggle like a seasoned professional. That was good. As far as anyone in Tomelac knew, I had always been an investigator of magic and witchcraft.

Garth watched in awe as I juggled up to five potatoes, sometimes closing my eyes as I kept them aloft. Whenever the road wasn't too bumpy, I would juggle two in one hand and three in the other, yawning as I kept them bobbing up and down. My hands hadn't done that particular trick in some time, but they never failed me.

The show always ended the same way. I would shout, "Bag!" and Garth would throw open the potato sack. Effortlessly, I sent each potato soaring through the opening, one behind the other in a perfect line. The final potato I would toss over my shoulder while looking the other way. Garth clapped every time.

Just after one of my shows, the driver knocked on the front wall and slid open the window. "Pyle, comin' up." The window slammed shut.

"Why's she telling us that?"

"Because it's uphill. Any place with stalls is going to be. She's just warning us we're about to be less comfortable." I pushed open the window on my side just as the wagon began climbing. Clusters of old trees gripped the ground, filling my sight with a dense thicket.

"Why do they put the stalls so high up?" pondered Garth. "Seems inconvenient. When I'm king, I'll have 'em moved low."

"King Garth, the Reformer," I muttered, but my mind reeled.

Believe it or not, I'd never thought much of Garth as a future king. Everyone assumed he wouldn't survive long enough to take the throne. But as ideas lit up Garth's eyes about moving outhouses to more convenient places, I realized he would likely be running our lands during my golden years. Sooner, if Ulder's enemies got to him. I leaned back in my seat and pictured Garth sitting on the throne, wearing a crown that kept slipping from his head and proudly holding the royal scepter, bent and dented from the times his majesty defended himself from flies.

And, for the first time, I wondered if Garth could actually be a *better* king than his father. Why not? They were nothing alike.

Stories of Ulder's savagery had spread to every end of every continent. I heard them long before getting my job as the court inquisitor, but never believed them. Kings were expected to build up frightening reputations, after all. I assumed none of the tales were true.

But I had been wrong. In fact, the truth was even worse.

During his first year on the throne, Queen Ria of Landri sent a messenger who claimed to have proof that Ulder wasn't a true Pendragon. The messenger's body was sent back, but Ulder kept the poor man's head in a pickle jar. It often attended state functions.

Outraged that Ulder would treat a messenger this way, Queen Ria retaliated by having two of Tomelac's diplomats sewn together.

Ulder then announced that Ria clearly lacked an understanding of human decency and protested by tying a few of *her* diplomats to an elaborate pulley and rope system. With this contraption, he would force them to act out his favorite plays.

Shortly after, all the remaining diplomats from both kingdoms resigned.

I found these stories humorous until I arrived at Tomelac's court. Rather than the epoch of civilization and bureaucracy I had hoped for, I arrived on my first day to see Ulder laughing at a blindfolded man struggling in a hangman's noose.

The man was accused of sorcery. Just a rumor, but one repeated often enough to turn the innocent fellow into Ulder's entertainment.

Ulder watched until the man stopped struggling, and, as I recall, a small boy named Garth stood at his side, imitating his father's laugh.

Our carriage crested the hill and lurched to a stop. Garth gathered his potatoes while I threw open the door and let myself out. I reached to stretch out my arms and took a moment to savor being more than two feet from the prince, who was still trying to figure out how to work the door latch.

We had parked at the far edge of the crossroads. The intersecting paths disappeared into pale dirt at the top, where three pine boxes stood tall at the center. To a weary traveler, the sight was inspirational.

Surrounding the camp were caravans of all sizes, including a few larger than I had seen before. I perked up when I noticed some of them were taking on passengers.

That was tempting. The entire ride so far had made me feel like a condemned man being driven to his execution, but for the cost of a few coins I could board a caravan and disappear. Problem solved.

Of course, it wouldn't work if anyone recognized me. Escape was only possible if I could remain anonymous for the next few—

"Erlin, is that you?"

I closed my eyes in frustration. When I opened them, I stood before a familiar face, the last person I expected to see here.

Staring right back at me was the beautiful woman I'd seen in Tomelac's court. Her mist-colored eyes held me in place, like one of the dissected moths on my wall.

"Aren't you Erlin, the inquisitor?" she asked loudly.

Chapter Eleven

I CLOSED MY EYES and recounted several words that are not found in any holy book.

"I saw you in Tomelac!" She walked my way, wearing a smile that told me she knew everything and wasn't going to tell me any of it. "Is this where Ulder sent you? Where's that boy you were with?"

A few people were looking our way. She'd been loud enough to draw attention, and I couldn't help thinking that she was doing it on purpose.

"Yes, that was me." My normal quick-thinking was impeded somehow by her presence. "I came...we came...to..." She waited patiently. I turned my gaze and found my inspiration at last as I gestured toward the tall pine boxes. "We were sent to check the stalls. Public service and all that."

"Oh? You're not Erlin the Inquisitor?"

"Never heard of him." I performed the lie I normally use when hiding my identity. "Between you and me, I don't think magic is real. I've certainly never seen it."

At this, one of her thin brows raised, only slightly.

I knew this look; she was trying to decide if I was filled with the same substance as the latrines. In my pocket, I squeezed my fingers around the earring. Her earring. Did she know I had picked it up?

"Back to work!" I faced the stalls and counted them off with a finger. "One...two...three! All here. The king will be pleased." I wiped my hands. "Time to go back."

"So soon?" Her knitted brow told me she was not finished dissecting me.

"My apprentice has a certain shyness. Can't go when anyone else is around. He's been holding it since we were an hour from Tomelac. I thought the stalls would work out for him, but he insists on waiting until we're back."

She crossed her arms.

"So..." I grasped for words. "This is simply a case of mistaken identity. I'm not—"

"Erlin!" Garth threw open the carriage door, having finally figured out which way to turn the handle. "Hold my potatoes!" The prince shoved the bag in my arms and dashed toward the middle stall.

My own inquisitor tapped her foot on the ground and then pointed at the bag. "Nice potatoes. He keeps those with him all the time, *Erlin?*"

"Yes. They're great for juggling," I replied. Thanks to Garth's intrusion, she held all the cards in this conversation, leaving me with nothing but my rapidly decaying wit and the fact that I speak to women about as well as I wrestle tigers.

"And what's your apprentice's name?" She narrowed her eyes this time, like I was being tested.

Nervously, I gripped the canvas bag and realized I could feel a stubborn bump along one of the potatoes. "Wart," I said, smiling. "The boy's name is Wart."

"And you need an apprentice to count outhouses?"

"It's government work. They think I'm bad at my job if I'm not expensive."

She nodded, still appraising me.

The woman standing before me presented a greater mystery than any I would find in Hanbury. I wanted to know more about her, but I found myself unable to focus whenever I took in her wide eyes and wry lips.

Needing to out-think her, I mentally poured cold water on my thoughts and attempted a more clinical understanding of my situation.

Finally, I noticed she was no longer dressed as a noblewoman. In Ulder's court, she had looked every bit the part of a rich man's wife or visiting royalty, but now a loose skirt whipped at her ankles and a shirt of goat's hair hung from her shoulders.

Behind her, I saw similarly dressed women going about their chores while men in leather vests smoked long pipes and threw dice into circles on the ground.

They gathered around tall caravans, each decorated with colorful lines weaving around every side. Two-thirds of the crossroads were surrounded by these colorful folks, and I couldn't help but notice everyone else keeping their distance.

I finally understood.

This woman was an Abrecan. All of them were.

Given the amount of traveling I do, it's surprising how little I'd seen of these people, but everyone had heard of the wandering spice traders who sold their wares as they traveled in a never-ending migration through Albion. No one trusted them, though no one could quite say why.

Around her eyes, lines gathered while she watched me realize what she was.

A stout man with a handlebar mustache punched my arm to get my attention. Judging by his leather vest, he was another Abrecan. "Z'at your friend up there?"

"I think of him as a co-worker."

"He gonna be in the middle box for a while?"

I shrugged.

He shook his head and walked away, clearly disappointed in me. I had half a mind to interrogate him, but the woman grabbed my arm. "Don't leave your friend," she insisted. I saw fear in her eyes.

"What are you talking about?" I hadn't told her I was trying to leave Garth behind, but she seemed very insightful.

She glanced up the hill, and then back at me. "Your apprentice. Wart. He looks...a little ignorant."

"He once got lost on his way to the moat, but why—"

Before I could understand what was going on, the man with the mustache returned with three large men who marched up the hill and knocked over Garth's stall.

Chapter Twelve

THE PINE BOX TOPPLED BACKWARD while every Abrecan on the hill rushed back to their caravans.

The outhouse tumbled over, landing upside down, and then teetered on its edge, threatening to roll the rest of the way down the hill. I winced at the thought of what was happening to Garth.

"What are you doing?" I shouted to the woman, but she disappeared in a flurry of skirts. The Abrecans were boarding their caravans in a blur.

I ran up the hill with a fever dream of grabbing the wooden box before it fell any further, but just as I arrived the outhouse leaned away from my outstretched hands.

It tumbled over and continued down the hill. The box moved slowly, impeded by outstretched branches and brambles, but never stopped its clumsy, end-over-end journey through the woods on a deadly course for a rushing river at the bottom.

It was obvious I couldn't stop the outhouse by approaching it from behind, so I ran down a narrow side path. The box was hitting every obstacle on its way down, which meant I had a slim chance of getting in front of it before Garth came crashing down into the water.

Unfortunately, stumbling down the path did not fill me with confidence, as I was immediately reminded of my days in the schoolhouse as a child, where I excelled at all studies that did not involve going outside. My heroics at the chalkboard were always forgotten the moment I would try to kick a ball but only succeed in slipping on a cow patty.

But the memory of my school days *did* remind me to keep an eye on my feet. The ground was littered with outstretched branches and wayward stones. I half fell and half ran down the trail, arms flailing, lacking all dignity. My only consolation was knowing no one was watching.

I risked a glance at the pine box and saw it somersaulting through the forest, barely ahead of me.

I ran faster, no longer cautious. If I hurried, I would *just* make it to the riverbank first, with *just* enough time to throw my shoulder into the runaway outhouse before it landed in the river.

My feet reached the waterline just ahead of the tumbling outhouse. I stood in its way and braced myself as the wooden monstrosity charged my way...

...but instead of pummeling me, the pine box landed on an even spot and came to a stop, upright and directly in front of me.

The impact caused the door to swing open.

I shut my eyes. But instead of being greeted by his royal highness, I was assaulted by a series of things that may have left his royal hiney.

It covered me from head to toe, and all of it was far too warm.

I carefully opened my eyes and noticed Garth walking toward me from the top of the hill, cinching up the waist of his breeches.

"Erlin, what are you doing down there?"

CHAPTER THIRTEEN

IT'S HARD TO EXPLAIN HOW I FELT JUST THEN.

"Were you...in the woods this whole time?" I asked, flicking you-know-what from my fingers.

"Well, I was doing, you know," He looked around and whispered, "the necessary."

"I know that, you—" I closed my eyes and took a deep breath. "Garth, we came here so we could do our business in a stall instead of crouching down like animals."

"The stall..." He gazed back up the hill at the two remaining pine boxes. "That's what they're for?"

"You must be joking. Why did you think we made a special stop?"

"I thought people just wanted a better view while they squatted down," said Albion's future king. "Say, do you know what you're covered in?"

"Oh, yes, Garth. Believe it or not, I am keenly aware."

According to rumor, anything found in a prince's bedpan would bring good luck. I knew this was a ruse invented by royals to calm horrified chambermaids after feast days, but, as I stood in the river covered in my worst nightmare, I was prepared to clutch any idea for comfort.

"Garth, run back to the carriage and tell our driver to take the south path around to the river. She'll understand. And tell her to hurry!"

It did me good to see him fall (twice) on his way up. I wondered if the Abrecans would see him, but they had boarded up their caravans in a blinding hurry and were already kicking up dust on the far side of the hill.

I stepped further into the river and removed my shirt, letting the cold water wash over me and my clothes. The shirt, I realized, was hopelessly soiled. I tossed it into the current and watched it drift away. It was only a few days to Hanbury; everyone would have to tolerate a shirtless inquisitor until I found a new one.

In my stumbling flight down the hillside, I'd scarcely had time to realize the gravity of my situation. Someone had tried to kill the prince. No fake names or simple disguises were going to keep him safe, which meant it was time to tuck tail and head back. There would be no investigation and no trip to Hanbury while Garth was in danger. The king would understand.

"Da won't understand," said Garth as I climbed into the carriage and explained my plan.

"I'm certain he won't want the crown prince in danger." The water hadn't cleaned the smell from my clothes. As I pulled the wooden door shut, the choking odor filled the cabin. "Someone just tried to assassinate you."

"I know! Da said this could happen. Said it happens to princes all the time."

I slid open the front panel and shouted to the driver. "Tomelac!" She nodded and cracked the reins. "Your father was right, but this isn't just any attempt on your life. The Abrecans were waiting for you, Garth. That means they know where we're going."

It sounded silly. The Abrecans were nothing more than wandering traders, and the idea of them killing a prince didn't make any sense at all. My mind was filling with questions I knew wouldn't be answered any time soon.

"But Da told me something about this!" Garth pulled up his shirt and pulled a twine-wrapped bundle of papers from his waistband. "Look, there's lots of them. Sick...falls in love...here it is!"

Garth handed me a thick, folded page, the kind used in the castle for brief messages. On the front were printed the words, *IN CASE OF ASSASSINATION*. I unfolded the letter and read:

INQUISITOR ERLIN.

IN THE TERRIBLE EVENT THAT MY SON, GARTH, THE CROWN PRINCE, BECOMES THE TARGET OF AN ASSASSINATION ATTEMPT, PLEASE DO NOT BRING HIM HOME.

"How many of these letters did he give you?"

"Dozens." Garth held up another bearing the words, IN CASE OF SHAPESHIFTING.

"I *have* to read that one." I snatched it from his hands.

INQUISITOR ERLIN.

IN THE TERRIBLE EVENT THAT MY SON, GARTH, THE CROWN PRINCE, IS THE VICTIM OF A WICKED SPELL THAT TRANSFORMS HIM INTO SOMETHING, LIKE A FISH OR A SQUIRREL, PLEASE DO NOT BRING HIM HOME. MY SON WILL NEED TO LEARN HOW TO WORK OUT THESE PROBLEMS ON HIS OWN.

"King Ulder has thought of everything." I handed the letters back to Garth, who tied them up again and returned them to their place under his waistband. Upon remembering where the paper had been, I felt a strong need to clean my hands for the second time. "I don't care what the letter says, we're cornered and Tomelac's the only place to go from here other than Hanbury, and the Abrecans are going that way."

I was mostly telling the truth. There was one other path, but I didn't want to think about it.

With a groan, the wagon rolled onto the main road. "We'll just drop you off," I decided, not wanting to face King Ulder while covered in his son's breakfast. I imagined leaving him at the front gate, paying the driver to start the week-long trip to the sea, and jumping onto the first boat I could find.

Something occurred to me just as I was ready to doze off. "Let me see those letters again."

Garth retrieved the bundle of missives, and I sorted through them until I found the letter I was looking for. *In Case of True Love.*

Inquisitor Erlin.

In the very unfortunate event that my son tells you he has fallen in love, please bring him home immediately.

CHAPTER FOURTEEN

I DIDN'T BELIEVE I COULD FALL ASLEEP, with my breeches, shoes, and socks smelling of latrine, but Garth and I kept the front slot open, hoping some of the foul odor would release through the little window, and eventually I nodded off.

The driver woke us a few hours past midnight and said, "You might wanna see this."

Garth and I, putting our sleepy heads together, gazed through the opening. The road ahead was dark, but, as my eyes adjusted, I could just make out the edges of the dirt road, barely lit by moonlight. Further ahead, a series of lights danced along the path like a line of fireflies.

"What it is it?" asked Garth.

"A caravan," I sighed. "Those are lanterns lining the sides of wagons. That's more of the Abrecans; somehow, they got ahead of us, and now they're cutting us off before we get to Tomelac. How did they get here so fast? I thought they rode in the other direction."

The driver shrugged. "They did. But no one knows the roads better than the Abrecan drivers."

"We're trapped then, right?" asked Garth. "There's nowhere else to go on this road. Isn't that what you said, Erlin? There's nowhere else to go?"

The driver looked inside and raised one of her eyebrows at me. Of course, there was one other road we could take.

"Take the path to Barton," I sighed.

"What's in Barton," yawned Garth.

I couldn't be sure. Maybe nothing. But I knew the habits of the country folk who lived outside the walls of Tomelac, and I knew their ways were as steady as clockwork. If tradition held, we would not be the only visitors making our way to Barton. I silently prayed that no one there would recognize me, but that sort of thinking never panned out. My life had become a magnet for bad luck, so I resigned myself to the wicked hands of fate.

"Barton is the only city we can get to where no one's trying to kill you," I explained.

He seemed to sober up, finally realizing the danger he was in. "That woman you were talking to...was she..."

"Part of it? Could be." I felt anger growing in my chest. "Maybe she only talked to me so I wouldn't notice what they were doing. We should have run the moment I saw her."

"Why didn't you?"

I hated it when Garth had good questions. "Won't happen again." I settled into the wooden seat and tried to recapture my slumber.

The be honest, I didn't feel like she was part of any ruse, but it was hard to figure out what else she could have been doing.

"I'll find her, and then Da will execute her. Just to be safe."

I was too tired to stop myself from bolting upright and looking him in the eye. "Oh, that's a *great* idea, your highness. We don't know what's going on, so why don't we start killing people? And when she's dead, you can kill me—after all, I might be in on it, too. As long as we're being thorough, why not kill our driver? You know. *Just to be safe?*"

He flinched. Though we rarely employed decorum when talking to Garth, he had probably never been spoken to this way.

"Da says we have to stop our enemies *before* they kill us! Besides, I should be mad at *you* for putting me in danger—that's against the law, you know! Endangering the prince is as bad as killing him yourself!" He crossed his arms. "I'm only trying to help you."

"By killing a woman who only *might* be guilty? Your highness, I do not appreciate violence for my benefit. Or anyone's benefit. It's one thing to use extreme measures when there's no other choice, but it's quite another to use violence before you've even *bothered* to figure out what's going on."

He had nothing to say to that.

I redoubled my efforts to fall asleep. "There's a proper set of stocks in Barton. When we arrive, you can have the magistrate slam me in there, if you like. It's your right, and I've surely earned it. Good night."

I didn't wake up when the wagon stopped, and I remained asleep while our driver parked just outside of town, tied the horses to a tree, and fell asleep in the front seat. An inn would have been nice, but this way we could escape at the first sign of trouble rather than being caught in our beds.

It must have still been night when we stopped. I woke up well after sunrise and noticed Garth was absent. I opened the door, just a bit, and glanced around. I'd lost him. For all I knew, he could have already been stabbed and hung on a wall. But a moment later I heard his voice as he approached.

"I got you some new clothes." He stopped outside the door next to me, holding a bundle of fabric. "Want to try them on?"

My eyes opened a little. His pie-shaped face stared back, full of eager kindness and not a trace of anger from our previous discussion.

Maybe I'd been too hard on Garth. His casual talk of killing someone had horrified me, but that's simply what everyone expected of him. Every noble and royal he'd ever met, just about everyone in his life, talked in exactly the same way. Threats of violence. Promises of punishment. Nobles kept the common people in line with anger and oppression, so it was only natural Garth would learn the same habits.

But now he looked at me with a face full of innocence. Like everyone else, I found it easy to laugh at his ignorant ways, but now I saw his ignorance as a blank slate. An opportunity. He was a boy with everything to learn, and his heart was not black like his father's. At least, not yet.

He handed me a tunic and a set of breeches, along with a set of small clothes. "Someone's on their way with a pair of boots."

I looked through the clothes and realized Garth had done something competent. "How did you do this?"

In his face, it was obvious he didn't understand my question. A better one would have been, *how did* you *do this?*

Garth recounted his tale of the morning. "Once we stopped, I remembered what you said about the potatoes, that it helps to give people money. But then I remembered what you said about not looking like someone who has money. So I went to a shop that had clothes and offered to pay with some potatoes."

"Shrewd." In the cramped cabin, I pulled off my dirty outfit and forced my way into the small clothes.

"But he told me he didn't accept potatoes."

"How dreadful."

"So, I fished out one gold coin—"

"A gold coin should buy ten sets of clothes," I said.

"I know! And I told him the same thing."

"Oh. So, you got some change back?"

"I would have, but, you know, taxes. Apparently, the king takes quite a lot."

It was a ruse, of course. Yes, Ulder's taxes were about as fair as the cat taxing the mouse, but the shopkeeper had gotten away with taking a full gold piece for a set of cheap clothes. I almost admired him.

"So, who's coming with those boots? Did they cost another gold coin?"

He frowned. "No. I had to look somewhere else for those. I walked up and down the street asking people if they sold shoes."

It was truly a wonder Garth was alive. "You are aware we need to keep in hiding, right?"

"Don't worry about that. I gave everyone my false name." He whispered, "Walt."

"Wart," I corrected.

"Anyway, I saw some people setting up tents, and I thought they might be starting up a market."

"It's not a market," I mumbled, but Garth didn't hear me.

"So, I asked if anyone had boots for my friend, Erlin."

"That's my real name."

"You never game me a false one."

He had me there.

Garth continued. "Then this man came over and asked if it was the same Erlin he used to know. He described you perfectly and even said he knew your boot size. I think he's an old friend."

"Fantastic." Everything was going wrong.

I stepped out of the carriage and tossed my stained clothes aside. "You've done well, Garth, with the exception of...well, never mind. You couldn't have known." In my bare feet, I stepped onto the grass.

The driver was laying in her seat, hat pulled down over her face.

I tapped her shoulder. "Um..."

"Geltrude," she grunted, giving her name for the first time. Drivers rarely needed to tell their names. They normally answered to the name of their profession, which was easier on everyone. "We're heading into town to get a bite."

Geltrude lowered her hat so it blocked out more of the sun.

"Right." I patted her shoulder. "Sorry to bother you."

I walked carefully, avoiding any obvious rocks. "Let's hope those boots fit."

"In a hurry?" Garth asked.

"The Abrecans won't take long to notice we didn't end up in Hanbury or Tomelac, so they'll be on our trail shortly. Now, tell me about this man who's delivering my new shoes."

"He's an odd one. Talks funny, like he's always reading poetry, and he dresses real strange."

"How strange?"

Garth shrugged. "Like...like a jester, I guess."

A jester. In Barton. Who knew my boot size. Sadly, that could only mean one thing.

My fears were realized when someone down the road shouted my name.

CHAPTER FIFTEEN

DAGONET.

In the center of the street was a man who didn't know he looked like an idiot. Dagonet wore a white ruff over his bi-color tunic that frilled around his neck and bounced as he walked. Hands on his hips, standing unabashed in his woolen tights, he loudly repeated my name.

"Erlin!" He gestured toward me while onlookers gaped, ensuring my first impression in town was a bad one.

Well, my first impression in quite some time. I was certain no one would recognize me.

"Our prodigal returns!" He continued in a voice he believed sounded dramatic but actually came across as a man trying to sing a woman's part. "Avalon truly smiles upon us—"

I closed the distance quickly. "Calm down, Dagonet." A useless request. At every turn, at every one of life's unexpected quirks, the Dagonet I knew would make more noise than a pair of newlyweds at sundown.

He rubbed his well-measured stubble. "Come back to the fold, Erlin? Need a place to practice your true gift?"

"True gift?" Garth looked Dagonet up and down. "Are you an inquisitor, too?"

"Yes, Garth," I said, shaking my head. "And when I become a truly great inquisitor, I, too, can wear pointy shoes."

Garth studied Dagonet's stupid footwear. "Is he going to Hanbury with us?"

"Hanbury? Stuck up and cold." Dagonet spat. Elegantly. "Demanding crowds with deep pockets—all sewn shut! Why the devil would you go to..." Realization set into his face. "What did the boy just call you? An inquisitor? What does that even mean? Do you work for the—"

I clapped a hand over his mouth. "Could we get something to eat?" I glanced around. Dagonet's theater company couldn't be far, but they were out of sight for the moment. "Something close?"

Dagonet crossed his arms. "Yes, but you know what I'm going to ask." He mumbled all of this into my hand.

"Fine. Buy us lunch, and you can ask me anything."

He clasped his hands. "Lovely! I know just the place."

He pointed across the street to a pub. A sign swung over the porch, and after some squinting I was able to form the squirrelly letters into words: *The Last Sip*. These words had been scrawled by, I assumed, a man who had never seen letters before and had been forced to write with his feet.

We had only gone a few steps when Garth gripped my shoulder and pointed ahead, further down the road. "They found us!"

The road had only risen slightly, but we'd gotten just high enough to see across town to a grassy field on the far side. In that field we saw a few gigantic caravans, like the wagons the Abrecans used, but even larger. The grassy area was brimming with men and women trying on bright clothes and helping each other apply makeup.

"Don't worry. Those aren't Abrecans. They're with Dagonet."

"Abrecans!" Dagonet shook his head and spat again.

We continued toward the pub, and I cringed as the newfound silence was broken by little bells on the tips of Dagonet's shoes. I allowed our path to keep us in the middle of the road for longer than was necessary. With any luck, a caravan or post rider might speed through and run over all of us.

To my disappointment, we survived our walk to the other side of Barton's only street. I entered the pub, barefoot, and was thankful to see a nearly empty room with nice tables. A proper place to eat for a change. Not fancy, but someone was going to bring me food while I sat and did nothing. Divinity itself. And I'd tricked Dagonet into paying for it. I knew what his questions would be and exactly how I would refuse, but I could humor him long enough to squeeze a meal out of him.

Garth tried to plop himself into the first table he saw, but I gently led him away from there and settled into a seat where I could put my back to a wall and watch the door. Garth, despite recently having survived an assassination attempt, hadn't learned the value of being paranoid, a personality trait I possessed in spades.

I also used the extra time to stall. Dagonet was brimming with questions that I didn't want to answer, and I didn't need Garth to learn about my past and then tell his father I'd been lying to him for several years. Between Dagonet and the Abrecans, my future wasn't looking bright.

Dagonet took a seat and leaned toward me, eyes digging into mine. "So. Erlin the...inquisitor? Isn't that what your friend said?"

"He's my apprentice. And...yes." Dagonet and I hadn't seen each other in about four years, since right before I started my work in Ulder's court, but he could already tell my job was nothing but a con.

"Tell me...what exactly does an inquisitor *do*, Erlin?"

"It's the most important job in the realm!" Garth spoke too quickly for me to interrupt. "He's brave, and he's the smartest man in Tomelac—in all of Albion!"

"Impressive! You sound *sooo* important, Erlin. Tell me more." Dagonet folded his hands and waited.

"Fine," I said. "Well, as I recall...oh, it'll have to wait—the barmaid is here!"

Garth and Dagonet turned their heads. The waitress was actually sitting on a stool, rubbing a tired foot she had propped up on the bar.

"No, she isn't." Dagonet turned back to me. "Now, I want to hear about how brave you are."

"Um, I'm *sure* she's about to get up..."

I was right. As I spoke, the waitress put her shoe back on and left her stool.

"...and head right for the kitchen. Just as I suspected." She disappeared into the back room. "Well, does everyone know what they want? Should I ask for menus?"

Dagonet stared at me like a pigeon watching a crumb.

The waitress burst forth from the kitchen and I nearly applauded. Dagonet was easily distracted, and if I could get him to stop hounding me about my job, I just might be able to get my boots and my meal and hit the road before he learned what I'd been up to for the last four years.

The waitress had taken a single step out of the kitchen when Dagonet turned to shout, "Three ales!" She spun and walked back through the kitchen door, which hadn't even had time to swing shut.

Dagonet leaned back in his chair, victorious. "So? Tell me about this exciting job. I've never heard of an inquisitor."

"It's complicated work." I said, adding a gesture to pad my speech. "I ask questions. Get answers. You know. Inquisit. Lots of inquisiting. Sometimes I inquire. That sort of thing."

My old friend held out his hands in frustration. "Inquisiting about *what?*"

"You don't know?" blurted Garth. "Erlin keeps our whole kingdom safe from magic!"

I buried my face in my hands and waited for Dagonet to stop laughing.

CHAPTER SIXTEEN

THERE ARE PEOPLE WHO BELIEVE IN MAGIC, and there are people who can read. Tomelac, along with most of Albion, has lots of believers and very few readers. The city hears no end of the evils of magic, and King Ulder takes the issue more seriously than his own gout.

Dagonet was laughing for a full minute before he could talk. "How long have you been hunting mages?"

"No time, old friend." I wanted to push the conversation elsewhere. "My apprentice and I need to be in Hanbury."

"Something about the Abrecans?"

"That's right. Say, you live on the road, what do you know about them?"

"Not much." He leaned back in thought. "They haven't been around as long as people think. Bit more than a decade, I'd say. I can't tell where they came from, but they're not the first traveling people to stop in our lands, and I'm sure they'll eventually roll on and peddle their wares in some other place. Are you worried about them? Think they might crush you in one of their pepper grinders? Force you to paint their wagons?"

"Shut up, Dagonet. We're in serious trouble."

"Is that so? I'll have you know there are three towns with arrest warrants for me and my troupe because they didn't appreciate our plays. We suffer for our work. Suffer!" He spoke the last word to the rafters, squeezing both hands into fists.

"Troupe?" asked Garth. "I still don't know what you do. Erlin never told me about his old jobs. Did you hunt wizards together?"

"Hunt wizards?" Dagonet could hardly contain himself. "Your master couldn't hunt a pheasant if it died on his doorstep."

He wasn't wrong.

"That's not true!" shouted Garth. "I was there when he killed Mirdal the Mad!"

Our drinks arrived in tall, froth-crowned glasses, and I abducted mine with both hands.

"You killed Mirdal the Mad!" Dagonet lifted his glass but merely gestured with it. "The hero!" Ale foam splattered the table. "Your stories must be as courageous as the time I found a fly in my soup."

"I was there!" Garth slapped the table. "In court!"

I nearly choked on my drink and silently begged the prince to stop and let me save some of my dignity.

But Garth couldn't even slow down. "Erlin walked in carrying the red robes, the ones Mirdal wore, with runes stitched on 'em and the skull painted on the back. He had it in his hands and my Da shouted—"

"Drink up, Garth!" I begged. "Don't want it getting warm."

He pushed his drink away. "Ma says I can't. Anyway, Erlin walks in carrying that robe and with red blood all over his hands, and everyone just stared because we knew what it meant. He'd killed Mirdal the Mad and carried his robe into the king's court to prove it!" Garth beamed.

That part of the story was true. Sort of. But Garth, as usual, only knew a piece of the puzzle.

Dagonet squinted at Garth. "Interesting. You were there, young Wart, when all this happened? Does your family spend a lot of time in the king's court?"

Dagonet had found the gaping hole in Garth's story.

"Wart's family has been farming for generations," I said quickly. "Potato farmers. Ulder holds a lottery for one lucky family to visit court every year to raise morale. That day when I, as you know, *killed* Mirdal the Mad, was the day Garth asked to be my apprentice."

"A beautiful tale." Dagonet waved his glass. "The potato boy goes to the castle and meets his destiny!"

I was starting to suspect Dagonet did not believe my hastily written tale. A pity, since I was rather proud of it.

"I'll never forget." Garth proudly held up his potato bag, trying to bolster my story with evidence. He even held out one of the juggling variety. "I knew I wanted to be his apprentice the moment he walked into court with that robe."

That was something I didn't know. Before being assigned to the other unlucky teachers in the castle, young Garth had apparently imprinted on me. I knew stories were powerful. Dagonet had taught me that. But I'd never considered how spinning yarns in court would have affected young Garth.

The prince was smiling at me. Dagonet was laughing behind his eyes while he finally took his first sip. And I was trying to melt into my seat.

"So, what do you do, Mister Dagonet?" Garth asked.

"My boy. In these hands, from these lips...dreams become real."

"You're a wizard?" said Garth, half in wonder and half in fear.

"In some ways, you're absolutely right." Dagonet turned away as a distant, visionary look overcame his eyes, even though he was staring at a stuffed beaver mounted on the wall. "Is there a more noble mysticism? Is raising the dead more potent than raising one's imagination?" He clenched his hands and raised them overhead, the image of a lunatic who believes he's milking a giant, invisible cow. "Upon the pantheon of architects and priests, gods and heroes, does anyone shine brighter than one who shapes our fancies into reality with the stubborn clay of our minds and—"

"Oh, knock it off, you dry ham." I said, "Wart, he's just an actor."

If you've ever taken anything from the squatty hands of a baby, then you know what Dagonet's face looked like.

(It was the castle's the last taffy treat, in case you're wondering, and his mother even never noticed.)

"Just. An. Actor." His pitch fell with each syllable. "And I suppose, Erlin, *you* were never—"

"Wart!" I clasped his shoulder. "Out the window! Someone's looking for potatoes!"

"I have some!" He hustled through the tavern and out the door.

Dagonet, dumbfounded, looked out the window and watched Garth trip down the tavern steps. "He just runs off when you say something like that?"

"I used to come up with clever things to distract him, but I found that just about anything works. Listen, I've worked very hard to keep anyone from knowing about my past. They take me very seriously in Tomelac."

"Surely he's figured it out by now, after everything I've said."

"One of the potatoes in his bag is actually a rock. He says it needs time to ripen."

Dagonet shook his head, then leaned closer. "As I was saying...*just* an *actor*?"

I knew he wouldn't like that.

He went on. "And I suppose *you* were *just* an *actor* when crowds screamed for encores? When towns whispered your name months before your arrival? Didn't anyone in Tomelac recognize you from your glory days?"

It had come up, but only once. The people in Tomelac are *far* too proper to enjoy a traveling theater group, but a stable hand once recognized me and asked to see my donkey impression. To watch me juggle. To see me stand on one hand and hop around. Mostly, though, he wanted to see my impression of King Ulder falling into cow dung. I was embarrassed, but also flattered. *The Calamities of Ulder* was my masterpiece, after all, but no one in Tomelac needed to know that.

Needing to keep my secret, I told the stable hand I was performing a special version of my play that evening in the great hall. When he entered, smelling of horses and interrupting one of Ulder's decrees, he was sent to work the stables in the remote village of Werne, where the year-round presence of mud forces the locals to ride pigs.

"It was just a roadside attraction," I said. "Not a big deal."

"Just a...roadside attraction." Dagonet frowned. "We invested so much in you."

"Oh, don't lay out a guilt trip, Dagonet. I'm eternally grateful, you know that, but don't fill the boy's head with lies about the grand theater and me being a countryside celebrity."

He grinned. Dagonet knew a lot more than that. In fact, Dagonet was the only person, other than me, who understood what really went on between me and Mirdal the Mad. It wasn't a story I wanted anyone to hear, and Dagonet knew it, which gave him a bargaining chip.

Dagonet folded his hands with a smirk. "So, the boy believes in magic?"

"Lots of them do in Tomelac." I lowered my head into my hands, realizing for the first time how heavy it had gotten. "Ulder is obsessed with his executions. Eventually he'll kill everyone in Albion and finally be happy, I guess, with no one left to accuse."

"Oh, yes, Ulder. Who believes you...you of all people actually *killed* Mirdal the Mad? If he only knew."

"I really hate him. He's worse than you think."

"Tell me everything," he said warmly.

I wanted to. Living a lie meant I never got to share my troubles with anyone, and an untold story is a heavy burden, but we were distracted by the noise of hooves, reins, and rattling wagons coming from outside. From the sound of it, at least three wagons were rolling into town. Big ones.

"Abrecans," Dagonet whispered.

I jumped, nearly knocking over the table. Garth was still out there, looking for someone who needed potatoes.

Chapter Seventeen

I MADE IT AS FAR AS THE DOOR.

I stuck my head out in time to see the three wagons rolling down the street. Abrecans hopped out and searched buildings on either side. In the lead wagon, next to the driver, I saw the stout man I'd encountered before, carrying a whip that looked as sharp as the ends of his mustache. His steel eyes scanned every corner of town.

It occurred to me that sending Garth outside wasn't the most brilliant idea I'd ever had, but it had served the purpose of keeping my secret from him. Now I simply needed to find him and get back to our carriage.

"That's your trouble?" whispered Dagonet, standing behind me. "The Abrecans are harmless!"

"This is serious!" I turned on him and grabbed his lapels. "Dagonet, you have to help us."

"My boy." He pushed my hands away. "I'm *just* an actor. Remember?"

He stepped through the door and walked away on jingly shoes.

Trying to stay hidden, I glanced out just far enough to look for Garth. I saw Abrecan men in their leather vests entering shops and snooping around houses under the watchful eye of their ironclad leader, but no sign of the prince.

Three wagons full of Abrecans methodically nosing around town would normally raise a few eyebrows, but no one seemed to notice. In fact, hardly anyone was even around. The few people I could see were walking further down the road, the same direction Dagonet had gone, where a crowd was gathering. Geltrude, our driver, walked past, following the locals to see what was going on, which meant if I *did* find Garth, we wouldn't be able to go anywhere.

There were too many problems happening at once, so I decided to work on one annoyance at a time. First things first, I needed to find the prince.

I turned around and dashed through the kitchen, where the server was asleep on the floor. Or that's what I thought. After a moment, I realized she was actually laying on her back in front of a beer barrel while trying to get the last drop from a spigot to fall into her wide, waiting mouth.

"Back door?" I asked.

She stopped slapping the side of the barrel and pointed to a door on the other side of a spice rack.

I rushed through, expecting to see more of the city, but behind the tavern there was only more of the countryside. I shook my head. This was how small towns worked, I remembered. Every building in Barton lined the road so vendors could quickly rush out of their homes and surround travelers with their wares, which meant there really weren't a lot of places to hide that couldn't be seen by a passing carriage.

It might be easy to imagine that Garth would have ended up on my side of this oddly bifurcated town. Wouldn't that be convenient?

But I knew better.

You see, I'm unlucky. And when you've been unlucky as long as I have, you don't even bother to ask which side the toast landed on when it falls off the table, you just assume you'll be cleaning butter off the floor.

The Abrecans were slowly and methodically crawling down the street. I darted ahead, behind a few buildings, and peeked out again. The leader's eyes faced forward, scanning everything and—as far as I could tell—never blinking. Tough guys don't blink, I've noticed.

"Erlin!" someone whispered.

Straight across the dirt road, I saw Garth pressed against a building. Maybe I'd been wrong about his survival instincts. Judging by the way he was clutching his bag of potatoes, he knew we were in big trouble.

I formed a plan to distract the Abrecans while Garth doubled back behind the buildings. If he could get to the wagon, maybe he could escape while I led the Abrecans on a chase.

I locked eyes with Garth and gestured toward the back of town, moving my hand in a circle.

Garth nodded back, very seriously, and I believed he had actually understood me until he spun around in place and then eagerly looked back at me, like he was expecting a treat.

"No!" I forcefully repeated my gesture. He responded with a confused sigh and then spun around again.

But this time, before he could stick his landing, I saw two pairs of hands shove something over his head and drag him away.

Chapter Eighteen

I wasn't sure why I ran into the road. It could have been the sight of Garth's helpless, clueless face, just before the bag went over it. It could also have been the fact that Ulder personally flayed people who let his family get hurt. Either way, I ran toward Garth.

Also, I didn't know what I would do when I got there. Battling two assailants was at least two more assailants than I could manage, but that didn't matter since I didn't even make it across the street before the mustached man in the lead wagon shouted at me. He unfurled his whip and cracked it high over the heads of the horses.

I flinched, knowing the caravan would flatten me like dough, snuffing out the candle of my life while I crossed the street to help the prince, who probably thought he was being forced into a game of hide and seek.

It seemed a pitiful end to my tale.

While few can have any lasting impression on the world, those who work for the king in Tomelac are given a headstone when they perish rather than being piled in the beggar's hole, burned, and then used to grow Petunia's plants. (She says the ashes are perfect for adding to the soil. I tell people she enjoys smearing fertilizing manure over her ex-lovers.)

So, while I've never been an ambitious man, I did once catch a whiff of aspiration as I walked past the graveyard in Tomelac and noticed the inscriptions on the headstones of the kingdom's departed servants. One read, *Here likes Oraf, General in the Ochre wars. Killed by a deer. A female deer.* Another, *Here lies Amaran, captain of the guard. We think. Body was returned headless.*

Some were left to rest under an inscription of their final words. For example, *"I've made a new stew for the king." -Edule, royal chef.* Which was followed by, *"This stew tastes funny," -Llayel, royal food taster.* Not a single one offered the deceased a shred of dignity, which is why I felt the need to prepare useful last words to utter if I ever saw the end of a sword pointed my way. Posterity is a harsh judge.

But other tombstones spoke of academic contributions. *Here lies Malorie, who wrote the first very heavy book.* Or, *Here lies Monmuth, who invented small letters at the bottom of pages.*

I had long imagined mine would read, *Here lies Erlin, slayer of Mirdal the Mad,* or *Here lies Erlin, who was terribly mysterious.* But as I dashed across the street to find out what happened to Garth, I realized it would more likely say, *Here lies Erlin, trampled by spice traders.*

But I had severely over-estimate how quickly a large wagon can build speed. The horses pulled and the caravan lurched forward, but I had plenty of time to scamper the rest of the way across the dirt road to where I'd last seen Garth.

It was easy to spot the footprints and see where Garth had been abducted and dragged away. I followed the prints, doggedly rushing along their path, which took me headlong into the gathering crowd.

I was thankful the large gathering would make it difficult for anyone to find me, but now I could only catch glimpses of the footprints here and there.

More distressing was the fact that someone had grabbed me from behind and pulled me away.

It happened too fast. My mind couldn't decide if I should panic over losing the crown prince or over the fact that a second person was pulling on my trousers.

"Gar—" I nearly shouted his real name when I saw him in the crowd, several armlengths away. I couldn't see his face, but he didn't seem worried. Apparently, being kidnapped by a crowd couldn't penetrate his childlike sense of wonder, even as we heard the *jingle-jangle* of the Abrecans' caravan getting closer.

As my trousers were pulled down, I felt my body fall backward. I was caught by a few strong hands and held in suspension while someone tugged my trousers off and someone else pulled my shirt over my head. As I was about to scream, I felt more hands smearing something onto my face.

More confused than anything else, I looked around and caught another glimpse of Garth wearing...

...feathers? Something familiar rang in the deep recesses of my skull. My head swung back, and I noticed the Abrecan men, wearing hard faces and those shiny leather vests, advancing on the crowd.

With no sense of where I had been dragged, I was forced through the back door of a wooden structure. More hands smeared my face while something soft was wrapped around my body and cinched tight.

Before my assailants let me down, a pair of boots were pulled onto my feet.

I stood blinking, standing wobbly on boots that were entirely too tall, and I heard Dagonet's voice from directly behind me.

"See, boy? I told you I'd get you some shoes!"

He shoved in the back with both hands, and I stumbled through a curtain.

Finally, I understood where I was, and why there didn't seem to be any people in town.

Before me, the population of Barton watched me while they sat on the grass, cross-legged and eager.

It had been stage make up they were smearing all over my face, and I now wore an over-sized cloak and a pair of boots that made me half a hand taller as I stood in the center of Dagonet's stage looking nothing like myself.

I was an actor again, in front of a rapt audience, and I knew exactly what to say.

"Line!"

CHAPTER NINETEEN

"IT'S A GOOD DAY FOR BATHING IN COW URINE!" Dagonet hissed from behind the curtain.

"It's a good day for bathing in cow urine!" I said with a royal gesture.

And then I remembered the next line of the play. And the line after that. The tricky dance, the eating scene, and the controversial-but-tasteful ending. Like a snowball rolling down a mountain and turning into an avalanche, the entire performance came hurtling back from the far reaches of my memory.

Mostly, I remembered the name of the play.

We were doing *The Calamities of Ulder*, my masterpiece, and I was playing the lead.

The crowd laughed when I bent over as a stagehand released a puff of smoke that appeared to erupt from my nether regions. And again when my crown fell from my head and I tore my breeches picking it up. Also, when I chased away envoys from Sacksony and Sirap by speaking only in loud flatulence (provided by another stagehand breathing tightly into his hand). Nothing had changed in the years I'd been away; audiences still wanted to see their leaders expel gas.

Just off stage, wearing a suit of yellow feathers, I could see Garth. Mostly, I could *hear* him cackling madly with every joke. And I eventually realized...he didn't know the name of the play or that I was lampooning his father.

After canvassing the town, several Abrecans settled in to watch the show. They even laughed, except for their leader. I stumbled when he locked eyes with me, but he gave no sign that he recognized me under my wig and makeup. Dagonet's people had done excellent work.

There was less flatulence in the second act of *The Calamities of Ulder*. As the king, I was visited by a wizard who leaned on an arcane staff. Dagonet had taken on this role, which meant each line was now twice as loud and twice as long. (This helped find me the motivation I needed to order his death.) "You're killing me because I use magic?" he cried out. "No," I bellowed, "It's because your staff makes me feel insignificant!" Most of the crowd appreciated my innuendo. A few scratched their heads until a neighbor leaned over to explain the joke. After a few moments, everyone in Barton was laughing at Ulder's wood envy.

I glanced in Garth's direction. He looked confused. A young woman stood tall so she could whisper in his ear. This woman was also dressed in feathers, bright blue ones. After her explanation, Garth shrugged, still confused. The joke was beyond his reach.

Just as I was enjoying my time on stage, once again delighting crowds and insulting kings, I remembered we had entered a crucial scene in which Ulder disappears into the woods to ask the heavens for a sign that he was divinely chosen to lead Albion. A few of the actors stepped to the edge of the stage, dressed as woodland creatures. Garth's new friend, the young woman dressed as a blue bird, whispered hasty instructions to him.

"I seek only a sign!" I roared to an expectant audience. "That..."

I paused. Here I would normally shout out the name "Ulder," but Garth had yet to grasp the subject of the play. I decided to skip it.

"...that I possess the wisdom to rule Tomelac! The heredity! The charm!" The crowd rubbed their hands together more and more with each word. They knew the next part. "And, of course, the *handsomeness* to rule!"

At that last one, I saw a flurry of feathers just before a pair of eggs flew harmlessly over my head.

I frowned and tried again. "I said...I possess the *handsomeness* to rule!"

This time, the eggs landed near my feet. Garth's new friend threw as badly as he did.

"As I was saying," I growled, "I am clearly handsome enough to—"

Garth, in a bird costume far too small, scurried in front of me and, with a look of pure delight, shoved both hands into my chest.

I stumbled, trying to keep my balance, but realized too late that someone had knelt behind me. Outwitted, I fell backward, tumbling over Garth's blue-feathered friend, humiliated by a schoolyard trick.

I opened my eyes to see both of them throwing eggs onto my face while the rest of the forest creatures jeered. When every egg was broken, Garth and the other creatures disappeared behind the curtain, leaving me to stumble to my feet and deliver the play's final line:

"Rejoice, good people—"

Cabbage exploded in my face.

Apparently, the ending of my play had evolved to include the audience. Looking out, I saw each person brandished a scrap of outdated food. I took a defensive stance as sour milk splattered my costume and a sheep's bladder bounced off my forehead.

"Good people—" I tried again, but two children hoisted a live chicken toward me. Its wings obscured my vision.

At a sign from Dagonet, the entire crowd threw everything they had in one final gesture. I raised my hands in tired acceptance as a shower of rotten food blanketed the stage.

"Rejoice, good people!" Runny eggs made it difficult to keep my eyes open. I spit out cabbage and continued. "And look upon your king!"

Chapter Twenty

I LEFT THE STAGE and decided the curtain call would have to happen without me. In the old days, I looked forward to doffing my wig and taking a bow in front of my fans, but that wouldn't do while the Abrecans were watching.

I gripped the curtain and peeked out. The jugglers and fire breathers gave one more demonstration, followed by the line of twirling dancers and then the acrobats. Garth rushed out to join the other minor actors, wearing an oversized bird beak that kept his face hidden. He darted back to safety after a brief bow, and none of the Abrecans seemed to notice. It was quite the risk, but hiding in plain sight had turned out to be very effective. The Abrecan men in their leather vests stood frustrated at the edges of the crowd, glancing around with their fists on their hips. I couldn't keep from craning my neck out to scan every corner of the audience.

"Looking for someone?" asked Dagonet, standing close.

"No. I was just—"

"Don't lie to me!" Dagonet removed my cape and the coat under it. "I know the moon-faced look of an actor gazing out from backstage, hoping to see a smiling face looking back at them. Who is she, Erlin?"

"Why are the Abrecans still here?"

"You're changing the subject, but I imagine they won't be satisfied until they know who was behind that brilliant portrayal, which is why I'm doing this." He pulled the wig off my head and plopped it loosely on his own, then put on the coat and whipped the cape over his shoulders.

The crowd cheered as Dagonet strolled out, the final actor to take a bow. He pulled off the wig and beamed at the crowd, who assumed it had been him playing the role of Ulder all along. A simple trick, but good enough to fool the Abrecans, who shrugged and began making their way back to their caravans.

And then I leaned out even more, foolishly exposing myself and hoping to catch the eye of a woman with long, dark hair who was probably trying to kill me, but she was nowhere to be found.

I always hated it when Dagonet was right.

"This is Wendy!" Backstage, Garth tugged at the feathers attached to his arms. He'd been crammed into a costume that wasn't designed for him. "She's a bird!"

The young woman in the blue bird suit pulled on his sleeves, trying to help him out. "I'm a wobbler!"

"Warbler!" shouted Dagonet, who was untangling a wig from a pair of netted stockings. "How many times must I say it?"

Garth succeeded in extracting one of his arms. "Wendy says she has to titter to look like a wobbler."

"Teeter!" I corrected.

"Warbler!" Dagonet raved.

The two of them continued to pull on his costume.

"I take it you haven't seen that play before?" asked Wendy. She yanked on the two strings that held his outfit together but only made it tighter.

"I've never seen any play before. What's it called?"

"The Calamities of—"

"Garth," I interrupted, "Has Wendy seen your potato collection?"

"Those were *your* potatoes?" Wendy asked. "I put them with the props."

"Some of them are good for juggling."

"Show me!"

Across the room, Dagonet shot me a look of weariness while Garth and Wendy, still halfway in their feathered costumes, threw potatoes at one another in a pitiful attempt at juggling.

I made my way to the other side of the narrow caravan, remembering as I stepped over loose planks that this gigantic carriage opened up into a stage. Being run and maintained by actors meant it threatened to fall apart at every sneeze.

"We owe you, Dagonet."

"Yes, you do." He grinned. "You know my fee."

I hung my head. "I'll play the role. If it hides me, I'll do it." What worried me was keeping Garth from understanding what had happened. I couldn't shout about potatoes every time someone started to utter the name of the play.

Dagonet clapped. "Excelsior! We'll do a lunch show tomorrow and two in the evening!"

"Just as long as we make our way to Hanbury." I was determined to solve Lord Tark's murder and then scurry back to Tomelac, praying it would be the end of Garth's apprenticeship.

"Hanbury? We've discussed this. My theater won't last a day there. No money to be made, and without money we don't eat."

"Maybe you'll be the first to break through to them," I offered.

Dagonet glowered. "Hanbury hates theater almost as much as Tomelac does. The important cities never have room for our acts."

I began to understand. "You know, maybe you don't have to perform *The Calamities of Ulder* every time."

"And what about *The Pushy Pendragons?* Should we stop doing that one, too? What about *The Deal with the Sídhe Devil? The Bare-Naked Lady of the Lake?*"

"I don't think I've seen that last one."

"You know very well that it's not art if it doesn't offend the rich!"

"Well, it's their pockets you want to get into. Surely you've got a play that won't offend anyone in Hanbury."

His chin lifted in an arrogant manner that is rarely employed by anyone who has not called themself an artist. "Get used to Barton. We'll be here for a while."

"What good is offending the rich if they aren't around to be offended?"

We slowly turned to realize that Garth had been the one to say those words.

Dagonet stammered. "What do you mean?"

Garth finally stepped out of his costume and stood before us in his small clothes. "I'm from Tomelac, and I've never heard of your plays. You said they're for offending rich people, right? But doesn't that mean you have to actually have rich people in your audience? Otherwise, your play isn't offending anyone."

I crossed my arms in satisfaction, feeling a bit of pride toward my pupil. Dagonet's face fell as he realized Garth, of all people, had found a chink in his armor.

Dagonet sniffed arrogantly. "We'll drop you off. I'm not entering that city as long as I live, but we'll perform in every nearby town until Hanbury's rich and famous are a laughingstock across the countryside."

CHAPTER TWENTY-ONE

SHE WAS WAITING FOR ME, a few towns later.

Garth and I hid with Dagonet's acting troupe for several days, putting on plays and blending in with the actors, and we had gotten pretty good at our parts by the time we rolled into the little town of Clement, the last stop before Hanbury.

Even though the sun was starting to set, Dagonet insisted we squeeze in a performance. It had been more than a day since we'd seen any sign of the Abrecans on our tail, so we were all taken by surprise when their wagons rolled into town while we were setting up.

"Is it the same caravans?" Garth asked, getting his feathers into place.

"Hmm." I pondered Garth's surprisingly good question while struggling with my wig. "This might be a different group. No one knows how many Abrecans there are. Oh, bother—the clips have come loose again." I was distracted by the idea of the Abrecans coordinating their efforts across the countryside. They could cover a lot of ground if they were well organized.

"Should we even perform?" asked Garth, who, at last, had developed a sense of fear.

"We *must* perform." I pulled on the boots that added three inches to my height. "If we run, we'll look scared, and every predator can smell fear. They need to think we're just another traveling crew."

Dagonet mumbled something about not being "just another" anything.

Wendy fiddled with the straps on the front of her bird costume. "What are you two talking about?"

"Wendy, you've got that backward," Dagonet droned. "The straps go in the back."

She dropped her hands. "Not again."

A long sigh from Garth told me he'd been losing the same battle.

Through a dirty window in the dressing caravan, I saw the Abrecans roll by. One after another, three large carriages slugged their way through the small town.

"Did any of them stop?" asked Dagonet.

"No..." I watched them pass by without so much as glancing our way. "I guess they've given up on finding us with you."

"Then let's enjoy ourselves!" He clamped my shoulders. "The women of this town have a wonderful tradition that I know you're going to *love!*"

I glared at him, quite certain I wasn't going to like it at all.

The eggs found my face on the first try. Garth and Wendy were getting better.

Clement was built on uneven ground where rocks jutted out all over the place. The city always seemed to be saying, "Oh, you were trying to walk? Here, have some dirt." This meant we couldn't use the stage, which required opening up two of Dagonet's caravans, each revealing half of the stage, and linking them together, because the rocky ground made it impossible to get the wheels into place.

The crowd didn't mind watching us act from the ground right in front of them. I think they were accustomed to it. When we would normally leave the stage by slipping through a curtain, we simply dashed behind the carriages that we'd parked around in a half-circle. It felt unprofessional, but the locals were just happy to see a play.

But I hadn't anticipated the effect this would have on the last act.

Once I rubbed the yolk from my eyes, I saw a few ladies get to their feet. I assumed more rotten food was headed for me, but none of them were holding any. I blinked away another bit of runny egg and suddenly a woman was standing directly in front of me. She slapped me across the face, hard, and I think someone in Tomelac could have heard the *clap* even if they were in Ulder's vault.

I know how to take a hit. I've known that ever since the day Petunia, the castle gardener, caught me relieving myself on her prized rosebushes. (It was her fault. The previous day, I'd returned from one of my trips to discover bats hanging from my ceiling, drawn there by plants she had snuck in while I was away. It was the guano that hurt my feelings most.)

The next woman slapped the other cheek. After that, two ladies held me in place while someone's great grandmother stabbed me in the belly with a crooked cane. I had no idea what Ulder had done to irritate these women, but I was paying for it in spades.

The misty-eyed woman was next.

She wore a plunging neckline and a long skirt—the very image of a countryside tavern wench. I marveled at her ability to slip into this new role as easily as I would have changed costumes backstage. As I shook eggshells from my wig, I realized she had, once again, caught me at a disadvantage.

Laughing as she walked, she threw up a slender hand. The crowd grew quiet in anticipation—but I knew the telltale signs of misdirection. In a flash, her other hand pulled a square of paper from her bosom and crammed it into my shirt pocket.

Before I could reach for the note, she spun me around by my shoulders and used one of her tall leather boots to kick me in the rear. "Rejoice, good people!" she shouted, as I stumbled away, "and take a good look at your king!"

She didn't even get the line right.

Chapter Twenty-Two

"What's it say?" Behind the stage, Garth pointed at the note in my hand.

"I don't know." I stared at the paper, which was still neatly folded. "And I don't think I *want* to know." That was a lie.

"Wasn't she the same woman we saw at the privies?"

"Yes." Unlike Garth, I knew that her presence could only mean trouble. I threw the note away onto the grass, vowing not to be a victim of her charms. "Dagonet, Wart and I need to run."

Dagonet was already removing my wig and donning it on his own head. "Well, Hanbury is only a day away. I suppose you'll make it on your own. Take off your pants!"

"No time! Garth, how quick can you get out of that costume?"

"Wendy's gotten pretty good at it. Watch this!"

She appeared behind Garth and tugged on his toggles. After one dramatic, swooping motion, Garth stood proud while the yellow bird suit fell to the ground.

I averted my eyes. "You...didn't see a need wear your small clothes under there?"

"That's why it's so fast now! My small clothes made it too tight—"

"Garth." I took a wig from a bust and pulled it down on his head. A decent enough disguise. "We're in trouble, so put on something. Anything. I'll make sure the roads are clear while you wake our carriage driver."

The carriage was currently parked in the grass, far behind the makeshift stage. Geltrude had shown no interest in seeing the performance more than once.

He pointed to the paper I'd thrown aside. "Aren't you at least going to read what she said?"

I shot him a glance that put the fear of his mother into him. Garth looked like he might argue, but instead he pulled on his small clothes, breeches, and tunic in what must have been record time. If nothing else, the actor's life had taught him the art of the quick change.

While he hastily put his shoes on the wrong feet, I glanced out from behind the caravans and looked up and down the main road, seeing nothing. The way to Hanbury was clear.

On the other side, the people of Clement were cheering as the actors took their bows. Part of me quietly lamented that Dagonet was bowing my place. Genius is never appreciated.

My thoughts were interrupted by the creaks and groans of our pitiful carriage shambling over a few stones as it made its way onto the road, just past the makeshift stage. I grabbed a wide-brimmed hat from the costume rack and scrambled toward the carriage with my head down, hoping no one could see my face as I opened the side door and climbed in next to Garth.

The moment my door closed, I heard the reins crack and felt the wheels kick into motion. "We'll drive through the night and ride straight into the big gate of Hanbury." I swept off my hat and smiled at Garth. "Well done, your majesty. You made quick work of my instructions."

"So...why didn't you read her note?"

"I'm not so simple as to fall for a woman's charms," I explained. Truth be told, I was trying not to think about how well the barmaid outfit had suited her. "That note was surely a trick. There's a good reason your father told you not to fall in love. Take my word for it, Garth, love will turn your brain into oatmeal, and with an oatmeal brain you'll never make a smart decision again. Women like her just want to trap you in their web."

"Sometimes...I think it might be nice to be caught in a woman's web."

I shook my head. "Women are nothing but trouble, Garth. Besides, when did you become a romantic?"

"Last night, when I was watching the stars with Wendy—"

The driver, who apparently understood our haste, cracked the reins harder than before. Garth and I threw up our hands for balance as the carriage bounced over a hole.

I heard the floorboards under me creak in protest as we took a sharp turn while a wheel on the other side momentarily lifted off the ground. Going this fast, we would surely draw attention.

"Garth, did you tell our driver we were in a hurry?"

"No, but I remember he told me it would be a short trip."

I shrugged. At least we would make good time, and the Abrecans couldn't bother us once we were in the city. Hoping to get a bit of sleep, I leaned back and pulled the hat down over my eyes. "Well, it sounds like...everything is..."

Like a mad courier rushing down a hallway with an important letter, a rather crucial observation made its way from the back of my thoughts.

I shot up, wild-eyed, and grabbed Garth by the shoulders. "*HE?*"

CHAPTER TWENTY-THREE

I CONSIDERED that perhaps none of Garth's tutors had taught him about the birds and the bees.

"Garth, our driver is a *woman*!" I screamed. "Don't you remember Geltrude?" I clawed at the small sliding door in front of us, but it wouldn't budge. "Do you mean to tell me there's a *man* driving our carriage and you didn't think that was suspicious?"

The carriage rolled faster and faster, barely holding itself together over the bumpy road.

Garth struggled with the door handle. "He said he was our new driver. Da's drivers change all the time!"

"Well, that's just brilliant, you idiot."

"If he's not our driver, then what was he doing there?"

"Trying to kill us, you stupid, stupid—"

"You can't talk to me like that! I'm the prince!"

"I'm the prince! I'm the prince! You be sure to tell that to the first person we meet on the other side, you useless—"

"You're not supposed to make fun of the prince! I'll have you—"

The carriage made a hard turn that threw Garth's body onto mine. "You'll have me what?" I pushed him away. "I know—lock me in the stocks! Burn me alive! Go ahead and threaten whatever you want. Just be sure to enjoy it—because we're about to die!"

I finally forced open the tiny window just in time to see a man leap from the driver's seat. A small part of my mind wondered why the horses weren't stopping on their own. A very long, downhill path appeared in front of us.

"Do you think this has anything to do with that woman?"

"Of course it does!" I tried my door, but someone must have tampered with it. The hinges didn't budge.

"Maybe you should read her message."

"I threw it away, Garth."

"About that..." Struggling in the shaking wagon, Garth reached into his pocket and produced her note.

"For crying out loud." After a few tries, I managed to grab the letter from his bouncing hand and open it.

ERLIN, DON'T USE THE CARRIAGE. ESCANOR'S POISONED YOUR HORSES AND HE'S WAITING FOR YOU AT—

Our runaway carriage hit a stone and the letter fluttered out of my grasp. The impact threw us upward and our heads hit the ceiling, making a crack in the thin boards overhead.

That gave me an idea.

For once, the cheapness of our rickety wagon would work in our favor.

"Get up!" There wasn't room to stand, but we got to our feet and hunched over with our shoulders touching the top of the cabin. "Up!" I ordered.

He understood. Together, we pushed against the overhead beams until a board creaked and snapped in half. Both pieces fell between us, exposing the blue sky and fast-moving tree branches. I stood tall and worked my way out of the hole we had made in the carriage roof, ducking under flying leaves as I wormed my way onto my belly.

Glancing down, I could see the reins resting in the driver's seat. Our saboteur had simply let go of them before leaping away, and the leather straps had gracefully fallen around one of the knobs.

There wasn't time to think. I reached down and found I could nearly grab them, so I stretched further, barely balanced on the shaky roof.

Up ahead, I noticed the gigantic hole in the road just before the horses stumbled through it. The carriage threw me forward.

The ground rushed up to meet me.

"Erlin!"

Garth's thick fingers gripped my ankle. With him as my anchor, the two of us tumbled over the top and fell into the driver's seat. I landed on my side, barely able to keep from rolling off, while Garth was nearly in a sitting position.

Miraculously, the reins were in my hand.

"Here..." I handed them to Garth while I tried to sit up.

Garth took the reins and pulled back, gritting his teeth, but the maddened horses continued their thundering race down the slippery hill.

"Maybe if I only pull to the right we can make that turn..."

"What turn?" I managed to sit up and finally noticed we were heading for a sharp curve, with nothing but a dense forest on all sides.

Garth tugged the reins. The horses' bloodshot eyes spoke of poison and fear. I was ready to jump for it when the horses actually responded and tilted our course a bit to the right. If Garth kept going, we could actually just turn in time to avoid—

Something moved in the road, just around the corner.

Without thinking, I snatched the reins and pulled back as hard as I could.

The enraged horses rebelled by running in different directions and snapping their harnesses, demonstrating that they had only been dragging us along as a courtesy. Both horses disappeared into the woods.

For a quiet moment, physics prevailed and the horseless carriage continued down the hill.

We didn't have long to appreciate the spectacle. The broken end of the wagon tongue, succumbing to gravity, fell and planted itself on the ground. I made eye contact with Garth just as the cabin flipped forward and hurled us into the air.

After a short flight, I landed hard in the middle of the road and realized that the shadow passing over me was the carriage itself, blocking out the sun as it tumbled overhead.

I curled into a defensive ball. The carriage continued until its glorious flight was interrupted by a tree. It smashed into a thousand splinters that rained on Garth as he was just getting to his feet.

In the silenced woods, we stood and admired the wreck. Tiny pieces of the carriage were spread in every direction, and the horses were long gone.

"Why'd you do that?" asked Garth. "I could have steered us around!"

"Yes. I think you could have." I turned down the path, where it curved to the right, and pointed. "But you would have hit them."

In the middle of the rough path, oblivious to the surrounding drama, half a dozen baby ducks were gathered in a puddle.

Chapter Twenty-Four

"Ducks?"

I motioned for him to walk with me. Hanbury was a brief ride but a long walk, and it was already getting dark. "Yes. Ducks."

Not very appreciative ones, I might add. We walked past and they didn't even look our way. Not a *Thanks for not running us over,* or a *Nice of you to almost kill the crown prince to save us.* Nothing.

"They're just ducks!" Garth had never been mad at me, but he was getting close to it now.

"I know." I had acted on instinct when I grabbed the reins. Looking back, it seemed like a dumb thing to do.

"We might have missed them completely! They could have been safe, and we'd still have a carriage with two horses!"

"And your potatoes."

I thought it was a funny thing to say, but Garth's eyes grew wide and he ran back to the site of our spectacular crash. I slouched after and watched him pick through the forest floor.

"Help me find them!" he said. "I paid a lot for those potatoes! I never got to try a throwing potato."

I wanted to finally explain that potatoes didn't work that way, but he was already mad at me, so I relented and followed him through the trees.

We walked through the forest, gazing at the ground. Potatoes, if you never noticed, look a lot like dirt.

"They're just ducks!" Garth picked up a potato and added it to his bag. We had already found quite a few.

"I know they're only ducks, Garth. I know very well what a duck is." I nearly stepped on a potato. I picked it up and approached him, dropping it in the bag. "And we could have killed them."

"You risk our lives...for a few baby animals?"

"Admittedly, it may not have been smart. I did it without thinking." Finally, I understood it myself. "Garth, preserving life is important. I don't like killing things, and I supposed I've developed a habit of trying not to be responsible for anyone's death. It's a good habit..."

I paused. Garth, bent over with his hand on a potato, looked at me and froze. I had misspoken.

As far as anyone knew, I was pretty good at killing people. Wizard, warlocks, and witches all died at my hand if they weren't carted off by the Inquisitors Guild (which also didn't exist outside of my stories).

Garth studied me. The gears in his head may have been rusty, but they were turning. Yes, Garth was simple, but I was realizing that his mind could grasp just about anything as long as he had enough time to think about it.

I held up a finger. Garth saw the warning in my eye and held still, for which I was thankful.

Behind us, near the road, we heard the unmistakable sound of wagon wheels.

Garth's eyes flared.

Frowning, I pointed deeper into the forest.

We rushed past trees, stumbling over roots and rocks, trying to get away from the sounds, but our footprints, I realized, had been left all around the wreckage.

"They're this way," came a voice from behind, confirming my fear. Someone was chasing us.

I noticed we were leaving large footprints and whispered, "Don't step on the ground!" Garth furrowed his brow, so I demonstrated by stepping on one of the large tree roots and then onto an old log. The forest floor was littered with enough stones and branches for us to make our way without leaving much of a trail.

The sounds behind us still grew louder. I glanced back and counted at least ten men blundering their way through the trees, but they were still too far away to see us clearly. Probably.

Since neither of us were athletes, Garth and I were soon panting, barely keeping our balance on shaky steps. I motioned for him to stand in front of a large tree while I stood in front of another. We caught our breath, out of sight from our pursuers, but also out of ideas.

Our pursuers slowed down when they reached the place where our footprints stopped. I heard them yelling in confusion. Glancing back, I could tell they were still advancing, albeit much slower.

As night fell, the mist rose through the forest.

Garth looked my way. He had a determined look on his face, and I knew we were both thinking that our only chance was to run for it, hoping to hide in the mist, but then my heart sank at the sound of riders coming from directly ahead of us.

Shaking my head in defeat, I watched a handful of women on horseback emerge through the curling tendrils of fog, wearing leather breeches and effortlessly making their way through the trees atop black horses.

And, of course, in the lead was the woman I'd been trying not to think about.

She gracefully pushed her horse along the mossy ground, staring at me with those mysterious eyes that seemed to know everything. I didn't even know her name. She led a second mount, a paint horse with a white splotch on its face, and even it moved with practiced grace.

The mist-eyed woman looked to Garth, and then to me, well aware she held our fate in her hands. Garth and I held our breath as Abrecans approached from both sides.

She then looked beyond me, toward our pursuers, and said, "There's no one over here."

The men behind us muttered as their footsteps faded away. I looked up at her with as much thankfulness as I could muster.

When the men were well out of earshot, the misty-eyed woman rode near to Garth and handed him the reins to the paint horse. "Can you ride, young Wart?"

"'Course I can!"

In a dizzying display of near competency, Garth approached the horse in the wrong direction, placed his foot in the stirrup, and plopped himself into the saddle, facing backward.

"That happens every time." He slapped the horse's rump, which was right in front of him. "I should get down and—"

The horse galloped away while Garth clutched at its backside.

"That's...not going to end well," I said, trying to watch where he went.

"Abrecan horses are the most well-trained in the world," she said. "Mollie will take him to our camp. Now climb up."

She reached down, and I realized she meant for me to ride behind her. For a moment I wondered if I could get there gracefully, but then I remembered I was following Garth's act and that no amount of clumsiness would be noticed. With her help, I climbed atop the sleek mount and settled in awkwardly behind the saddle. Behind her.

"Hang on," she said.

To what? I felt like I was supposed to wrap my arms around her for balance, but the thought of it made me feel like a shy child. Not to mention, I wasn't sure if we were being rescued or kidnapped. Being close to her was turning my brain into oatmeal.

Before I could figure anything out, she clicked her tongue and spurred the horse into a trot.

I wobbled and wavered the entire way, never quite sure what to do with my hands.

Chapter Twenty-Five

I GRIPPED THE BACK OF THE SADDLE with my fingertips to keep my balance. We rode silently through dark trees alongside the other riders, occasionally glimpsing Garth ahead of us. To his credit, he hadn't fallen off.

Which was nearly more than I could say for myself.

When her black stallion took an unexpected turn, I leaned the wrong way and tilted toward the ground. I grabbed wildly at the saddle and slowly pulled myself back up.

"What are you doing?" she asked.

"Saw a four-leafed clover back there," I said with as much confidence as I could fake.

"If this is your first time, just say so."

"Don't be ridiculous. I'm just superstitious."

That raised one of her eyebrows, but she shook her head and focused on the path. "Watch out!" A stray branch emerged through the moonlight, and she ducked under it.

My eyes widened at the sight of the oncoming branch. Lacking any useful sort of reflexes, I closed my eyes and threw up my hands, knocking the branch down.

"You've never done this before," she said, adjusting her legs. "Just admit it."

"Of course I have."

"Just never back there?"

"Well, this *is* the first time anyone's asked me to do it this way."

"At least you've got a tight grip on the rump. Not everyone does that on the first try."

I took some pride in that. "How much longer?"

"Nearly there. Are you getting tired?"

"No, I'm fine. Like you said, I've got a good grip on the...uh, rump."

"Just put your arms around me, stupid."

Trying not to appear eager, I wrapped my arms around the woman I'd been thinking about every time I closed my eyes.

She whipped the reins and I held tight. Her steed carried us through a break in the trees into a wide, open field. In my pocket, I felt her earring press against my leg. I wondered if I would ever find a way to return it to her, or if it would remain with me, a part of her I always kept.

We rode over a grassy hill covered in dew that glistened in the moonlight and descended upon a camp surrounded by Abrecan caravans. Tall leather tents pointed their tops toward the stars. On one end, several horses were tied to a series of low-hanging branches of an ancient tree.

And at the base of that tree lay Garth, shaking his dizzy head as he sat up.

We rode to him, and I made an idiot of myself attempting to get down. I've long believed horses to be untrustworthy. This one stepped forward just as I was pushing myself off, forcing me to land on two shaky feet, arms akimbo.

Garth, half-standing, reached for my wavering hand, thinking I was trying to help him up. "Thanks."

"Garth, no—"

He grabbed my hand and both of us fell, tangled up in one another.

"It's hard to believe someone's trying to kill you." The misty-eyed women tied up the horses in a series of quick motions. "Seems like it would be easier to ask both of you to fetch water and see how long it takes for you to fall down the well."

I pointed a finger back at her and opened my mouth to protest...but she had a point.

I heard her gasp as a series of anxious noises traveled through the camp, along with the sound of wagon wheels approaching.

"Get up!" she hissed. "Escanor's coming!"

That name again. Escanor. The fear in her voice made Garth and I jump to our feet.

"My tent!" She rushed us to the other side of the camp and threw open a tent flap. "Now! And don't make a sound!"

The tent was large enough to stand in. We walked inside and watched her pull the flap shut and wind together the wooden toggles that held it tight.

"Keep quiet." She rummaged through a bag and produced a long skirt, then shot us a penetrating glance. "Well?" She pointed past us. "Turn around!"

Apologizing, we spun the other way like chastised children while she changed out of her riding clothes.

Something wasn't right. I tapped my foot on the bare ground and tried to focus.

My instincts were telling me I was overlooking something important, but I couldn't put my finger on it. While I should have been concerned about being in the enemy camp, or fully distracted by the beautiful woman behind me, something else tugged at my mind that I couldn't develop into a full-blown thought.

"Does Escanor make camp here?" I asked, trying to return to a practical matter.

"No," she huffed. "I think he's just stopping by to see if...well, to see if we've found you. You can turn around now." She was peering through a gap in the tent flaps, wearing the long skirt. "Escanor's going to talk to the men around the fire, then he'll look around and leave. He won't enter any tents without good reason, so just keep quiet."

Escanor. The name burned in my mind. I have a terrible memory for names, but I had a feeling he was going to be a very important person in my life.

I snapped my finger as the lingering thought finally made its way to the surface. "Where do you sleep?"

"What?" She spun around so quickly the skirt rose like a cloud as the hem circled her bare feet.

I gestured around the tent. It was filled with clothing and supplies, but the ground was mostly bare.

"Oh!" She tucked her hair behind her ears and smiled big. Too big. "I...must have forgotten to set out my bedroll! Busy night and all."

I'd like to tell you I figured out what was going on at this point. I'd like to tell you I followed my suspicion to its logical conclusion and understood the danger I was in.

I'd like to tell you that, but there were too many thoughts rushing through my mind for me to focus on any single problem. For example, I didn't know if we were being rescued or if this was what it looked like to be kidnapped. I had no idea where we were or how we would we get to Hanbury. And my eyes kept darting to the leather breeches she'd tossed aside.

"I have to go out there." She began undoing the toggles that held the tent flap. "Stay here and don't move."

"Ma'am?" Garth's voice was as quiet as a mouse.

She stopped her work and turned to him.

"Thank you," he said, looking flustered. "Other than my mother—and Erlin—no one's ever been nice to me before."

That surprised me. Garth had spent his life in the lap of luxury, surrounded by servants. Apparently, he could tell the difference between hired help and people who actually wanted to help him.

I saw pride in her eyes when she made a slight bow and said, "My name is Morrigin." She slipped into the night, closing the tent behind her.

Morrigin.

I made sure to remember that name, too.

CHAPTER TWENTY-SIX

INSIDE THE TENT, we heard the visiting wagons roll into the camp.

I had wanted to keep the tent flaps completely shut, stay quiet, and wait out the night as Morrigin had asked, but once we heard the sound of horse hooves and jangling reins, Garth and I couldn't keep ourselves from peeking out.

The new wagons parked at the edge of the campsite. I was glad to see they didn't unhitch their horses, because it meant they weren't staying long.

The first to enter the camp was Escanor, the broad, mustached man who'd already tried to kill Garth twice. He strolled into the middle of everyone and began chatting with the men sitting around the fire. Their conversation had an air of familiarity, but it was obvious they didn't know each other. It was more like watching soldiers who wore the same uniforms but had never met.

Not much was known of the Abrecans. I'd always assumed they were a tight-knit organization, but the group Morrigin traveled with didn't appear to have anything to do with Escanor or his companions.

Morrigin, in her long, flowered skirt, tended to the fire and poured coffee into the men's cups, always keeping her eyes low. I wondered if Escanor could tell she was listening to his every word.

After his visit had gone on for an hour, Escanor swept his eyes across the camp. He settled his gaze on every tent for a few moments. When he looked at us, I put a hand on Garth's shoulder for him to be quiet. Neither of us breathed until he shifted his eyes to the next tent.

When he'd looked everywhere, Escanor threw his coffee into the fire and left. "If you find them, kill them!" was all he said.

###

With him gone, I felt a tiredness seep into me. Garth yawned and stretched.

It seemed impossible, but Garth and I eventually settled into the lumpy ground and fell asleep. When we awoke, there was no sign of Morrigin or her possessions.

In fact, there was no sign of anyone.

Wagon wheels woke us from our slumber. Garth and I sat up at the same time, realizing in our sleep we had drifted toward one another for warmth. Avoiding eye contact, we rose to our feet and looked through the tent flap.

"Did you notice if Morrigin ever came back?" I whispered.

Grath rubbed his eyes. "If she did, I never noticed. Maybe she slept somewhere else."

"Doubt it."

I swept open the tent flap and showed him the empty grassland that spread out before us. Now that the sun was out, we could easily see the walls of Hanbury rising in the distance.

"Did *you* hear them leave?" he asked.

"No...wait. I hear someone coming."

We held still and listened. We'd grown accustomed to listening for horses and wagons, and we both knew a few large vehicles were headed our way.

The wagon wheels stopped somewhere out of sight, but very close by, and then a high-pitched man's voice broke the silence.

"Erlin? Oh, Erlin? The show must go on!"

Dagonet? I wondered if he would go away if we stayed quiet.

Garth jumped to his feet. "Wendy?" In a mad dash, he ran past me and tripped over the tent entrance, landing on his face.

I approached the caravan and sized up Dagonet. "How did you know we were in there?"

"That woman told me."

"Woman?" I asked. "I don't know anyone out here."

"Of course you don't!" Nearly cackling, he climbed down from the driver's seat. "Just like you haven't been looking for anyone's face in the front row. You can't lie to me."

I needed to change the subject, but I also needed to know what had happened. "So...this woman, whoever she is, came to you? While we slept?"

"Must have ridden all night. Told us exactly where to find you. Smart woman."

An urgent thought occurred to me. "Geltrude!"

"Is that her name? She told me it was Morrigin."

"No. Our carriage driver was named Geltrude."

"One of my actors saw her take a ride back to Tomelac after talking to a strange man."

I rubbed my chin. Escanor hadn't killed her, just convinced her she'd been called back home, or replaced with a new driver. There was nothing unusual about replacing drivers on long trips, and the Abrecans were certainly clever enough for a forgery.

"Now!" Dagonet rubbed his hands together. "About this woman."

"I've got to be in Hanbury. *Days* ago, Dagonet."

"It's just over the rise, but the Abrecans are camped out there."

Which ones? I climbed up into the driver's seat and stood tall on the bench. From there, I could see a few Abrecan caravans parked near the main gate. Men in leather vests, patiently smoking long pipes, watched everyone coming and going.

"Why aren't they in the city?" I asked.

"They're not allowed," said Dagonet from below. "Merchant's guild in Hanbury is quite strict. But don't worry, we'll get you in. Just sit inside and we'll roll you through the gate!"

So many things were wrong. The Abrecans would recognize Dagonet's crew and realize we were inside. And it wouldn't be impossible for the Abrecans to sneak in a few men to come after us. But something else tugged at my mind.

"Dagonet. Why are you doing this? You promised never to set foot in that city."

"You convinced me, dear boy, to expand our services! The people of Hanbury need the cold slap in the face that only comes from true art!" He thrust a finger in the air. "Wearing words as our weapons and acting as our armor, we'll topple their pedestals and—"

"She's paying you, isn't she?"

"Boatloads."

CHAPTER TWENTY-SEVEN

GARTH VOLUNTEERED to take down the tent. Even though I was in a hurry to get inside Hanbury, I stopped to watch because I knew this would be a spectacle not to be missed.

Dagonet and I chewed on strips of bacon while Garth, inside the tent, took down the tall stick that held it up in the center, bringing everything down around him.

"Will you take the whole caravan in?" I asked, as Garth shouted something we couldn't hear.

"Just the two that make up the stage," said Dagonet.

The Garth-shaped lump under the collapsed tent crawled in a small circle.

I squinted at his progress. "Think it'll rain?"

The canvas wrapped around Garth's wriggling form, trapping him in a cocoon.

Dagonet began unraveling an orange. "Hopefully. We need it."

###

We helped Garth after the bacon was eaten.

Garth inquired after Wendy, but she was not with the company. Apparently, her family was wealthy and required her presence at important functions once in a while, in return for allowing her to travel with the actors. I asked Dagonet why she would bother living in a creaking caravan with countless others, piled onto each other at night and sharing bread scraps for dinner, but the question was lost on him. "Who *wouldn't* fly the banner of truth in the face of lies?" was all he could muster for a response.

Garth and I sat in the large wagon, pressed against the others. As the wheels moved and the caravan lurched, Garth gripped his precious burlap sack close.

No one stopped us as we rolled through the wide city gate.

I could tell Garth was disappointed to be hiding inside, where we couldn't see Hanbury's rising walls or the bright banners that fell from the top of the battlements all the way down to the grass. Royal blue, bearing images of fighting dragons. Riding into Hanbury was quite a spectacle.

Along with the big iron gate and the endless banners, I knew Abrecans were gathered around the entrance, watching everyone coming and going. I could feel their eyes on us as the creaking caravan rolled through.

A hand was extended toward me. I turned to see a young man with a peach fuzz half-beard leaning in my direction. "My name is Ywain." The lad seemed nervous. He held up an orange cat in the crook of his other arm. "And this Leo. We're big fans. Big fans!"

I shook his hand slowly. "Of...what exactly?"

"Of what!" Ywain looked at his tired companions, cramped inside the bouncing carriage, and then turned to poke me in the chest. "Of *you*, of course!"

"Of me!" I repeated, somehow already weary of this man. "Of course. It's always...nice. To meet a fan."

He sat next to me, shoving someone aside. "I saw you when I was young."

"That long ago?"

"You were magnificent!" Ywain swept his hand through the air. "You strolled along the stage with the grandeur and gravity of Ulder himself!"

Dear goodness, this man really was a fan. Of me.

Ywain continued. "Dagonet was preparing me for the roll before he found you in Barton."

I recalled Dagonet had been quite pleased to discover me. A little *too* pleased. The other actors shared amused glances, and I knew immediately that young Ywain was rich enough to help Dagonet pay his bills but not talented enough to have a speaking role.

"My father, the Duke, used to talk of Ulder as if he were a great man. He stormed out when we saw your play, but I knew that—finally—someone was telling me the truth!" The cat, Leo, thrashed around trying to escape. "With each word, you slayed Ulder's legacy." The cat took the opportunity to try and wiggle free, but Ywain's hold was too strong. "And when I saw you take your bows, that's when I knew...I wanted to be just like you."

"Wonderful." I slapped my knee. "Are we there, yet?"

"And when Dagonet told us that the Amazing Erlin had been found, I knew it was destiny!"

The wagon did not slow while it took a sharp turn. Costumes and wigs tumbled from over my head and covered the passengers on the other side. I'd rarely met an actor who could drive well.

"Well, I certainly hope I didn't steal your part."

"Steal it?" Ywain shook his head. "You *invented* it! And me!"

"Let's not get hasty."

"I watched the master at work in Barton. And now I'll watch him again, here in Hanbury!"

I held up a finger. "Ah, that's where you're wrong. Wart and I are finished with the theater for now."

Ywain backed away, his face turning pale. "You...you won't be with us anymore? But that..." His suddenly looked like a man watching a miracle happen. "Do you know what this means? It means *I* get to play the lead!"

I had, believe it or not, already puzzled that out. "Congratulations. Want to give me your best Ulder?"

"Huh?"

"Show me your impression. Let's run through a few lines of the play, young man."

"Really?" Ywain stood, grappling with Leo. "Yes, I'll just...run through a few lines." He cleared his throat. "It's a..." Ywain halted, his face filled with despair.

He looked at me with sincere apology as he tried to remember the play's opening line.

"Go ahead," I whispered.

He stood taller. "It's a...it's a..."

The other actors were covering their mouths to hide their laughter.

"Good..." I whispered. "It's a *good*..."

He nodded quickly and tried again. "It's a *good*..."

"Day..." I provided.

"It's a good *day*...ffff..."

I nodded encouragingly, mouthing out the next word.

"It's a good day f..." He watched my mouth move. "...or.... It's a good day for!"

"That's right," I said. "It's a good day for..." I gestured for him to continue.

"Oh, there's more." His eyes darted back and forth. "It's a good day for—"

The curtain behind us swept open. In the suspense of watching poor Ywain try to recite a single line, I hadn't noticed we'd stopped moving.

Dagonet stuck his head inside. "We're here! Time to unpack!"

"It's a good day for..." Poor Ywain was standing at the precipice of discovery when his cat leaped from his arms. Actors parted as it dashed out the back. Ywain, still muttering half of his line, ran into town after it.

Chapter Twenty-Eight

We piled out into a city square, complete with cobblestone streets and tall buildings on every side. Men and women hustled all around, like we'd entered a life-sized ant hill. Wars were fought from Tomelac, but any of the kingdom's official business that needed to be written down, thought through, or added up was handled in Hanbury. It was widely believed that anything that couldn't be screamed into submission—like facts and figures—should be kept away from King Ulder.

I stood next to Dagonet and stretched my back. "How did you get a spot in the town square?"

He grinned. "I didn't ask, dear boy."

I looked around. A few constables were already pointing fingers. "They'll take your show down in the blink of an eye."

"Nonsense. I've got a play about crooked lawmen that always throws off their confidence. Then I'll follow with a play about wealthy priests and another about accountants with sticky fingers. The important people will be offended, but not before I've drawn a crowd."

"Don't you have any nice plays?"

"My dear boy, art that does not offend is like a magic spell that doesn't work—just a bunch of silly words!"

He clapped his hands and the actors moved quicker, pushing the giant wagons into place. Dagonet was trying to get set up going before anyone had time to stop them.

"This one's a bit heavier than usual," said an actor, pointing to the wagon they were trying to push into place. "I think someone's still in there."

Dagonet glared at me, and I realized it *had* been awfully quiet since we arrived.

Sighing, I walked around to the back of the carriage and poked my head inside. "Garth, what are you doing?"

"Just looking around," he said. And he was. Garth stood in the center of the carriage, giving everything one last look. "Do you miss it?"

"Which part?" I gestured for him to get out. "Not getting paid? Sleeping ten to a room?"

Garth climbed down with difficulty, but only because he felt like he was leaving a part of himself behind. "All of it. I think this was special, being a bird in that play. You don't miss it at all?"

I didn't answer him. I also knew he was remembering his time with Wendy. The two of them had shared something special. I also believed the two of them shared a single brain cell.

Garth opened his potato sacked and poked around. "There it is." He pulled out the book we'd been reading. "I've been going over this every chance I get."

In all the excitement, I'd forgotten about the old book with the open eye on the cover. I hadn't thought about The Restless Ones in days.

We walked back to Dagonet, and I shook his hand. "Goodbye for now, friend...you *do* know these snobs will eventually find a way to run you out of town, right?"

Dagonet beamed. "I wouldn't have it any other way."

###

"Are we going to investigate Lord Tark's body now?" said Garth, hoisting his burlap sack over his shoulder.

"I don't think we'll see him," I said. "I'm sure they've buried him."

When we'd first run into Dagonet and his company, I had bemoaned the sudden lapse in our schedule. This trip with Garth was more dangerous to me the longer it lasted, and I had every intention of getting it over with as soon as possible. But eventually I realized that being held up by the Abrecans was going to play right into my hands.

Even though I'd been on a few actual cases, my work never often amounted to more than pretending to solve a problem that had never existed. After being told silly magic was responsible for their problems, people will believe silly magic was the answer. So once the terrible rains stopped, or the cattle plagues killed off their last bull, or the barrel of tasteless ale finally ran out, the people had no trouble believing the problem had been solved by the herbs I had them hang over their doors or the shapes I had them paint onto their cows. It never occurred to them that the problem had simply run its course. (Or that I had stayed up late and valiantly drank the last drop of their sour ale.)

And by the time Dagonet rolled us into Hanbury, I was certain the rumors of Tark's death would have been replaced by more recent, juicier gossip. A murdered lord would be talked about for years, of course, especially one killed in such a dramatic fashion, but the mystery surely was stale by now. All I needed to do was spin a story explaining there was nothing to worry about. I could tell them I'd found the Restless on the road and dealt with them, or that I'd stolen one of their own magic artifacts and used it to banish them from the countryside. So long as Garth was out of earshot when I spun my lie, I might even be able to get back to Tomelac with my reputation intact and Garth none the wiser about my deception. I was a few lies away from returning to my old life.

A girl, barely ten, ran toward us. Across her chest was a purple sash. "A herald," I said to Garth. "They're still expecting us after all this time." That didn't bode well.

"Are you here to see the dead body?" she asked, with the excitement one normally only sees on a child's face on their name day.

I knelt down to speak with her. "Are you Lord Tark's herald?"

She nodded. "I'm Lily. Are you the *ink visitor*?"

"Inquisitor," I corrected. "Who are you?"

She planted tiny fists on her hips. "Lady Broom sent me. So, are you here to see the body or not?"

Lady Broom was the wife of Lord Tark, and I assumed she had been running the city since Tark's murder. "The dead body. Yes, that's why—" Before I could continue, I realized something was afoot. "Little girl, how did you know I was the inquisitor?"

"That was easy," said Lily. "Lady Broom told me to look for a stupid boy and a pretentious man."

I glanced back at Garth to see if he registered the insult.

He clapped my shoulder. "Sorry, Erlin, but she's right about me. I do like to pretend."

Lily pulled on my hand. "Come on! They said I couldn't see the body until you came."

"Little girl!" I found myself pulled along the cobblestone street. "Surely Tark's body is lain to rest by now." I couldn't imagine, after all this time, it was in a state to be investigated.

"Not him!" she said, shaking her head at me. "They killed Lady Broom this morning!"

Chapter Twenty-Nine

I was vaguely aware of the little girl tugging on my hand, but at that moment a parade of bulls could have flattened me and I would barely have noticed.

First Lord Tark. Now his wife.

As I stood petrified in the center of a busy street, I felt a dark pulse running through the people of Hanbury, caught the cold chill of their words and the sharp sibilance of the same name on every tongue: "The Restless Ones."

It was like a veil had been removed to reveal the fear that shuddered through the city. The Lord and Lady were murdered. Hanbury was in disarray. Someone was trying to destabilize the country, and I'd just led the crown prince right into the middle of it.

Not that anyone would be able to tell. His shirt was on backward, and he was eying a potato that had a finger-length growth on the end.

"Would you eat that?" he asked. "I mean, if it was served to you?"

Until now, I had been certain that Garth's staggering, stammering, and general inability to appear wiser than a potted plant would ensure our safety, but here in Hanbury I was no longer sure. News travels slowly in the countryside, and gossip about royals rarely makes it far past the city gates, but in a major city like Hanbury it was very possible that someone would recognize him.

"Are you *coming?*" said Lily, tugging on my arm. "My brother's a page, too, only *he* got to see Lord Tark before they took him down, and if we don't hurry, Lady Broom won't even be runny anymore!"

"I don't give a flying Dutchman!" I finally shook her hand free and made a shooing motion. "I know the way, Lily. Go tell Lord...Lady...oh, bother, go tell whoever's in charge that I'll be there shortly. With my new apprentice, Wart."

Frowning, Lily stomped away from us.

I needed to think, and as usual I was going to have to do the thinking for both of us. Luckily, I spied a shop not far down the road with a sign that read *Odd 'n' Ends*. I dragged Garth inside, where we were no longer surrounded by passersby who might all be assassins.

Away from the bustling streets, I felt a bit of clarity in my mind. I'd always preferred dark rooms for thinking. Not much light penetrated the little shop, which I understood as a trick to make sure the low-quality wares were not easy to see. The store surely had a strict policy on returns.

There was only one thing I was certain we'd need. I glanced up and down the rows of goods and didn't see it, so I approached the shopkeeper, a burly man who glared over a tall counter as if he were sizing me up for a wrestling match.

"Good man, I need a bucket," I announced.

"Three copper," he said, barely moving.

"Three?" I was planning to pay only two. I suspected he was planning to receive only two. We could have agreed on this out loud without the needed for verbal combat, but it was the way of commerce to lie while silently agreeing. "Can I at least see the bucket first?"

"Why? It's a bucket. You never seen one before?"

"How do I know it doesn't have a hole in the bottom?"

"Cuz if it had a hole in the bottom, I'd call it a water clock and charge triple."

He had me there. But I had him, too. "I'd pay three coppers for a nice bucket, but if I can't look at it then it's a gamble. Two coppers."

His hands pressed against the counter, as if his mind were grasping for a precipice, but we had reached the logical end of our discourse. Trying not to smile, I reached into my pocket and dug out a pair of coins.

The shopkeeper grunted. "Not sure why you need a bucket. Got bigger things to worry about with the Restless walking around here. Don't look at me that way, smart boy, I've seen 'em."

"You've seen the Restless?" Garth blurted out, entering the conversation with the grace of a collapsing building.

"'Course!" The shopkeeper disappeared into the back room. "Can't miss 'em."

"Garth," I whispered, "what are you—"

"Dark eyes?" Garth shouted.

"Sure enough." The shopkeeper replied from the back. "Dark as night."

I squeezed Garth's shoulder. "The Restless don't have—"

"And bats?" shouted Garth. "You saw bats? In swarms?"

"Naturally." The shopkeeper emerged. "A big batch of bats covered the moon just last night."

He handed the bucket to me, and I silently reached for the handle. My eyes were on Garth, who was stroking his chin.

Garth leaned over the counter. "And I assume you heard them speaking in an unknown tongue?"

The shopkeeper nodded slowly and then leaned his face close to ours. "The coldest, darkest tongue you ever heard."

"That'll do." Garth turned away. "Come on, Erlin!"

###

"What do we need a bucket for?" asked Garth when we were outside.

"All in good time." I was still trying to make sense of his questions about the Restless. "What was that all about? Black eyes and bats? Speaking strange languages?"

"He was lying!" said Garth. He reached into his burlap sack, dug around for a few moments, and then triumphantly pulled out the old book. "There's nothing in here about dark eyes. Or bats! Or any of it!"

"Then why did you bother that poor man?"

"To see if he was lying! Remember that time you told me that everyone's always lying?"

I nodded. In truth, I had no memory of saying that, but it certainly sounded like me.

Garth continued. "Well, I wondered if he was telling the truth, so I made all of that up to see if he would agree with me. It was like the play you were in. Remember? The one about the king?"

Until traveling with Garth, I hadn't noticed the play didn't often refer to the King by name. The title, *The Calamities of King Ulder*, was common knowledge, but Garth didn't possess any common knowledge.

"Yes," I said. "I remember that play."

"Well, there was a scene where the king is fooled into marrying a dog because everyone convinced him it was a rich queen who was famous for shapeshifting. Remember how the king went along with it so he wouldn't look stupid? It's like that. I wanted to see if the shopkeeper was lying."

I guided us around the next corner toward the Tark Manor, where the Lord and Lady of Hanbury lived. Or where they *had* lived until recently.

"Garth, that's...remarkable. You went to a play and learned something."

"I didn't understand all of it." Garth stowed the book back inside his bag. "But when I wore that costume and stood at the edge of the stage, it was like

I was watching my own life from up high. It looked different."

Just then, we heard people scattering, and I turned to see a shape rushing toward us. My fears of an assassination were relieved when I noticed the crowd merely parted to make way for a small, orange shape. Running behind the orange shape was Ywain, valiantly chasing his cat.

"Erlin!" he shouted, running our way. "It's a good day for bathing in...uh..."

"Cow dung," I said, turning as he ran past. He had nearly gotten it. "Well done, Ywain." He disappeared down another street, and I turned to Garth. "You've done well, too. I'm impressed with your research, and with your new perspective."

Garth looked up. "I learned a lot when I was a bird."

CHAPTER THIRTY

TARK MANOR TOWERED OVER US. Every one of the pointy roofs ended in a tall spike, which was how the rich reminded the rest of us they were the ones in charge. Oh, you can afford a home of your own? That's adorable. Did you notice my tall spikey things are bigger than your entire house? Did you pay your taxes? I'm raising them because one of my spikey things fell down and I simply can't go on until it's back. Oh, did I just drop a vase? That'll cost you. Don't worry; things are bad all over.

The guard at the front gate straightened up when he saw us approach. A small helmet tottered on his head. He held out a hand and shouted, "That's close enough!"

I produced the letter Ulder had given us, showing him the seal. "I've been sent by the king."

Garth and I had been stopped a good distance away, so the guard had to lean over and squint. "I can't read that from here, and I'm not s'posed to let anyone get closer."

Ordinary people can solve problems. Ordinary people can casually work through misunderstandings and even untangle complicated knots. But there's always people who can't do anything but make situations worse, and those people invariably find themselves in middle management. Fortunately, working in Tomelac had given me a lot of experience in dealing with obstructive bureaucracy.

I opened the letter and held up the drawing that showed the gristly sketch of Lord Tark, murdered. "Does this look familiar?"

A lump rose in his throat, and he waved me over. I tried speaking to him as we came near, but he pointed us inside while wrestling with his gag reflex.

We strolled across the courtyard. I recalled an interesting statue that was just coming into sight as we passed a cluster of trees, but Garth surprised me.

"Do you think they still have the one with the dragon?" asked Garth.

I stopped in my tracks. "What did you say?"

"The dragon statue. It has big eyes and looks nice. Not like the pictures in books that make them look all mean. I think his name's Pyro."

"Who told you about that statue?" I asked, fearing I already knew the answer.

"I saw it," he replied. "Just last year. Da took me."

For the second time that day, I felt my chest clench as my situation worsened. Garth had been here before. I don't know why I assumed otherwise, since royal families often travel to big cities, but Garth wasn't exactly someone you let accompany a head of state to an important function. More than once, he'd asked visiting queens to refill his flagons, and at one ill-fated dinner he'd misunderstood the meaning of a holy man's fancy robes and ordered him to juggle for the court. I understand the priest gave it a valiant effort before Garth reassigned him to kitchen duty. It was nearly a week before someone noticed the visiting priest was missing, and another week before the Queen Mother noticed the archbishop was scrubbing dishes in the kitchen.

"Last year?" I asked. "You were here that recently?"

"We saw Lord Tark and everything!" said Garth. "Lady Broom took us on a tour."

I couldn't think of anything more colossally stupid than to bring Garth here, when people might recognize him. Royals were often kidnapped for ransom, and that was the best-case scenario. Ulder had enough enemies to fill an entire country (a country about the size of the one he managed, to be precise) and it would be difficult to find anyone who wouldn't see Garth as an opportunity for revenge. I had tossed wheat rolls at the back of his head in the banquet hall a few times myself, so I could only imagine what would happen if Garth was recognized by someone holding a sharp object.

I studied Garth, trying to remember what he looked like a year ago. Sadly, it was clear that not much had changed. He stood taller, but his pie-shaped face and confused expression were uncannily the same as when he'd been younger. The king had been a fool sending him to Hanbury.

"COME ON!" came a shrill voice.

I felt a powerful tug on my hand and saw the young page, Lilly, pulling me along.

"Lilly, this is very important," I said, struggling more than I thought I should just to keep a small child from dragging me away. "Do you know who this is?" I pointed at Garth.

Lilly frowned. "I don't know who *anyone* is."

"Well, his name is Wart. He's my apprentice from Barton. Now, if you be sure to tell everyone his name is *Wart* and that he is from *Barton,* then I will usher you into the room with all the blood." It was the most grotesque deal I'd ever made.

Clutching the bucket under my other arm, I let Lilly drag me, with Garth stumbling to keep up, through the double doors and past dumbfounded guards. I flashed my letter as we passed while Lilly yelled, "This is the ink visitor and his friend from Wart. His name's Barton!"

"Close enough," I mumbled.

We passed through a hallway lined with armed guards, all a blur as Lilly rushed us through the keep and up several flights of stairs to the very top. I'd never been in this part of the manor, which was obviously the Lord's personal chambers.

Lilly slipped past the guard standing at the last door, forcing me to crash into him.

"Sorry," I said, getting my bearings. "I'm the inquisitor from Tomelac." I weakly held up the letter, but the guard turned his attention to the room.

"Lilly!" he screamed. "You know you're not supposed to be in here!"

"But in the ink visitor promised!" Lilly wailed as the guard lifted her. She flailed her legs in the air as he carried her out, and both feet kicked me in the chest as they passed by. Her protests could be heard until she was all the way down the stairs.

Both of us taking a deep breath, we entered the room.

I noticed an ornate bed and several tall shelves brimming with shiny books, the sort no one actually read, and a few mahogany wardrobes surrounding a tilted vanity mirror.

But straight in front of me, in the middle of a stone wall, hung the body of Lady Broom, impaled on a torch sconce.

I gazed at her terrible wounds, frowning at the long gash that exposed her organs, and then my eyes followed the elaborate pattern of blood traced onto the floor. The guard was right to remove a child from this place.

From the corner of my eye, I noticed Garth tense up. His hand went to his mouth and his back shuddered.

"Here," I said, handing him the bucket. "I bought this for you."

CHAPTER THIRTY-ONE

I SUPPOSE it was the most disgusting thing I'd ever seen.

Not only because we were seeing parts of the human anatomy that are normally kept politely under the skin, but also because the whole thing was disgusting to my morals. My mind couldn't accept this level of brutality.

Garth filled up the bucket and then used his foot to nudge it behind a bookcase before looking again. This time, he shuddered at the sight of Lady Broom, but he kept himself upright.

My teeth had clenched hard enough that my jaw was hurting, an old habit from childhood. I couldn't remember the last time I'd been that angry. Breathing slowly, I closed my eyes and turned my brain toward the comforting, cold thoughts of logic. I couldn't figure out why the world was so dark, but I could figure out this murder scene, and maybe set one thing right.

I opened my eyes and saw things differently.

The body couldn't have been hung with more precision. I had assumed I would be seeing the act of a madman, but this was the work of an artist. Not merely a murder, but a spectacle.

The gears in my head began to spin.

Even though I was a fraud, an inquisitor who never asked questions and didn't believe in magic, I was never one to pass up a mystery. I'd come across my convictions the hard way, by investigating fantastic stories until I was convinced it was all tricks and superstition. I'd heard the same bedtime stories as everyone else when I was a child, but instead of shrugging my shoulders as I got older, I began taking time to look into each little fairy tale. The neighboring village with the talking mice or the tall trees in the distant forest that whispered about the future. It wasn't good enough to enjoy the stories. Not for me. I always needed to see it for myself.

And every investigation had left me disappointed. My keen mind had found the thread that unraveled the truth in every situation long before the mystery could take root in my mind, and this time would be no different.

Not a murder. A spectacle.

I was *supposed* to see it. I was *supposed* to be here looking at it. Everyone in the kingdom was supposed to be shocked to their core by this.

Everyone's seen a child who's only pretending to be upset. I spent as little time around children as possible because they are famously sticky, but even I knew how to tell a true grievance from a contrived one. As I looked closer at the incredible care taken to display the body, I become more certain this was a staged tantrum.

This murder, as well as the previous one, was a distraction.

"We need to leave," I said.

Garth's feet may as well have been stuck in clay. "I...Erlin, this is..."

"I know. It's impossible not to stare because of how it makes you feel. But...we're *supposed* to look at it. There's something else going on that we're *not* supposed to see."

"And we need to...go look at the thing we're *not* supposed to look at?"

"Yes." But I, too, found myself unable to tear my gaze from Lady Broom. Her death was displayed in such a way that it cried out for justice, but the cool calmness of my logical mind told me that justice was going to be found elsewhere. "Let's just step away and look around..."

I paused.

Something scraped the ground behind us. I spun around to see a man holding a crossbow.

By the billowing curtains, I gathered he'd just snuck in through the window. He must have been waiting out there for a long time.

The assassin didn't waste time. He raised the crossbow and squinted while he aimed.

I'm not a protective sort—particularly where anyone rich or famous is concerned. I'd personally laughed at Garth's expense more times than I could count, and seeing a crossbow bolt split a royal in half would normally make my day. But when the assassin took aim, I found my feet moving on their own. In the direction of Garth.

I sighed as deeply as I could, believing it would be the last time I would bemoan my place in the universe, and pushed my weight toward Garth to shove him out of the way.

Unfortunately, I wasn't the only person feeling protective.

"Erlin, look out!" shouted the prince.

We fell against each other, grappling for dominance and both failing to move at all.

Just then, the assassin pulled the trigger. The crossbow released the bolt with a resounding *twang*.

CHAPTER THIRTY-TWO

POTATOES FLEW EVERYWHERE.

There was a *rip* as I heard the bolt tear through several things, followed by a *thud* (and then a few tiny *thuds*) and then a *whump* that shook the bookshelf behind me.

Garth and I fell in the confusion. The sound of the bolt's impact threw us both into a panic, and I had no idea what had been torn asunder. I glanced up at Garth and we both patted our bodies looking for holes. No blood. No wounds. We both shrugged.

I looked up to see a quivering crossbow bolt that had impaled my book about the Restless into the wall (along with two plump potatoes which lined up along the shaft like they were ready to be cooked over a spit).

The assassin stood in place, a new bolt half-loaded onto his weapon. Our eyes met, and he froze.

Crossbows are funny things. You can shoot through a wall with one, or right through a fancy knight's precious armor, but you can't do any of that *quickly*. This guy had walked into the room with his weapon already loaded so all he had to do was aim and pull, but now he had to gently put the new bolt in place and then yank back on the string until it locked into place. It wasn't easy work, and—judging by the red lines embedded deep in his fingers—he'd struggled to do it the first time.

Still surprised I wasn't hurt, I rose to my feet. The assassin stood at the door, over fifteen paces away, his hand resting on the tense string while he debated whether or not he had time to pull it into place.

The crossbow had missed, but it was enough violence to send my heart racing. I had no idea what to do. I was stuck in a problem well beyond any of my books.

I recalled the statues I'd seen of great warrior men and did my best to impersonate them. I leveled my eyes at the assailant and curled my fingers into a fist. Eyes narrow. Shoulders square. Knees bent, just a little.

I felt silly, but it worked. The assassin bolted out the door.

Garth asked, "Should we go after him?"

I shook my head, certain we wouldn't know what to do if we found him. In fact, what we needed was someone to rescue *us*.

"The bell!" I pointed to the silk rope hanging near the bed, which was probably connected to a bell that rang for servants. "Pull on it!"

Garth ran to the edge of the bed and tugged hard.

There was nothing.

I began to wonder if Garth was more hopeless than I'd realized. Even a noble could ring a bell with competence. But when he tried again, we both saw the rope fall to the ground, having been cut clean to prevent anyone from calling for help.

"They won't have done that to all of them," I reasoned aloud. "We just need to find another room hooked up to the same bell."

Every rich person's house used the same signals. One ring of the bell always meant "Get in here," and two rings meant, "Get in here before there's a mess to clean up." But a series of urgent tolls always meant there was a torch wielding mob at the door. Enough tugs on one of those ropes, and the guards would lock the place down tighter than Ulder's vault.

"Come on!" I ran into the hall and gestured for Garth to follow.

I was pretty sure the assailant had run to the left, so we went to the right, around a sharp corner that ended at a stairwell. We stepped as quickly as we could down the steps to the next floor down, which was still several stories high, and came out in the middle of a long hallway. I ran, glancing into each door until I found another fancy chamber with silk ropes hanging near the bed. We rushed inside.

"Get in there and pull the rope." I stood guard at the door as he ran in. "Don't be shy, Garth. Give it a good pull, and then give it a few dozen more."

I didn't hear anything. Garth stammered, trying to say something. I slowly turned around.

The assassin stood ten paces from Garth, crossbow in hand. My bad luck had brought us exactly to our assassin's hiding place.

But the assassin didn't look confident. There was no sign of a predator who'd stumbled onto his prey. In fact, he looked scared. Of me.

"Erlin the inquisitor?" he whispered. The crossbow fell from his shaking hands.

Garth finally pulled on the rope. The bell clanged at least ten times before he stopped. Meanwhile, the assassin kept his frightened eyes on me.

The hallway filled with the sound of guards, who soon filled the room. "Nobody move!" someone shouted.

The assassin pointed a shaky finger at me as he backed away. "I'm not stayin' anywhere near that madman." And then he jumped through the window.

I rushed over in time to see him fall onto a wagon. The wagon's top had been removed and the bed filled with hay; the assassin had barely landed before a whip was cracked and a pair of horses pulled him away.

"Why did he do that?" asked a guard.

"I know why," said Garth, proudly. "He was scared of Erlin."

Chapter Thirty-Three

As far as I knew, no one had ever been afraid of me. I had tried to intimidate Petunia, the scheming court gardener, when I arrived in Tomelac, but it had been useless. She, alone, had seen through my act, or at least enough of it to know I was actually harmless.

I spent so little time dealing with the public, I'd never run into my own (apparently) fearsome reputation.

"Sir, I asked if you'd ever seen him before," said the guard near me, a man wearing his helmet crooked who'd apparently been interrogating us.

"Never. But he just landed in an Abrecan caravan."

"You'll be safe from them in here," he said. "Now, your name?"

"Erlin."

His jaw fell. "The inquisitor! They told me you were here, but I didn't recognize you."

"It's a gift." I'd often been thankful for my average appearance.

"My name's Tallbottom. Private Tallbottom. Like I said, don't worry about the Abrecans. We don't let them into Hanbury."

"How exactly does that work?" I asked, having been long fed up with their approach to this problem. "You don't let their wagons roll through the gate, but what's to stop one of the men from taking off their leather vest and wandering in? Because that's exactly what's happened!"

He straightened his helmet. "They're not s'posed to do that."

"I'll let them know the next time I see them. Can you at least order the Abrecans to park their wagons away from the gates?"

"Sure. That is...in theory. It's something this estate can do."

I raised my eyebrows, awaiting more of a response.

"Well, we *can*," he said, "but only the Lord can order that."

I was ahead of him. "And if the Lord is dead?"

"Then the Lady has to order it."

I took a breath to summon my patience. "And if the Lord *and* Lady are dead?"

He pulled off his helmet and scratched his head. "Well, I don't know. No one's ever killed 'em both before."

"Did Lord Tark and Lady Broom have any children?"

"Oh, yes." He replaced the helmet and smiled. "They did."

I leaned closer. "And?"

"Oh. I see. Very clever. Well, his lordship's sons are away."

"And his daughters?"

THE ONCE AND FUTURE IDIOT 179

"Married."

"And the castle steward?"

"Resigned after Lord Tark died. Said she couldn't go on after what happened."

"Then who's in charge of the manor?"

"The steward never told us who was next in command, so we're just doing our jobs, like always."

"Fine...how about the city constable?"

"Constable Clary? He was here this morning!"

I clapped my hands. "At last. Tell me, where can I find Hanbury's constable?"

"The constabulary building. Past the gate, two streets, and then it's on the right."

"Well done." I said, turning on my heel. "I'll have a word with this Constable Clary—"

"Wait—you want to speak with Constable Clary?"

"Yes." I stopped in my tracks. "At the constabulary."

"Oh, you won't find Clary at the constabulary."

I felt myself wanting to make another fist. "Pray tell, where can I find the good constable?"

"Oh, he isn't the constable no more. Clary was here this morning, you see, and he was so shook up by Lady Broom's murder, her being strung up and cut open like her husband, that he swore off violence and joined a monastery."

"So...there is no constable in Hanbury?"

He tilted his head. "Now that you mention it, I suppose not. How about that?"

"Would you say, Private Tallbottom, that there is, in fact, no law and order whatsoever in Hanbury?"

"I hadn't noticed 'till you said it, but I suppose we are a bit lawless right now. Do you think anyone else will notice?"

"I think it's a bit late for that."

"Just as well. Time for my rounds."

With a face beaming with the sort of happiness that only comes from ignorance, Private Tallbottom strolled out the door, whistling as he went.

###

"They've got rooms for us here in the manor," said Garth, as I was leading us away from there, through the courtyard and past condescending spires.

"Not a chance," I said. "That staff is dafter than..."

Dafter than the crown prince is how the saying went, but I held my tongue.

"Let's just say I'd rather trust a bull with a carton of eggs," I said. "Besides, Tark Manor is where the next assassin will be looking for you."

"You wanna leave town then?"

"No, the Abrecans are gathered at the gate. That's certain death." I kept us in shadow and clung to the walls as I followed my nose to the part of town royalty never saw. A ramshackle tavern eventually rose above us, with enough floors that we could look out a window and see most of the city if we got a room on an upper floor, which would also keep us as far as possible from the smell that was already gagging me. "This is the last place anyone will look for you."

The doorway was only covered by a haphazardly draped cloth. I tried to squeeze past without touching it. Inside, a bard sang his poor heart out to a room that was determined to be louder than his lyre. A few eyes looked our way, sizing us up with dark looks. But these were not the eyes of assassins or killers, only pickpockets and cutpurses looking for an opportunity. I motioned for Garth to stay close as we made our way to the desk.

"One room," I shouted.

A surly woman leaned my way and held out her empty palm. I dug into my pocket and made of show of looking very hard for any coins, lest anyone think I expected to find any. In that sort of room, financial confidence is the quickest route to being robbed. (I employed similar logic when I lied to the tax collectors about how much Ulder paid me.)

After a long search, I placed a coin in her hand. She carefully bit into it and then laid down a copper key with the number *12* stamped on it.

As Garth and I headed for the stairwell, I had an idea. I turned to the woman and asked, "Is there a courier?" It seemed like asking a stray dog for a glass of champagne, but she nodded and pointed to a man in the corner who sat in a chair, fast asleep.

"Kenneth'll get y'er message anywhere in town," she said.

The man called Kenneth looked up, interrupting a snore as he wiped his nose. He staggered my way, and I felt his breath just before I smelled it.

"One copper," he said, holding out the hand he'd used to wipe his nose. "Two, if you need me to write it."

Holding my breath, I managed to toss the coin into his palm. "Just show me to the inkwell."

Chapter Thirty-Four

We climbed up the rotted stairs up to the highest floor. I had my concerns about our courier. Each time I repeated my directions he would reply with a crooked salute, and then I watched him wander out of the building like a man using his feet for the first time. I had to run outside to give him the note he'd forgotten.

"Remember that assassin?" I asked, as Garth and I were settling into the room. "Did you get the impression he was...afraid of me?"

"Of course he was—you're Erlin the Inquisitor! You've killed more mages than anyone! I bet they're still talking about the time you knocked that warlock out with his own crystal ball. Or the time you tricked a whole coven into cooking themselves! It's a good thing I'm not here alone."

Garth clearly felt safe with me around, which was a shame, since I'm usually about as dangerous as a banana peel.

"When do you think they'll empty the bedpans?" he asked.

"I'm afraid we do that ourselves."

"How?"

I pointed to the window. "Garth, do you have any idea who's trying to kill you?"

"The Abrecans. Say, where are they going to lay my clothes out in the morning?"

"Focus, Garth. The Abrecans are traveling traders, not killers."

He sat on the edge of the bed. "Someone...else is making them kill me? Someone who knew I was going to Hanbury!"

I snapped my fingers. At long last, the wonderful clarity a teacher experiences when their student has reached a bit higher than last time. I savored the moment, knowing this feeling of accomplishment would have to last me for a long time.

"Well done." I paced the narrow space in front of the bed. "Now, do you know anyone that really hates you? Anyone at court? Or any visitors that have threatened you?"

"That gardener woman seems prickly."

"She is. I don't think she's a killer, but it wouldn't hurt to throw her in prison when we get back, just for a day or two."

A knock on the door. I held up a hand to quiet Garth and approached the door. "Hello?" I said, using a different voice.

"Wart?" someone shouted. "Erlin?"

I threw open the door. "Shut up, Ywain, and get inside. My note told you to be discreet!"

Ywain, looking embarrassed, scurried inside, holding a paper bag under one arm and a squirming, furry mass in the other.

"Is that a different cat?" I asked.

"Leo ran off." Ywain held up a black cat with white paws. It glared at me, begging for understanding. "But my grandmother's recipe worked on Oscar here."

"I can't tell you how happy I am for you both. Show me what you—"

"You've got a recipe for cats?" asked Garth. "You mean you...eat them?"

"Oh, heavens no!" Ywain dropped the bag and held his new cat closer. Oscar was not happy. "My grandmother, bless her soul, taught my mother a recipe that she'd learned from her mother's grandmother before my mother's grandmother was born."

The room spun as I mentally pieced together Ywain's family tree.

"What do they taste like?" asked Garth, who, as usual, understood the conversation as well as the floorboards.

"It's just an attractant." Ywain dropped the cat and reached into his pocket. He produced a small pouch. "Cats can't resist. Grandma's grandma told mom's grandma that her grandmother made it with apples, morning glory shoots, spider wort...onions..."

The cat, Oscar, was rubbing its face against Ywain's shin, its dark eyes fixed on the pouch.

"They love it," said Ywain. He picked up the cat again. "And it lets me train them, too. You'd be surprised what cats will do when they get the right presents. They're smarter than you think."

I picked up the other bag, the larger one Ywain had walked in with, and looked inside. Dagonet had packed it with a few things from his troop. Wigs. Makeup. Even a robe with a hood. I reached inside to see what else I could find.

"Wart," I said, ending a conversation I hadn't been listening to, "I don't want you to leave this room again without this." I pulled out a false grey beard and tossed it to him.

Garth held it over his mouth. "Will this work? Won't I need to talk like an old man?"

"I can help you!" said Ywain. "I like to really get to *know* my characters. Spend time in their minds and imagine—"

"Thank you, Ywain." I pushed him toward the door. "Take a different route back and thank Dagonet for me."

I shut the door as quickly as I could, leaving just enough time for Oscar to scamper through.

When I turned around, Garth was settling into the middle of the bed.

"Erlin," he asked very seriously, "something's been bothering me. Do you mind if I ask you a question?"

"Of course. I'm your teacher, after all. What is it?"

"Where are *you* going to sleep?"

Chapter Thirty-Five

THE NEXT MORNING, Garth and I stepped through the nameless inn's lower floor and confidently walked the streets of Hanbury as if no one was trying to kill us.

Garth had taken well to the disguise. Using the tools Dagonet had sent, I turned Garth's golden locks into a grey mop. Then I attached the beard with sap, using enough to keep Garth from pulling it off by accident. I knew using too much sap could make removing the beard very painful, but sacrifices sometimes must be made for the greater good.

As for me, I've never been very outstanding. Not too tall. Not terribly large or small. I was fond of my ability to blend into a crowd, so a monk's robe and a pair of glasses were enough to hide me. Garth and I strolled into the alley, stepping over a few of last night's patrons, and headed for the front gate.

"I thought you said we'd be hiding," whispered Garth. "You know, staying in the shadows and taking the back alleys?"

"Only if you want to get caught. The Abrecans will be looking for us in the shadows. Not to mention, the back alleys are where you dumped your bedpan. Dagonet was right; hiding in plain sight is the best way." I spied a vendor setting up a cart. "I think a sweetroll is in order."

This excited the prince. We approached a yawning vendor who handed over the warm treats with the sort of grumble that only accompanies the serenity of early morning.

"Think we can get out with Dagonet? Like how we got in?" asked Garth.

"That's not a bad idea," I said, "but I'll bet they're keeping an eye on Dagonet."

We walked further until the city square was in sight. Dagonet's troop was still camped there, all sleeping inside their oversized carriages. A few beggars slept on nearby benches, and I was certain at least some of them were Abrecans pretending to be drifters, ready to pounce if we tried to hide with the actors again. Even with our disguises, someone could recognize us as if they looked *real* close.

"Hullo? What?" came a gruff voice.

I turned and saw a sight that pinned me in place.

Ahead of us stood a man in a full suit of armor—even a helmet with a slotted visor pulled down. He carried a sword and shield covered in faded royal decorations. The armor itself was practically a museum piece, with dents and cracks in every conceivable spot.

I removed my smudged glasses and squinted to get a better look.

He reached his fisted gauntlet to rap the door of a business, and the antique armor squeaked with each movement, like he wasn't a man but a machine that needed to be taken apart, oiled thoroughly, and then put back together.

"What?" He rapped on the door. "Quite the imposition, I say. Sun's up! Get down here, you lollygagging miscreant! No respect for a king anymore!"

I knew that voice. It was—

"Pellinore!" shouted Garth.

I punched the prince's shoulder. "Quiet!"

Pellinore was not a subtle man. His cranky demeanor and bad hearing made his agitated discourse a common, eye-rolling experience in Albion, where Pellinore's position as king of the Manly Isles never seemed to keep him very busy.

The helmed head turned our way. "I say! What! A familiar face!"

"By Avalon." I threw the glasses back on my face, but it was too late. "This is all we need."

Like a noisy wind-up toy, King Pellinore of The Manly Isles stomped our way, clanging like a pile of pots and pans. I half expected to see springs fly loose from every joint in his armor.

"Bother these greaves," he said as he got close. "Can barely step." He reached for the visor and pushed up, unable to raise it. "Blasted thing. Rusted shut and hasn't moved in months. Can't show good manners!"

Through the slits in his visor, I could see his wrinkled face growing frustrated.

"It's not a problem, King Pellinore. By the way, have you met my assistant, Wart?"

Garth had been on the verge of saying something to Pellinore, who liked to visit Tomelac and could often be heard wandering the halls looking for his room.

"I'm Wart." Garth extended his hand, but Pellinore ignored him.

King Pellinore had recognized me from a block away, but he hadn't so much as glanced at Garth. Being old-fashioned, he would have ignored anyone who looked like a servant. Pellinore was a king, after all, a king who truly believed he was on important business.

"What brings you to Hanbury, Pelly?"

He hated that nickname, so I used it all the time.

"Blasted taxidermist, that's what!" He raised his hand with a metallic screech. "I ordered a stuffing of the most rare animal he could find to place in my manor, and do you know what that rascal sent me? A deception! Is anything worse than a liar?"

"I can't think of anything. What did he send you?"

"Last week, he delivered a monstrosity! The stuffed creature looked normal at the bottom, four feet with hooves like a deer, but he'd attached those to a lion's body! To top it all off, it had a neck taller than a tree, like a giant snake. And spots all over! Most questionable beast I ever saw!"

"And you're here to make him answer for sewing three animals together?"

"No one takes King Pellinore for a fool!"

Indeed. Looking through his slotted visor, I could see the wrinkles around his eyes growing as he focused on Garth, trying to discern if he looked familiar. He looked away and gave up with a shake of his head. I relaxed, but only for a moment as a new sound invaded the alley: a barking dog.

Around the far corner galloped a pile of white fur, a dog with no discernable eyes and the body of an old mop, dragging the wet ground as it shambled our way in a clumsy hurry. Caball, Pellinore's dog, rarely left his side. His barks would have raised the dead, but what troubled me was its dogged beeline toward Garth. The prince's habit of feeding Caball under the table had made them close friends.

I glanced at Garth, flaring a warning in my eyes, and Garth straightened up. I could tell he was itching to wrestle Caball to the ground and call him stupid, adorable names. Dogs have a strange power to make everyone less intelligent, which meant Garth's puny brain didn't stand a chance while Caball was around.

"Knock it off!" shouted Pellinore, as Caball rushed into Garth. "You don't know him."

Caball barked a curt response.

"Nonsense," shouted the old man. "You can only see hair."

It was true. Caball's bangs were more effective than the slits on Pellinore's helmet.

We heard a soft bell ring, like the kind you hear when you enter a store. Pellinore tried to turn his head but only managed to look slightly sideways while the metal parts of his armor screeched. Taking tiny steps, he pivoted his armored body around until he was staring at the taxidermist shop, where the proprietor was halfway through the front door.

"You there! What!" shouted Pellinore.

The taxidermist, wearing an apron covered in loose animal hairs, saw Pellinore and his eyes went wide.

"Stop, crook!" Pellinore, hand on his sword, tottered down the street toward the frightened shopkeeper, with Caball barking all the way.

Chapter Thirty-Six

GARTH AND I took our sweetrolls to a cluster of benches where we could watch the city gate from a distance. Each time the gate opened, we saw the Abrecans on the other side, watching from their nearby caravans, like jewelers peering through a glass.

To be on the safe side, we sat far enough away that we had to peer in between a few buildings to get a good look. Garth was even playing into his role as a hopeless drifter by collecting sweetroll crumbs throughout his false beard.

"We'll never get out that way," I mumbled.

"I don't understand why you're trying to leave."

I turned my head toward him slowly. The near-death experience at the hands of the assassin, followed by a near-death experience of the inn's unclean sheets, had not deterred the young prince. I saw, behind his false beard, a resolute face, determined to return to Tomelac the victor.

A couple walked past. Garth and I kept our heads down.

"It's worse than the time they killed Lord Tark," said a man, shaking his head.

"You weren't here before that," said the woman. "People haven't been this scared since Mirdal the Mad."

I smiled at the memory. Yes, Mirdal had been here. Years ago.

Garth perked up, as he always did when Mirdal was mentioned. He always told the story of standing by his father's side as I entered the great hall that day.

"Did you fight Mirdal the Mad here in Hanbury?" he asked.

"I guess you could say that."

"How did you beat him that time? Maybe we can do the same thing."

"Hmm. Good question, Garth." I thought back to those days. Garth didn't know what he was talking about, but he knew the stories—often better than I did. "I...believe we set him on fire. I saw him sneak into a building, so I locked the door and threw a torch in the window."

Garth, as always, beamed with pride. But...then a shadow of a doubt crossed his face. Something I hadn't seen before. His mind was no longer carried away by the romantic notion of my battles with Mirdal, the warlock who—in my stories—always slipped away just when his death seemed certain.

"What do you remember about that time in Tomelac, Garth, that time you first saw me?"

"You stormed into the great hall." He was thoughtful. Quieter than usual. Like he was really trying to remember the story instead of just reciting it. "You...had a robe in your hands. It was covered in blood. And it had the big letters and squiggles all over it, so we knew it was Mirdal's. People had been seein' Mirdal all around, so when you walked in and held up that robe, we knew you had...killed him."

Garth remembered it exactly as it had happened, but he'd understood none of it.

I'd never told anyone the truth about Mirdal the Mad. I wanted to let Garth in on the secret, but secrets quickly find the light of day when they're entrusted to anyone important.

"What was that you were sayin' before?" Garth asked. "Back in the manor, you said we were *supposed* to be looking at Lady Broom while she was dead."

"It's some kind of decoy," I said. "A trick. Someone's just trying to get our attention."

Truth be told, I hadn't quite worked out what was going on. I had a wise habit of stopping my curiosity just short of getting myself killed, and at the moment my survival instinct was begging me to get out of Hanbury.

I continued. "Someone was waiting in Tark manor so they could kill you, but no one's supposed to know you're here. Maybe someone in Ulder's court wants to murder you, to get back at him for something, and they saw an opportunity when he assigned you to this case."

Garth didn't understand. His eyes tightened as he tried to follow, but I knew it was hopeless.

"All I know," he said, "is that we can't leave until we figure out who killed Lord Tark and Lady Broom."

He nodded decisively. Then he whispered: "Prince's orders."

I felt my chest tighten. "What did you say?"

"There's a killer on the loose. A magic one. And your job is stoppin' bad people like that." He crossed his arms in a no-nonsense way. "Prince's orders."

It was clear he'd never given orders before.

It's a rare person who doesn't horde power. A child who notices his first ounce of influence will exercise it over their parents at every opportunity, and politicians do the same (only with less maturity). Garth could have been ordering me around the whole trip, but this was his first time to actually tell me do to anything. The way he shifted around in his seat, it was like he'd just tried on a new pair of pants and couldn't decide if they were too tight.

I let out a long breath. "Yes...sir."

"We already know the Abrecans are involved," he said quietly. "I think we should have them arrested."

"It's not that easy. Ah, sir." I thought of the woman who had helped us and my discovery that not every Abrecan was out to get us. "We can't simply blame the entire Abrecan community."

A voice from behind made both of us jump.

"No," someone said, "you certainly shouldn't do that."

Chapter Thirty-Seven

We slowly turned around in our seat.

Someone was seated in the bench directly behind ours. We hadn't heard them arrive. They'd made as little noise as a leaf falling from a tree. Underneath the headscarf, I saw a pair of blue eyes and a resolute mouth.

Morrigin.

Garth and I exchanged a worried glance. How much had she heard?

"Come around over here," she said to me, patting the seat next to her.

Garth nodded at me and then narrowed his eyes at her; he wasn't sure about Morrigin, but he wanted to see what she was up to. I stood, stretched, and made my way to her bench.

No matter how many books you read, no amount of studying can prepare you for the challenge of acting confident while you sit next to an enchanting woman, but I managed to settle into the bench without falling down or embarrassing myself.

She was dressed as a simple maid with a book laying open on her lap, its pages filled with recipes.

"Closer," she whispered. "Why are you on the other side?"

I scooted and closed the gap, but just then she moved in my direction and our hips collided. Being in the same room as an assassin hadn't made me so nervous. I could tell Garth was laughing at me.

"Pretend we're reading this together," she said softly, pointing a slender finger at a page about cupcakes. She leaned close. "Listen...the Abrecans *are* responsible."

"Aren't you one of them?"

"It's not that simple..."

Footsteps. A guard patrol was headed our way.

"Put your arm around my shoulder, Erlin."

"Good idea. I'll just...do that." I wondered if I should slide my arm across her back or simply raise it up like a drawbridge and bring it back down. She made an impatient sound, and I realized not everything befits an academic approach.

Having settled on a method, I flattened my hand across the back of the bench and pushed it past her shoulder blades.

"We're not all like Escanor," she said.

"I see." A delicate moment. I had slid my arm behind her, but now needed to rest my hand on her shoulder to complete the illusion. After some consideration, I balanced my wrist on her shoulder and let my hand dangle casually, like a man who knew how to do such things.

"Escanor has forgotten the way of the Fortunate Ones," she said. "I know you don't know what that means, but some of us remember the old ways. Some of us don't want to kill Garth."

"Why would the—"

She put a finger to my lips, silencing me. I had spoken too loud. "How did they know Garth would be here?" I whispered around her finger.

A thought occurred to me. I had first seen Morrigin at Ulder's court on the day Garth and I were given this mission. I moved in closer, studying her eyes for a trace of deception.

"I know what you're thinking," she said, "but I didn't tell anyone what I heard in court that day. Trust me. I don't know how Escanor knew about—"

She stopped talking and gave me a stare that sent ice through my veins.

With horror, I realize sliding closer had caused my hand to slip down further than I intended, and now my fingers rested upon the crest of a rather mountainous region.

I cringed as each finger left its incriminating perch. Her cold gaze was unrelenting.

Told you. I *never* know what to do with my hands.

Morrigin slapped the book shut. "Have you seen the red-roofed building at the north-east corner of town?"

"I've walked past it," I said, keeping my arm behind her. I wasn't sure if I should remove it completely or maintain the ruse. "Red shingles. Green shutters. Hard to miss. I hear it's a record building."

"Be there in ten minutes." She left, my mind reeling with each of her loud, booted steps.

"You can put your arm down now," said Garth.

I removed my arm from the back of the bench and set it in my lap, feeling very conspicuous.

"Bold move, Erlin." He eagerly leaned over to my side of the bench. "Sometimes the knights try that with the ladies in court."

"It was an accident, Garth."

"Sure it was. You just dangled your hand all the way down there by accident. Uh, huh. That's what Sir Kay always says. 'It was an accident.'"

"Garth, I'm not a ruffian. I didn't *mean* to. I was just sitting here—"

"Oh, yeah, kind of like that assassin didn't *mean* to shoot at us. He was just sitting there firing his crossbow for practice when we just happened to walk in."

It was just my luck that the only lesson I'd taught him was sarcasm. "I'm a gentleman."

"Oh, sure. A gentleman who just grabs—"

"Garth!"

CHAPTER THIRTY-EIGHT

I DIDN'T INITIALLY head to the red-roofed building like Morrigin had told me to. I had no reason to trust her. After all, she *had* been in court the day I'd been asked to take Garth to this city, and it *was* a group of Abrecans trying to kill us. I also wanted time to gather any remaining dignity before seeing her again.

But sometimes you see something that changes your mind about an important issue. Maybe it's finding out that the king's taxes are an unfair burden on the needy, or like that time I lowered a bucket into a well and found a hand inside when I pulled it back up, finally realizing why no one else in Tomelac used that particular well. These moments give us insight and clarity.

This time, my epiphany came when I saw Escanor walking down the street, straight toward me.

He'd shed his leather vest and other clothes that would identify him as an Abrecan. I thought we made eye contact, but he looked past me, past Garth, and hurried into a shop. Our disguises had worked.

They say any port is the right one in a storm, so I turned us around and headed for the record building.

I still lacked any reason to trust Morrigin, but she was our best hope now.

We kept to the shadowy side of the street as we scurried to the building Morrigin had told us about. Tall building, almost a castle, with red roofed turrets. Above the double oak doors, thick letters had been carved: *Charyot Manor.*

Garth and I stopped at the entrance so I could adjust his disguise. Inside, people might see him closely enough to realize he wasn't an old man with an old beard full of a food, but a young man with a fake beard full of food.

"It's fallen off a bit on this side," I whispered. "Let me adjust it."

"I didn't notice," he said. "Ow!"

"Sorry." I pushed the beard against the sticky paste that held it to his skin. Rather hard. "Still not there..." He winced as I squeezed his jaw on both sides. "Almost," I said, jabbing at his face with my finger. "There."

"Thanks, Erlin."

"Don't mention it."

I raised my fist to knock on the door, but I feared Escanor could be anywhere. Not wanted to waste any time, I simply threw open the door and ushered Garth inside.

We stepped in and faced a sea of unmoving faces.

I expected to be approached by an angry butler or a frightened serving maid. Surely the master of the manor would be down soon to shake a finger at me. Or perhaps burly guards would shove me back into the street while grunting in the language only known by mercenaries. Instead, I simply gazed out into a sea of wide-eyed bureaucrats.

The entrance opened immediately into a large room. Boxes, catalogs, and bookshelves lined every wall, and rows of desks piled high with papers roamed back and forth through the main area. Men and women peered through monocles or reading glasses (and sometimes both) as they pored over parchments and unrolled scrolls. Drawers were thrown open and books were laying out as far as we could see, like we'd interrupted a treasure hunt.

And everyone was staring at us.

"Looks like they recognize the inquisitor," whispered Garth. But I could tell I wasn't the center of their attention.

Someone snapped their fingers, and, as one, the company of paper pushers resumed their work. Murmurings and the sounds of shuffling of paper filled the room.

"There you are," came Morrigin's voice. She stepped through the room alongside a stocky, white-haired man wearing bifocals thick enough to make church glass. "This is Erlin and his assistant..." She trailed off, looking for me to fill in the blank.

"Wart," I announced. "We call him Wart." Then I added in a loud whisper, "On account of his feet."

"This is Zephyr," she said, gesturing to the older man. "He...runs the manor. It's his castle."

"What is this place?" asked Garth, as if we were on a lark and not hiding for our lives.

"Just a place for keeping records," said Morrigin, but she said it *too* sweetly. "Books and scrolls on everything."

"Don't lie," I said. "Everyone here is an Abrecan."

Once again, the room stilled.

It had been obvious to me that the Abrecans were more organized than I had previously realized. It was generally assumed they rode from one place to another, hawking their wares until there were no pennies left in town. But it had become clear they were more than wandering merchants traveling on a whim. And as I noted how connected these bureaucrats were to one another, working with a silent understanding that ordinary co-workers never grasp, and how easily Morrigin moved amongst them, the true purpose of this building quickly became apparent.

"You use this place to keep organized," I continued, watching Morrigin and Zephyr freeze as I explained. "And these accountants keep you rich. It's an incredible operation."

Morrigin and Zephyr exchanged a long, silent glance, then shrugged.

"Zephyr?" said Morrigin, "We need a room with...distractions."

"The observatory, my lady," he replied, gesturing overhead. "It is at your disposal."

"This way." Morrigin headed for a set of stairs in the nearest corner of the room, and we followed after.

After three flights of stairs, Garth was panting and leaning on me. He breathed a stinky sigh of relief when Morrigin reached the top and he realized we were done climbing. On the top floor, she led us through a long hallway.

"The bookkeepers live here," she told us. "This is their living quarters, so try not to snoop."

She glanced back as she said it, catching me as I peered into a slightly open door. I turned my head forward with an apologetic grin.

"Let's go." She stopped walking and pointed down the hall at the very last door. I walked past her and realized she was going to watch me the entire way to make sure I didn't peer into anyone else's room.

But I'd already seen something. The rooms weren't bedrooms at all, at least not the one I'd glanced. Sure, there were shelves filled with books and personal items and a few dressers, but none of them were fully furnished bedrooms.

I wish I could tell you I understood what all of this meant. I really do.

We pushed through the door at the end of the hall and stepped into a tall room with a glass ceiling. Across from the door, between a pair of open shutters, stood a telescope mounted on a windowsill.

"Does it work!" shouted Garth.

"Of course it does." Morrigin pointed to it with a smile. "In fact, it hasn't been tested in a while. Go ahead. It's no good if it can't see to the next town over the rise."

That made no sense. The next town wouldn't be visible *because* of the hill in between here and there, but that didn't stop Garth from cramming his face up to the eyehole.

Morrigin cocked her head to the side, nudging me toward the far corner of the room, away from Garth.

"He's going to break that," I warned.

"I know. Maybe we can talk plainly while he's distracted. How much time do we have?"

I looked over my shoulder and saw Garth peering into the eye hole while reaching around to wave his hand in front of the lens. "I'd be surprised if we have five minutes."

"You took your time getting here."

"We saw Escanor," I whispered.

She cursed. "How did he get past the gate?"

"I assume the same way you did." I had been wondering how she managed it.

Morrigin waved her hand, irritated. "He probably stuffed himself into a crate or hid in a barrel. We need to stop him. Will you help me?"

"Of course."

Behind us, we heard a gasp. I turned to see Garth grab the telescope just before it fell over the windowsill. He clutched it to his chest.

"You must have a lot of questions." She looked at me, waiting.

"I assume Escanor, or someone working for him, killed Lord Tark to draw me here."

She nodded.

I continued. "It's obviously a trap for Garth, but how did they know he would be coming along?"

"I don't know."

I couldn't decide if she was telling the truth. But it didn't matter, because I had an idea. Liar or not, she was on my side. "If you can get Escanor to meet you somewhere in the morning, I think I know how to take care of him."

Her eyes widened. I dare say, she was impressed.

Morrigin and I whispered out a plan to trap Escanor into taking the blame for the murders of Lord Tark and Lady Broom. The rest of the Abrecans would avoid suspicion, and Garth and I could return to Tomelac safely.

It was incredibly clever, but there's always something I forget.

Chapter Thirty-Nine

That night, I slept better than any night since I'd been saddled with the responsibility of Prince Garth. I stretched and yawned before getting out of bed and slid into the robe that served as my disguise.

As I pulled on my boots, the blessed silence was stolen by a half-snore noise from Garth's throat as the boy awoke in a fit.

"You'll need to stay in here today," I said. "It's too dangerous with Escanor about."

He nodded and rubbed his eyes. I had been prepared for him to pout about this, but he didn't mind at all. After all the excitement he'd shown about watching me work, and the way he could recall of my dramatic adventures, I believed he would be disappointed not to be there when I solved this case and arrested the magician responsible.

"It's going to be quite a show," I continued. "I think we'll have them right where we want them. Like the time I caught those warlocks hanging upside down in the black tower. Remember that one?"

"Mmmhmm." Garth sat up in bed and settled against the wall. "I'll wait here."

I eyed him suspiciously. "Just going to sit in here all day? You'll be fine?"

"Yeah, I've got my telescope." He reached over the edge of the bed for his burlap sack, which now jingled and jangled with metal sounds.

I'd forgotten about that. Of course, the telescope had ended up tumbling over the edge of the window and crashing to the street below. We came across the wreckage on the way back to our lodging. He'd picked up the pieces and was now holding the largest and smallest lenses together like a sandwich and pressing them against one eye. "I think I can fix it." He picked up the bronze tube and tried to cram the large lens into the small end.

Knowing the crown prince was going to need all the time in the universe to complete this project, I happily stepped out the door to meet Morrigin.

###

"Tighter," said the blonde, speaking around her gag. "It'sh too loose."

Behind the wooden pole, Morrigin tugged on the ropes.

"That'sh better."

Four women, all chosen by Morrigin, were tied to up in an old stable at the edge of town. They apparently were the same women who had ridden with her the night she rescued Garth and me, and they were quite willing to work against Escanor.

We used red paint to draw large open eyes on every wall, a symbol everyone in Hanbury knew was linked to the Restless Ones. Anyone walking into this old stable would panic at the sight of the festooned women and cultic images, believing they had stumbled upon a horrific crime that confirmed everything they believed about the Restless. It was a perfect trap when you added a mob of panicky idiots, and it was time to set the spring.

"One of the ladies told me where Escanor is staying," Morrigin told me, when the painting was all done. "It's a tavern a few blocks away. I've sent him a message to meet me there at noon so I can tell him where you are."

"Is he alone?"

"No." She pursed her lips. "But I'll tell him to come alone so you won't get spooked. He'll believe that. He's got no reason to be afraid of you."

I took that personally. "Almost time then," I said. Something had been weighing heavily on my mind, and I decided to ask. "Morrigin, Escanor is...one of you. An Abrecan. Won't the others be upset that you're getting him arrested?"

"There's hundreds of Abrecans. Only a handful are loyal to Escanor. When he's in prison, the rest of his men will scatter."

"If you're ready, I'll fetch Tallbottom and tell him he's about to make the arrest of his career."

She smiled at me. "You're doing a brave thing for your friend."

I could think of two things wrong with that sentence.

###

I'd last seen Tallbottom when he interrogated me at Tark Manor, just after the assassin had tried to kill Garth. But this time I needn't go that far. As I rushed through the streets, I noticed a light on in the constabulary. A constable was better than a manor guard, so I walked inside, hoping the town's elusive lawman had returned to his post.

"Anyone home?" I ventured. The front door opened into a corridor. At the end, I saw a few prison cages, all empty.

"Inquisitor?" came a familiar voice.

I took another step and entered a small room with a desk. "Tallbottom?"

"You remember! How do you like my office?"

"You...you're the new constable?" I asked.

"Well, I s'pose," he said, leaning back in his chair as he decided how to explain. "I came here to check and see if Constable Clary had come back, and that's when I found this note that says he won't be coming back."

Tallbottom handed me a scrap of paper that read, *I won't be coming back.*

"That's when I realized no one was stopping me from sitting behind his desk and pretending *I* was the constable. And then I decided nothing was stopping me from wearing his badge. And then—"

"And then you realized you could take over his job and get a higher pay," I finished.

His eyes widened. "Higher pay?"

"Listen, I need the constable right now."

Tallbottom settled further into his chair and gestured for me to begin.

"How would you like to catch Tark's murderer on your first day as constable?"

Then I told him exactly what Morrigin had said. That Escanor would be headed for the old barn at noon. That he was an angry man with dark hair and breath like a tobacco pipe. That his right hand bore a tattoo of a small blade and a thick scar encircled his right bicep. (Morrigin had supplied those last parts.)

Tallbottom stood and slapped his hands on his desk. "I'll get some men!"

He ran past me, leaving the constabulary door open as he blew his whistle in the street.

###

I strolled back to the stable with a spring in my step. I didn't know where he was, but I knew Escanor was walking right into my trap. It would do me good to see justice done, and Garth would tell his father about our triumph forever, ensuring the security of my job as long as I lived.

I made it back to the stable and opened the door to look inside one more time, just to make sure everything was still in place.

And that's when our plan fell apart.

I only intended to take a quick peek, but as soon as I opened the door someone kicked it open from the inside and pressed a hayfork against my neck, just under my jaw.

"Garth?"

The boy was wild-eyed and shaking while he held the farm tool in both hands.

"Garth, what on earth are you doing?"

"Not this time, Erlin! I'm not letting you hurt anyone!" he shouted.

Behind him, the women were untied. They shrugged at me.

"Did you untie them?" I grunted.

"Like I said, you're not hurtin' nobody today!"

"I don't hurt people," I said weakly. One of the oversized tines was pressing against my throat.

"You do too!" Garth said, and I saw a tear in his eye. "I've been watching with my telescope! I watched you tie them up!"

"It's not that simple—"

"You can't just kill these women because they dress like Abrecans! Everyone deserves a trial—you taught me that!"

"Garth. You don't understand."

"*You* don't understand. *I'm* in charge, and I'm not letting you hurt these women. If it was right to save the baby ducks, well, then it's right to save these people, too!"

The situation was grim. Escanor was near, and he would kill us as soon as seeing us. Tallbottom would never see my trap sprung. And Garth was nearly killing me with a blunt hayfork.

But I couldn't keep myself from smiling. This boy, the crown prince, who had failed every test given to him by every one of his instructors, had just passed life's most important test.

"Garth," I said softly, "you've just ruined every-thing."

CHAPTER FORTY

JUST THEN, Morrigin strolled around the corner with Escanor.

"What's she doing with him?" asked Garth.

I felt the thick prongs leave my throat as he lowered the hayfork. About a block away, Escanor and Morrigin stood side by side, frozen in place. She stared at me with confused eyes. I'd never seen her when she didn't appear confident.

Her cold expression quickly returned. "Moonriders!" she yelled. With a look of resignation, she stepped away from Escanor.

I hadn't heard that word before, but it quickly became clear what she meant. The women inside the stable ran out and—alongside Morrigin—formed a protective line in front of Garth. One of them took the hay fork from him and held it out, looking more menacing than Garth could have ever managed.

Escanor put two fingers in his mouth and whistled. A handful of men stepped out from behind nearby buildings, grinning as they pulled knives from their boots or from inside their jackets.

"What are you doing, Morrigin?" shouted Escanor, strolling confidently toward us.

"Some of us honor the Old Ways, Escanor. Not everyone's forgotten."

"How can we forget?" he replied. "We know the mistakes of our fathers, and I know how to fix them."

"Not this way," she said. "Never this way."

The four women standing in front of us, the ones she called "Moonriders," nodded in agreement.

I had no idea what they were talking about, and I didn't care. The prince and I needed to be elsewhere, but Escanor had a few more men than Morrigin and there wasn't any place to go.

"What's all this then?" came Tallbottom's voice.

Tallbottom, leading half a dozen guards, walked into the street, right in between the two groups.

Thinking fast, Morrigin pointed into the barn. "He tried to hurt us! Just look!"

Tallbottom's eyebrows rose when he saw inside the barn. He took a quick glance at Escanor's men and their brandished weapons and then put his hands on his hips. "Just what in Ava—"

Again, Escanor put his fingers to his lips and whistled. This time he whistled in three bursts, which he repeated. A signal to someone. Each burst was loud enough that I wanted to cover my ears. I've never understood how some men could do that.

"I don't know what you're up to," said Tallbottom with a frown, "but I'm the constable here, and no one..."

Constable Tallbottom trailed off as a screeching noise reached our ears, followed by a loud crash and a series of screams. Escanor smiled wide as the realization hit all of us: his men outside heard his signal and had broken the city gate. Somehow. Already, we heard people riding horses through the streets. Escanor's men were on the way.

He and Tallbottom stared at one another while the constable debated where his attention needed to be.

"Come on," said Morrigin, grabbing Garth's arm.

###

She rushed us through the streets while confusion filled the air.

With Escanor on our heels, we followed Morrigin back across town to Charyot Manor. All of us needed to catch our breath once we ran through the door. The bureaucrats quickly spun several heavy door locks into place.

Zephyr, the man with the monocle, came running down the stairs. "Is he here? Is he safe?"

Morrigin pointed to Garth, who had wearily collapsed against a bookshelf.

"I'm fine too," I said.

"We need to get out," said Morrigin.

Zephyr considered, his mouth forming a thin line. Then he said, "Top floor. My room is at the very end. You can climb out over the wall. I'm sorry, it won't be easy to—"

"It's exactly what we need," said Morrigin. "Let's go."

The door shuddered as someone pounded on the outside.

"No," said Zephyr. "Not all of us." The little man ripped a sword from the wall, the sort of thing that was obviously meant as a decoration and not an actual weapon. It wobbled in his sweaty grip. He tucked the weapon under his arm and took a moment to button his top button and tuck in his shirt before holding the sword in both hands. "He'll have to get through us."

Around the room, the rest of the bureaucrats were picking up their own weapons. Scroll cases. Umbrellas. Books listing the many kinds of birds. The bookkeepers lined up behind Zephyr, looking as stern as any military formation.

"One more thing," whispered Zephyr. "Take this." He reached inside his coat and produced a small piece of paper folded neatly into a square. "One of the clerks finally found it just after you left yesterday." He looked at her carefully. "I'm afraid you'll have to visit...her. Can't avoid it."

Morrigin took the paper as if she were being handed something very heavy. She stared at it, like she might open it and read what it said, and then handed it to me. I shoved it into my pocket, alongside her earring.

Morrigin put a hand on Zephyr's shoulder. "We can't thank you—"

"It's the Old Way!" he said, as another pounding left a crack in the door. He fixed his eyes on Garth and said, "Now get him out of here!"

Morrigin paused to speak again, but she said nothing. She grabbed Garth's hand and dragged him up the stairs.

I followed, feeling as if I'd been forgotten, swallowed up by something more important.

We climbed to the top of the stairs and followed Morrigin to the last room of a long hall. She rushed inside and threw open the window. I could tell it pointed away from the city gate.

Morrigin pointed through the open window, her intent clear. "Climb onto the roof. Maybe we can get down from there."

Maybe? It sounded insane, but just then we all jumped at the sound of Charyot Manor's front door being broken in half.

However, my mind was at work on a different problem.

This was Zephyr's room. I saw a wardrobe and a few cabinets pushed against the walls, but otherwise his personal chamber was empty. It clawed at my mind.

Once again, dear reader, I wish I could tell you I understood what all this meant, but a moment later Morrigin was shoving me through a window with her boot.

CHAPTER FORTY-ONE

I WENT FIRST, with Garth right behind me.

The roof slanted, as roofs do, and I found I was unable to stand in place. My only option was to step quickly, obeying the tug of gravity, toward the ledge and hope my instincts would take care of the rest.

Zephyr had been wise to send us here. The end of the roof overhung the city wall, and just below I could see a road leading into the forest. After a short hop down, Garth and I stood atop the wall, right in the middle of the path where the guards walked their patrol.

"Now what?" asked Garth. "Didn't he say we were supposed to climb down somehow?"

It was a good question. Being a fortified city, there were no ladders to get down. Behind us, Morrigin was shutting the window and just starting her descent along the shingles.

"The banners," I remembered.

Every side of the city was decorated with them. Nearby, one banner was attached to the top of the wall with a metal rod, like a curtain. I stepped close and glanced over the edge. My stomach swam at the sight of the ground so far below.

Shaking my head, I grabbed the banner in both hands and swung over the top, trying not to think about how much it would hurt to fall nearly three stories. Or how it would feel to survive only to have Garth land on me and finish the job.

Hand over hand, walking backward down the city wall, I made my way toward the ground, counting steps to keep my mind occupied. I didn't want to look at the ground, but looking up reminded me that Garth was fumbling his way right above me, so I kept my eyes closed until my feet touched the grass.

We stood at the corner of the city, where the north and east wall met in a sharp edge. The main gate was on the south side, far away from us.

"Where's Morrigin?" asked Garth as he finished his descent.

I looked up. "I assumed she was next." There was no sign of her. "No time to wait. Let's head for the trees."

I only took half a step before we heard a big wagon coming our way. Or maybe several.

"Can we still make it to the woods?" asked Garth.

"They'll see us, but we may not have a choice," I said. "At least we know a wagon can't follow us if we move through the trees." I hoped my words sounded more confident to the prince than they felt. Whoever was riding our way could easily dismount and follow us wherever we went, and they would probably move faster than either of us. Most people did.

THE ONCE AND FUTURE IDIOT

"What are you two still doing here?" came a voice. Morrigin stood behind us.

"How did you get down so fast?" I asked.

"Quietly," she replied. "Why aren't you running?"

"Where—*exactly*—should we go, General Morrigin? Would you like us to run into the woods and survive on beetles until they hunt us down?"

Morrigin frowned, realizing we were cornered. "Maybe I can talk to them." She rounded the corner to face the oncoming carriages. There were three of them barreling down on us, but I soon realized they weren't driven by Abrecans.

It was Dagonet and his troupe.

"Well, don't just stand there, boy, climb up!" he shouted from the front of the lead wagon.

I ran toward my old friend as he slowed down. "How did you find us?"

"Find you? We're escaping those lunatics! They tied the gate to their own horses and pulled it apart! Now climb up and hold on. I don't have time to stop!"

Not waiting for a reply, he ordered the driver to take off.

I grabbed onto some of the straps that held the wagon together and pressed myself close to the canvas covering. Garth scrambled for the driver's seat and Dagonet extended a hand to pull him up. Morrigin climbed alongside me just as the vehicle sped up.

"It's going to be bumpy!" shouted Dagonet.

The wagon bolted down the sparse path through the woods.

I looked back and saw Morrigin watching the city, where the Abrecans at Charyot Manor had surely been overrun by Escanor. A tear wandered down her cheek until it was buffeted by the wind and blown away.

Chapter Forty-Two

DAGONET STOPPED once the city was out of sight.

His wagons were a wreck by then. Charging through the woods, between trees and over rocks, had taken its toll on the vehicles, which had only ever been cared for by clueless actors who were fortunate to remember which side to hitch the horses to.

Garth, Morrigin, and I climbed down. I opened and closed my weary hands, tired from gripping the sides of the wagon. I soon learned I had been luckier than the poor souls riding in the normal part of the wagon, who emerged rubbing their backs and sporting new bruises.

"Did anyone follow us?" Dagonet asked.

"I didn't see them," said Morrigin. "But there aren't many roads out of Hanbury. Won't take them long."

"You didn't have to come back for us," I told Dagonet.

He waved it off. "I needed to get away from those bullies. None of them were behind the city, so that's where I went."

He was lying. Dagonet could have ridden back the way he'd came, but he wasn't about to admit he'd been worried about me.

"This road continues for a long way," said Ywain, approaching with a map in hand, "but we can turn onto a stone road up ahead. We won't leave a trail on it."

The actors groaned at the idea of riding over stones, but it was a good idea.

"Well done," I told Ywain.

He beamed. "My family's in the cartography trade. Been reading maps since before I could walk."

"I thought they were in the business of making potions that worked on cats."

"That's just a hobby on my mother's side! My family's run the cartographer's guild for generations."

"And you're the youngest sibling?" I ventured.

"How did you know?"

"Just a guess." It was obvious Ywain had older siblings taking care of the family business, leaving him with the burden of time and inheritance, but no obvious way to fulfill either. Unstimulated men of privilege find their way to the theater when they lack the dignity and will to be writers.

Garth had wandered off, so I followed him. His head slumped and his shoulders sagged as he stumped away from the group. No stupid questions. None of his usual diversions, like throwing rocks at birds or trying to talk to squirrels. I should have been thankful.

"Garth," I said softly.

"Be quiet, Erlin."

I silently remained at his side. The young prince could get himself killed without a grownup to make sure he didn't wander into a bear cave.

"I'm not very smart," he whispered. "I know that I'm stupid. Everyone says it."

He looked at me, and all I could do was return a weak smile.

"For once, I thought I could be useful," he continued. "I put the telescope together. I had to hold up the big glass part on the end, but it worked. A little. And from our room at the inn, I saw you tying up those women in the stable, so I thought..."

"You thought I had captured the villains and was putting them to death," I finished. "Don't feel bad, Garth. You didn't know."

He continued like I hadn't said anything. "I untied them all and then waited for you, because I wanted...I wanted to show you that I understood what you meant about the ducks. I didn't want you to kill anyone. It seemed like I was doing something smart, but that was the stupidest thing I've done in my life."

"No, it wasn't," I said. Then I pondered why that was supposed to make him feel better. "You didn't know. Garth, you tried to help people you thought were in danger. That's a good, smart thing to do. It was noble."

"But the Abrecans!" He pointed back toward the city. "The good ones, I mean. That mean man probably killed them!"

"We don't know that," I said, but Zephyr had looked exactly like someone who knew he was facing death. "You tried to help people, Garth, and it went wrong. That happens sometimes when you try to do good. It doesn't always work, but it's important to try."

He wiped a tear. "Will you tell me something?"

"Of course."

"Why did you draw those symbols on the wall? I don't understand. It's like you're just pretending that someone was using magic."

Because magic isn't real, I wanted to tell him. He was close to understanding this on his own, close to the panic that goes along with realizing you've built your life around a faulty worldview, but I wasn't interested in pushing him down that slope right now.

Morrigin approached, taking quiet, careful steps, aware of Garth's fragile state. "We need to leave soon."

Garth turned to face her. "Why are you always trying to save me?" he asked directly.

She flinched, then looked at me. "Have you read that piece of paper, the one Zephyr gave me at Charyot Manor?"

To be honest, I'd forgotten about it. "No. Should I?"

She pointed at Garth. "He should."

I took out the folded paper. It was not ordinary paper, but made from a thicker stock, something meant to last a long time. I wanted to read it, but instead I handed it to the prince.

Garth unfolded the page, and I watched his eyes move back and forth.

He looked up at Morrigin and said, "This isn't right."

"Our records are very reliable," she said.

I heard a bird call while Garth pondered.

Garth shook his head. "My mother told me, over and over, that this happened the following year. She wanted me to know!"

I glanced at the page, hoping to figure out what they were talking about, but the bird called again, and this time I finally realized it was not a bird. Standing near the carriage, Dagonet had cupped his hands around his mouth and repeated the sound. He was signaling us to get back.

We ran over and noticed the actors were loading themselves back into the carriages. "Dagonet, I've told you that if you do it *too* perfectly no one can tell it's not an actual bird."

He made an elaborate gesture. "I will not apologize for perfection!"

"I take it they're catching up?"

He pointed toward the city. "Someone thinks they saw something that way." Turning, he pointed ahead of us. "So, *we're* going *that* way. Toward the road Ywain mentioned. Well, some of us are."

Without explaining himself, Dagonet climbed up into the driver's seat. I started to climb up next to him, but Morrigin pulled me down and pointed to Garth, who was sullenly walking into the back of the carriage. "He needs you."

I knew it was useless to argue with her stoic eyes, so I followed Garth into the carriage while Morrigin took the front seat.

The carriage took off again, with Garth, me, and part of Dagonet's troop crammed into the back.

When we turned onto the stone path, I clearly heard the other pair of wagons continue rolling on down the dirt road. I smiled. Dagonet was letting his other two wagons leave a trail while we hurried along a different route.

The trip was silent. I watched Garth, who folded and unfolded the paper Morrigin had given him, reading it over and over with a look on his face that made my stomach hurt.

CHAPTER FORTY-THREE

WE BOUNCED PAINFULLY along that stone road for over an hour before we turned hard to the right and began down another dirt road. This wasn't something Dagonet would have done, so I assumed Morrigin had become his navigator. She was up to something. We were heading east and would soon be at the far edge of Albion, near the Sea of Glass.

By the time we stopped, night had begun to fall. We didn't build a fire for fear of being seen. Everyone slumped off the carriage while trying to rub warmth into our bodies. All but Garth. The young prince wandered away from the rest of us with his eyes down, not caring about the shivers that shook his spine.

Ywain emerged and looked around like a puppy that had lost a ball. "Where can I...you know...go?"

"Anywhere!" said Dagonet. "It's nothing but trees."

"With everyone else? In plain sight?" Ywain looked intently into the forest. "There. I'll just climb down that ridge a bit."

He ran off, his breeches in a bunch.

Dagonet rubbed his temples. "He's going to get eaten, isn't he?"

I nodded. Then I noticed Morrigin heading our way. "Where did you bring us?" I asked before she could say anything.

She paused for a moment, her mouth growing small while she decided how to respond. Finally, she pointed back the way we'd come. "It's dark. If Escanor comes looking for us this way, he'll never see our trail until morning."

It all sounded smart, but the way she avoided eye contact and fidgeted with her hands told me Morrigin was hiding something. Something big, I assumed. Normally Morrigin was as unreadable as the trees, but she was fretting too much for me to believe she was telling me everything. Whatever she was hiding, it was more important than her usual lies.

"What's our destination?" I whispered. "That man in Hanbury, Zephyr, he said you needed to see *her*, whatever that means. I don't like you yanking the prince around by your own whims."

She frowned. We'd never discussed it, but it had been obvious for some time that Morrigin knew exactly who Garth was, and I believed it was time for us to stop pretending.

Before she could respond, Dagonet interrupted. "I'll need to drop you off soon. My understudies have the other two carriages, and I'll need to catch up before they drive into a lake. Where *are* we going?"

I looked to Morrigin and raised my eyebrows.

"We need to talk to Garth," she said.

Garth sat cross-legged on the ground. He'd spread the paper out over a tree stump and stared at it, like it was a meal gone cold. Morrigin and I quietly took our places around him, trying to gauge his mood.

I took a quick glance at the page before Garth pulled it away and stowed it back into his pocket. I only saw it for a moment, but the format looked familiar.

A birth record? I'd seen plenty of them while researching which lords and nobles were lying about their lineage. That sort will pay half of their salary for a good forgery, just to make sure no one knows they grew up in a house without a maid.

The paper Garth was hiding bore every hint of such a record. At a glance, I had seen the royal seal and the telltale branches of an ornate family tree.

"I'm sorry, Morrigin," said Garth, staring down at the tree stump. "I know they were your friends back there. I didn't know what I was doing...and I think I got them..."

Morrigin's face nearly fell. The marble facade that seemed stronger than the mountains tremored for such a brief moment I thought I'd imagined it. The brave bookkeepers we'd hardly even met back in Charyot Manor had been more than just her friends. I wasn't sure I understood the Abrecans, but Morrigin's closeness with her people went beyond friendship, beyond family.

"Escanor did that," she said finally. "Escanor hurt them—not you. You were trying to *help* people. You have every reason to be proud of yourself. I certainly am."

I put a hand on his shoulder. "And so am I."

Garth looked up at me, intensely, deciding if I was telling the truth. I *was* proud of Garth. Proud of him for standing up to me, someone he respected. Proud of him for trying to save people instead of letting them die. Proud of him for so much.

But that didn't take the sadness from his face.

"What is that?" said Morrigin. She turned her blue eyes toward the forest.

"I hear it, too," I whispered. A clanking sound. Slowly advancing. And a voice that I couldn't quite make out.

Garth knelt and squinted through the tree line, then smiled. "Is that Caball?"

"Who's...Caball?" asked Morrigin.

"A dog," I said. "And bad news."

I pointed to the woods with a shake of my head while Morrigin, confused, continued to watch.

"What!" came a raspy cry from the woods.

Chapter Forty-Four

King Pellinore finally stumbled into view, crashing through the brush in his antique armor. The knee joints seemed to always give him the most trouble. His sword clanged against his thigh in an uneven rhythm as he clamored our way, hopelessly trying to keep up with his shaggy dog, who had already set himself on a collision course with Garth.

"Caball!" The smile returned to Garth's ruddy face just as the dog collided with him. The pair fell in a heap.

"It's Pellinore's dog," I said.

"*King* Pellinore?" Morrigin stared at the armored figure who was clunking our way.

"The same."

"Unhand that beast!" shouted Pellinore, pulling out his blade. Unlike his armor, the sword gleamed in the light and didn't show a trace of rust. The sharp edge was nearly audible as it cut through the air. The clumsiness of Pellinore's walk was all but forgotten as he stalked protectively toward his dog.

"It's Garth!" I shouted before he could close the distance and run the boy through. "Don't stab him, you old goat!"

Pellinore squinted at the prince, his grey eyes piercing through the slits in his visor. "Garth? What?" Recognition finally dawned on his face. Or what I could see of it. The sword disappeared back into its sheath. "Quite right, Caball," he called toward his dog. "Well done." Pellinore tapped the front of his helmet. "Quite a *nose* on that pup. Knows his friends from his foes, even in the dark."

"What are you doing out here, Pelly?" I asked. By now, half of the actors had gathered around. Pellinore was a spectacle even to them.

"That questionable beast! What!" He pointed a finger into the air. "Recall the shopkeeper in Hanbury?"

"The...taxidermist who sold you that stuffed...thing? A few animals all cobbled together?"

"Would you believe he told me it was not a fake?"

Despite all that was going on, Pellinore had my full attention now. "It has to be fake. You said it had the head of a snake, right?"

"Grafted onto the body of a lion and the hooves of a deer!" he added. "I nearly ran the rascal through, but for the integrity in his eyes. A king knows to look for these things, you know."

"And I take it you've made finding this creature your new obsession?"

"I'll track down the questionable beast and mount it on my wall! There's no escape—Caball and I have seen its tracks."

Morrigin scowled. "Wouldn't they just look like normal deer tracks?"

I shook my head at her. Pellinore was unstoppable when he had an idea. Best to let him meander. It wasn't unusual to see Pelly wandering the halls of Tomelac on his many visits, cantankerous as a woodpecker in a dollhouse, pacing around with his head full of odd ideas that he mumbled to empty suits of armor.

I noticed something hanging from his belt. A horn, covered by a simple cloth. "That horn...is it full of—"

"Fewmets!" he said proudly.

I groaned. The reason I avoided hunting parties (other than the hunting) was because hunters often traveled with a horn full of fewmets—that is, animal droppings—hanging from their belt. When they came upon droppings in the woods, they would gather around and compare it to the stuff in their horns to find out if they were tracking the right creature. The warmer the better, I was told, but I'd always held to the opposing view.

"Well, I'm starved." Garth sat up, still wrestling Caball with one arm. "I'd love a few meats."

"No!" I threw out my hands to stop the inevitable.

Garth got to his feet just as Pellinore swept the cloth away and held out the horn.

Since Pellinore's beast obviously was the invention of a desperate shopkeeper, I had hoped Pelly's fewmets also did not exist and that his gesture would merely reveal an empty horn. But I was wrong; the fewmets were about to become real.

The smell pushed me back. "Put that away!" I shouted, as the smell made my knees wobble. The actors stepped back in a wave.

"It's just animal droppings, city boy," announced Pellinore. "Every hunter knows the value of fewmets. It's how we know the beast is near!"

"How in blazes did you get fewmets from a mythical creature?" I asked.

With a screech, Pellinore lifted his metal visor, scaring a flock of birds out of a nearby tree. "Well, these fewmets are not from the *same* creature, mind you. Sometimes a hunter uses similar fewmets."

It was true. At banquet I'd once been seated next to a hunter who told me he'd tracked an elk with the use of deer fewmets because their droppings were similar. The story made me gain appreciation for his craft, but not for the meat pie I had been eating.

"But what's similar to the fewmets of the...questionable beast?" I asked.

"Well, nothing," said Pellinore. "That's why I had to put a few fewmets together. A deer, a lion, and a snake. Combined, they should be nearly the same as the droppings of the questionable beast stuffed on my mantle!"

Combined, I thought with a shudder, trying not to imagine the alchemy King Pellinore had gone through to smush three different animal droppings together.

Morrigin furrowed her brow. "I have questions."

"There's no lions around here!" I blurted out, as if that were the most absurd thing I had been told that day.

"The shopkeeper's cats were happy to oblige. Had to use more than one. Then I heard about a fellow who kept a snake as a pet. Odd fellow. Some men aren't in their right minds. Finding the deer fewmets was simple. Then I crammed them all together. Ingenious!"

The actors groaned. A few climbed back into the carriage.

Caball yipped.

"Quite right, boy." Pellinore flipped his visor down. "Time we got back to work! Bring your nose over here." Pellinore held out the horn. The shaggy dog gave it a sniff and then flattened his body and put his nose to the ground. "Caball's got a scent!"

"Did he follow a scent to get here?" I asked.

"Of course not, Inquisitor. I ran this way after we heard the other carriage near the bridge." He pointed in the direction we had just come from. "Quite rude. All that racket will scare any game this direction."

Morrigin gripped my arm.

"Other carriage?" I asked, understanding her urgency.

Pellinore pointed to the big wagon the actors traveled in. "Like that one. Better decorations, I must say. Winding along the path back there."

Dagonet whistled loud. "It's time to go. Sounds like they're right behind us!"

Morrigin frowned. "Escanor got lucky."

I had a feeling there was more to it than that. He knew where she was going.

"We need to climb aboard," I said to Garth, who was waving at the dog as Pellinore wandered into the woods.

"No." Morrigin put her hand against my chest.

I felt her fingers, warm against my body, and I almost couldn't look into her blue eyes. "What do you mean?"

"Yes," said Dagonet, leaning in close to her. "What *do* you mean?"

"I'll go," she said. "We'll meet them. Don't argue, Dagonet. They'll catch up sooner or later. I'll tell them I hitched a ride with you. Then they'll search you and see that Erlin and...Wart aren't with us. They'll believe me."

"What about us?" asked Garth.

"You and Erlin keep moving east. Just over the hill, you'll find footpaths that lead to the shoreline. Stay eastbound and take those paths to the shore. The Moonriders will find you there."

I shook my head. "You're going to get hurt."

"It's the only way to keep him safe. What matters is—"

"*You* matter, Morrigin. It's not just about saving other people. I don't know why you even care about him, but you're worth saving, too."

Her blue eyes widened. I don't think she'd been told anything like that before.

Morrigin grabbed Dagonet and rushed him to the carriage. I watched them climb aboard and take off, heading further down the path. I knew if we stood too long that the Abrecans would drive by and see us, which would ruin Morrigin's plan, but my feet refused to move until the carriage was out of sight and I knew there was no chance I would catch another glimpse of her.

Garth and I waited a few more moments before we silently turned away from the road. Like two men headed for the gallows, we faced east, as Morrigin had instructed, and took a step into the unknown.

At least, I realized, *Garth hasn't been in a talking mood lately.* I wasn't interested in any chatter. Some quiet time would help me.

A sound caught my ear.

In front of us, someone stepped out from behind a tree.

It was Ywain, struggling to tie his breeches while balancing a rucksack full of maps on his shoulder.

He looked around and said, "Where is everyone?"

Chapter Forty-Five

"...AND MY MOTHER'S AUNT'S DAUGHTER had a cat that rolled over when she sneezed!" said Ywain, continuing a story I hadn't been paying attention to.

"Your mother?" Garth asked.

"No. The cat."

"I mean, was it your mother who sneezed, or the cat?"

"Her niece sneezed and then she rolled over."

"Your mother rolled over when her niece sneezed?"

"No!" Ywain threw up his hands. "It's quite simple. My cousin trained her to roll over when she sneezed."

"Where does your aunt play into it?"

"It's her daughter."

"The cat?"

"Watch your step here," I interjected, hoping to distract them with the deep hole we needed to step over.

I'd nearly lost my mind during their previous conversation. Garth had asked if it was difficult playing the king, and when Ywain asked, "Which king?" Garth began a series of questions about the identity of a *witch* king. An hour of questions followed, with neither realizing the discrepancy.

The hole wasn't very deep. Ywain and Garth shared a confused shrug as they took the tiny step over it. In my mind, it was an excellent hole because it was just deep enough to end their conversation.

"Found it," I said, pointing to foot trail that curved in front of us and wound through the trees. "Morrigin was right. And it looks like it heads east."

I couldn't understand why moving east was so important, but at least I knew Escanor was going in the other direction.

In fact, I honestly had no idea what was going on at all. I wanted to know what was on the piece of paper Garth kept looking at, and I wanted to why half of the Abrecans were trying to kill Garth while the other half were trying to save him. And I wanted to know if Morrigin was still alive.

Mind you, I'm normally very comfortable with ignorance. It's hard to be upset about life when you don't know what's going on, which is why Pellinore's dog could be the happiest creature in all of Albion.

Unfortunately, my sense of responsibility was emerging. I'd spent my adult life numbing myself to maturity and obligations, but my adventure with Garth was unraveling years of hard work.

Of course, Garth wasn't entirely to blame.

Since that blasted, raven-haired woman first appeared, I'd been feeling all sorts of confused. Since the moment I saw her in the court of Tomelac, I always felt a pang of loss when she wasn't around.

Morrigin fluttered in and out of my life, like a scrap of paper in the wind, tantalizing my mind with an interesting verse or a snatch of clever wit, only to be thrust away by a new breeze before I could read a complete sentence.

"That man back there," said Ywain, "is he really a king?"

"Oh, yes," I replied. "King Pellinore is, er, technically, the king of the Manly isles. Up north."

"Technically?"

"His sons decided to make their kingdom a little more modern and let the people make decisions for themselves. His citizens vote on changes now. Even elected a senate. These days, poor Pelly hasn't got a scrap of work to do."

Anywhere he went, Pellinore always made a scene. A real character. Dagonet had seemed quite taken with the old man. I noticed him quietly impersonating Pellinore's little movements and studying his speech, all things he did to learn about someone so he could write them into a play. It wasn't every day you met an oddball like Pelly.

"What's that?" said Ywain, stopping in his tracks.

This was a problem, since a few low-hanging branches had forced us to walk in a single-file line with Ywain in the lead. Garth, who was only a step behind, piled into him.

I was next. Sadly, my mind was trapped in the memory of Morrigin's blue eyes when I crashed into Garth. As the three of us collided, my teeth clamped shut with a loud *clack* that jarred my skull.

My empty skull, I thought. *No brains up there anymore. Just oatmeal.*

"It's only a barrel," said Garth.

Sighing, I pulled myself from my lonely thoughts and looked to see what the brilliant minds were gawking at.

We were approaching a crossroads. The narrow dirt path we walked intersected with another just like it, thirty or forty yards ahead. And at the center, where the two lanes met, stood a wooden barrel.

"Only a barrel," Garth repeated, but his words were less confident.

I couldn't grasp any reason for it, but a barrel all by itself, untouched by the wilderness and thieves, just didn't sit right with me.

Garth snapped his fingers. "Say, that reminds me of something I was going to ask you."

I could only imagine Garth's question. I braced myself.

"Is it true," he asked, "that you stuffed Mirdal the Mad into a barrel, and that's why no one found his body?"

I close my eyes, silently cursing.

After all Garth had seen, all the deception and ruses, the idiot boy still believed.

"Him?" Ywain cried. "*He* didn't kill Mirdal the Mad!"

"Yes, he did!" Garth spun on him. "I was there! He walks into the room like he owns the place, carryin' that red robe, the one with all the funny symbols on it—"

Ywain interrupted. "Dagonet told me all about it! Erlin didn't kill anyone. He just—"

"Ywain!" I interrupted just in time. "That barrel, it...looks dangerous. Go check it out. I'll bet you're brave."

Ywain set his jaw and turned his eyes toward the barrel. "I am brave." He took a quick step and then stared ahead, like he was daring the barrel to move.

"What's he mean?" whispered Garth, who turned around to talk to me.

"Nothing."

I watched over his shoulder and saw Ywain take a few more steps. At this rate, I wasn't certain he would reach the barrel before King Ulder died of old age.

"But he knows something!"

I kept my mouth shut, but my nerves were lit.

"Why would he say that?" Garth continued, as Ywain inched closer and closer to the barrel. "Everyone knows you killed Mirdal. Everyone! Why would anyone say that you—"

"BEACUSE ONLY IDIOTS BELIEVE IN MAGIC!" I screamed.

A little too loud.

I had only wanted to shut him up and didn't realize what I was saying until it was echoing across the hills.

The woods became still. My shouting had frightened every creature into hiding, as if the monumental truth I'd just yelled into Garth's face had disturbed the peace of the realm. It was certainly going to cost me my job.

Everything was perfectly still except for the barrel. I saw it move.

It wobbled a bit.

"Did you see that?" Ywain whispered back.

"No," I lied.

Just then, the barrel turned into Escanor.

CHAPTER FORTY-SIX

EVERYONE THINKS they'll be ready for this sort of thing.

Not this sort of thing *specifically*; watching a barrel transmogrify into a person isn't a situation you plan on. It's just that no one believes they'll panic and scream at the sight of something impossible. But, believe me, when you see something that can't be real, the first thing you lose is your dignity. Every bit of it.

At that moment, I was surprised my dignity didn't make a mess in my small clothes.

An arm came first. Pushing out on one side of the barrel just as two stubby feet appeared beneath.

It was about the time the tip of his head emerged I realized I had fallen down in shock. Instinctively, I pushed myself away from the scene. Ahead of me, Garth and Ywain were frozen in place, still on their feet, but all three of us were screaming.

Well, "screaming" might be a bit generous since we were crying like children. Garth and Ywain ran into one another and fell. Unable to rise, they clutched one another. All of us yelled. I mean cried. We cried a lot.

Escanor finally looked like Escanor. He reached into his leather vest and retrieved the stubby pipe. With a grin, he clenched it between his teeth and then reached into his vest one more time.

This time, he brought out a knife.

My mind raged with questions and fear, but a small part of it found the situation suddenly comforting. Here was something I understood: a mean guy who wanted to hurt me. Familiar territory.

"Spread out," I whispered to Garth and Ywain. "Left and right. And stay down."

They looked at me, shrugged, and then crawled in both directions.

I stared at Escanor, not blinking, and cocked my head to the side as I cracked my knuckles. Every actor knows how to play a tough guy. It's easier than it looks. Escanor took one look at me and believed I meant business.

Of course, my chances of winning a fist fight were similar to the odds of Garth remembering to put his socks on before his shoes. Fortunately, I had a plan. A cunning one. But, as I watched Escanor approach, careful as a snake, I realized my plan relied on Garth's memory, and suddenly I wondered if I should make a fist or two and try winning that way.

He stalked my way, walking in between Garth and Ywain, who were cowering on either side of the path.

"You're a good-looking man, Escanor," I shouted with confidence.

That shook him. Just a little. He stopped his walk for a moment, still a dozen paces away, and tried to figure me out.

I went on. "You look good enough to be the king." Behind Escanor, I saw Ywain and Garth rising to their feet, but I couldn't tell if they knew what I was up to. "I'd even say you had the...*handsomeness* to rule!"

I waited. In the distance, a cricket chirped. Then another.

"The *handsomeness!*" I repeated. "I say you have the *handsomeness—*"

Escanor winced as a pair of rocks hit the back of his head. In the play, this is where a series of eggs would land on Ulder's face. Garth and Ywain had finally gotten my cue.

While Escanor stumbled in confusion, I stepped forward and kicked up a cloud of dirt up in his face.

But Garth was struck by true inspiration. He got on his hands and knees behind Escanor and smiled at me.

Pride swelled in my belly as I realized that—for once—I would not be on the receiving end of this schoolyard prank. I gave Escanor a hard shove and watched him tumble over Garth.

"Well done, boy!" I helped Garth up, and the three of us ran. "Let's go! He won't stay down for long."

We raced down the path, further east. Every time I glanced back, Escanor was racing toward us. I guessed we could keep running for another minute before reaching the end of our endurance, which wasn't bad for an ignorant prince, a bad actor, and a fraudulent inquisitor.

"Look out!" screamed Ywain, who was in the front.

The path turned left, but to the right was a steep hill—nearly a ledge. Morrigin, I realized, had told us to go this way because a wagon could not follow. But one wrong step would send us tumbling down a long, steep embankment. I couldn't see the bottom.

I glanced down the incline and wondered if the best course would be to fall. We could try to slide down and get ahead of Escanor, which would be easier than running. My legs were already wobbly. If we kept running, Escanor would be on us soon with his knife; tumbling down the hill might even the odds.

But we never found out.

A blur rushed toward us from the trees. I had only a moment to notice.

It was Morrigin. Somehow.

Escanor shouted a word that became a violent grunt as Morrigin's riding boot collided with his jaw.

Being a stout little man, Escanor wobbled from the force of her attack and from the surprise of it, but he didn't fall backward as Morrigin had obviously hoped. He grabbed her wrist.

"It's a long way down," I said, rushing toward Escanor.

I'm no scrapper, but I know a thing or two about balance. After watching actors who have had too much to drink, you develop a sixth sense for when they're *just* about to fall. An actor trying to spin on point only needs to be off by a hair to ruin their act.

Escanor was off by more than a hair. Too much weight on one foot. It normally wouldn't have mattered since he was strong enough to overpower Morrigin, but it only took a simple shove of my shoulder to knock him over.

Escanor tumbled away while I wrapped my arms around Morrigin. I was thankful to feel both of her hands holding on to me. Escanor lost his grip and fell down the embankment, rolling over and over while he screamed.

"He'll break every bone in his body," said Ywain.

Morrigin shook her head. "Look again."

I couldn't believe my eyes, but Escanor was changing again. In a few moments, he had completely transmogrified back into a barrel and was rolling easily down the slope and off into the distance.

Chapter Forty-Seven

You know that little hole in the top of a barrel? Not the entire top part, but the small hole that you could just get a spoon into? Turns out that little spot is called a "bunghole."

As Escanor rolled away, I could hear him yell, "You'll never make it to Kingsport!"

But he was transmogrifying as he rolled. It was difficult to tell, but I think he'd already completed one half of his transformation.

Which has led me to wonder for quite some time if Escanor was talking out of his bunghole.

Either way, his words set Morrigin on edge.

"What's in Kingsport?" I asked, letting my practical concerns outweigh my need to make sense of a universe that had suddenly stripped away even more of my comforting ignorance.

"The Moonriders," she said. "We need to hurry."

I should have still been in shock that a man had turned himself into a barrel and then back. And part of me was. It would be a long time before that memory would not haunt me.

And I could have been distracted by the fact that I'd just won a fight, and I had done so in front of a pretty woman. Mind you, she had done a lot of the work, but I remained the victor of said fight and was already prepared to tell the story if Morrigin ever forgot how it happened.

And it might have been wise to have paid a little more attention to Escanor's path down the embankment, where he, once again shaped like a barrel, rolled down, down, down, until the grassy slope touched the ground below. He had picked up enough speed by then that he rolled onward, eventually disappearing somewhere out of sight.

But none of that was on my mind. Something else was more important.

I still held Morrigin. Until this moment, putting my arms around her would make my heart race too quickly for me to focus on any practical matter, but even as I looked into her eyes, my mind was keenly focused on a specific complication. A single problem, rising out of the mess of my life like a single thread from a complicated knot. I knew if I tugged on that one thread, the rest of the mystery would unravel.

"How did you get here?" I asked.

She stepped away from me, away from my grasp. "We have to hurry."

"How, Morrigin?" My hands felt very empty. I thrust them behind my back. "You should be *wheels* away by now."

She looked desperate. "Dagonet and I found the other Abrecans from Escanor's crew. We found them right away. After they saw you weren't with us, they turned back to Hanbury, and I started running this way. Dagonet is going to on to Troyes."

Troyes. The city sounded familiar, but I couldn't place it.

I shook my head, realizing she had avoided my question. "Morrigin. How did you *get* here?" I couldn't piece it all together right away, but I knew her story didn't add up.

"Don't do this, Erlin," she begged. "Escanor knows where my ladies are going and we need to get there first." She pointed a finger at Garth. "And he's in a lot of danger right now."

Shaking my head, I gestured for us to move on.

###

Kingsport came into view an hour later, a seaside village with busy docks reaching out into the sea like long fingers, each with Ulder's seal burned onto the wooden slats.

"Why's it called 'Kingsport?'" asked Garth, because apparently he'd been using his skull to store old doorknobs.

"Because...it's the *King's* port," I said patiently.

"I get it!" Garth patted me on the back. "You're a good teacher. The *king's* port...hey, Ywain. You know why it's called 'Kingsport?'"

Next to me, Morrigin was scanning the city, looking very concerned.

"Do you see them?" I asked.

"No." She frowned.

"Hard to tell from up here," I offered.

"I don't see *any* horses. They're not here, but Escanor somehow guessed we were going this way. He might have gotten in their way somehow."

"Tell me what's going on," I insisted. "I can't go on like this, following you around and hoping the prince is safe. I don't even know why you're helping me. Can you tell me anything?"

Morrigin thought for a moment. "Kingsport isn't where I'm taking you. It's just a stop on the way." After a moment of indecision, she looked me squarely in the eye and said, "We're taking a boat to Avalon."

Chapter Forty-Eight

Kingsport wasn't a walled city, but it was still as well-fortified as any place I'd been. Guards kept a hard eye on every traveler, flanking the roads in pairs, while men in tall towers gazed over the land and sea, ensuring Tomelac's goods were sent and received safely.

But no one bothered us as we entered, and Garth, with his dirty clothes and his sad face downcast, wasn't recognized by anyone. I strolled toward the docks alongside Morrigin and noticed she watched the waves with as much joy as a child. The happiness was mostly hidden behind her stoic mask, but I saw her loosen her shoulders and let down her brow. Just a bit.

"Think they sell fruit here?" asked Ywain.

"They sell everything in port towns," I told him. "Why fruit?" I should have learned by then not to ask Ywain questions, but curiosity runs deep in my veins.

"My mixture!" Ywain threw open his rucksack and looked inside. "I've got most of my ingredients, but I need a few."

"For your...cats?" I asked, not really wanting to know the answer.

"Cats?" asked Morrigin, perking up. "You have cats?"

I made a mental note that Morrigin was a cat person. This boded well, for dogs tended to require more maintenance and I was notoriously lazy.

"I can train them!" said Ywain. "My family—"

"Train them?" I didn't believe it. "The cats I've seen you with are useless lumps trying to escape."

"You didn't see Oliver in action!" said Ywain. "We kept finding mice. I'd say, 'stay' and he would stay—even though he was hungry. Then I'd wait a few seconds and say, 'kill!' and he'd pounce! He only needed a few minutes of training, thanks to my recipe, but the ingredients haven't been fresh lately. My last cat was barely affected."

Ywain dashed over to a fruit stand to continue his hobby.

I looked to Garth and saw his face was fallen. I had hoped the spectacle of the barrel would distract him, but Garth still felt bad about his mistake in Hanbury. That was understandable. Even the best kings had to deal with disasters. I had made sure the prince knew I was proud of him for trying to help people, but nothing was going to lift his mood.

He walked absently along a pier, ignoring us, and then sat down on the edge, dangling his feet over the water. His eyes fell toward his lap, and he didn't even seem to notice the sea.

Morrigin and I stood nearby, but far enough away for him to be alone with his thoughts.

"How are we getting to Avalon?" I still didn't believe it. "No one knows the way."

"The harbormaster does." Morrigin pointed to a wooden building near the coast, in the center of the docks. "His name's Gus. Gus Fishborn. He'll help us."

"So, the harbormaster in Kingsport is..."

"Yes." Morrigin's smile grew. "He's an Abrecan. His job is keeping the secret of the location of Avalon, and he takes us there sometimes."

"And you've been? To Avalon? I didn't even think it was real."

"Yes. It's a place I need to go sometimes. But I've never understood boats, so I wouldn't be able to find it. Gus will pilot our ship. That one, in fact."

She pointed toward the docks at a black-hulled sailboat. I saw enough room on the deck for a handful of people to sit comfortably. My brain had no words for the different parts of a boat, but I noticed it had a second sail, which presumably gave it an advantage over the boats with only one. Then again, for all I knew this was to keep either sail from getting lonely.

"It's called the *Sable*," Morrigin explained. "Gus is proud of it."

"Can't wait to meet him."

I wondered why Morrigin was not in a hurry to get to the harbormaster, but when I looked closer at the building, I noticed a lot of movement in the windows and assumed Morrigin wanted to wait for a quieter moment when she could speak to Gus without being overheard.

"Do you see the garden on top?" she asked, pointing to the harbormaster's building. "It's how we find each other."

I could just see stalks and a few colorful buds peeking over the top of the roof. "You look for rooftop gardens?"

"Moon gardens," she corrected. "Those plants bloom at night, mostly on full-mooned evenings. Gus will sit out there at midnight, and any other Abrecan will know he's one of us."

"You have people like him in every major city, don't you?" I asked, but she only smiled her little smile, her eyes lighting up with the secret. "In fact, you've probably got someone in Tomelac."

She shrugged.

"I wonder who it is..." There was a garden on a rooftop just outside of Tomelac. I mentally ran through the list of people I knew in the capital, but none of them struck me as Abrecans. "Must be someone you trust, not one of Escanor's people."

Morrigin confirmed my theory with a wink. Mesmerized, I forced myself to tear my gaze from her mischievous grin before I looked like a fool. I certainly felt like one as I began floundering for more to say. I could tell she was proud of herself for pinning me with her clever glances.

We watched the water and let a peaceful breeze embrace us. Her hand touched mine—I'm certain by accident—and both of us tried to hide our smiles.

Along a pier, I saw a dock worker unloading a barrel, and my stomach churned at the memory of Escanor's transformation. It didn't make sense, and it certainly couldn't have been magic.

"Magic isn't real," I told myself, repeating my life's litany.

Morrigin stared like she was about to accuse me of something. The ocean rose behind her, but I stayed lost in those blue eyes, like a drowning man not sure if he wanted to be rescued.

Garth's voice was barely loud enough to hear. "Erlin..."

The distress in his tone was unmistakable.

He stood at the edge of the same pier where we'd left him. His brooding expression had been replaced with a look of terror.

"Is..." Garth pointed down, into the water. "Is that what I think it is?"

We stood on either side of him and looked at the water just under the next pier. Something had been hidden there, just under the water. It took a moment for my eyes to focus.

Horses. Morrigin gasped. Several dead horses lay on top of one another.

Chapter Forty-Nine

"No!" Morrigin spun and turned to the city, her mouth a thin line of anger.

I didn't have to ask. These horses obviously belonged to the Moonriders. Morrigin's women were already here, but something had gone wrong. I wanted to point out that we were only looking at horses—no dead women were under the boards—but Morrigin was not interested in talking. Her eyes were fixed on the wooden building at the center of the pier.

"We need to go," I urged. "I don't know what's happened, Morrigin, but it's obviously dangerous. We can get on that boat and—"

"Not without Gus," she protested. "He knows the way to Avalon."

"Avalon?" Garth stood, forcing himself between us. "Did you say—"

"I'll go," I said. "You and Garth stay here and see if you can get the boat ready."

She obviously wanted to argue, but I was right. Morrigin knew what was going on, and I didn't. That made me expendable.

"I'll shout something if I'm in trouble," I told her. "Just be ready to sail."

###

I hurried to the small building at the center of the docks and pressed my face up to the dirty window. Inside, I saw what must have been Morrigin's worst nightmare.

The women she rode with had been tied and gagged and placed on the floor. A man's body lay in the middle of the floor, face down, surrounded by a pool of blood that had escaped a wound in his skull. Gus, the harbormaster, I surmised. At least the Moonriders were still alive.

I couldn't tell who had done it. There were no Abrecan wagons nearby, but they could have entered the city another way. Maybe by a boat.

I decided to walk around and look for clues, anything to tell me what had happened, but I didn't want to draw attention to myself since that would only make me the next victim. I needed to look normal.

And it's easy to walk like a normal person when you're not thinking about it. We do it all the time. But you've got another thing coming the moment you deliberately try to put one foot in front of the other while acting casual, because it suddenly becomes clear you don't actually know how walking works. This causes you to think very, very hard about where you place each foot. Soon, you'll realize you've stopped swinging your arms, which, if you recall correctly, is a thing people do as they walk. So, there you are, staring at the ground so you can place one foot evenly in front of the other, all while swinging your hands like a baboon. Smiling, always smiling, because you don't want to look weird or anything.

I rounded a corner of a nearby building and jumped when I saw an armed figure walking my way, but I calmed down at the sight of his armor. He was one of the king's men, not an Abrecan. One of Ulder's knights, probably here to protect a shipment.

"If it isn't the inquisitor," came a booming voice from behind me.

I spun around. Blocking out the light was Sir Kay, one of Ulder's favorites. Not the most likely knight to win a spelling bee, but his faithfulness to the king was unquestionable. That made him rather annoying.

We were not supposed to use words like "crony" or "lapdog" to describe Kay and the others who did Ulder's dirty work, so I'll just tell you that Sir Kay was so invested in pleasing the king that his majesty had no need to call for a doctor to find out if he was growing polyps.

"What are you doing here?" I asked.

"Could ask you the same thing," returned Kay. "Aren't you taking care of the prince?"

"King's business," I said, crossing my arms. "Can't talk about it."

A sword, large as a tree, slid out of Kay's scabbard, making as much noise as possible on its way out. "Funny. I'm on the king's business, too."

He hefted the sword as if to add, *And I get to bash your brains in if I want.*

The soldier behind me put a hand on my shoulder. "Ulder sent us to keep the prince safe. So where is he?"

I noticed a flaw in their logic. "Why would he send you to look for him in Kingsport if we were headed for Hanbury?"

The two soldiers looked at one another, and then Kay shrugged, signaling there was no longer any need to lie to me. Despite that, I still had no idea what was going on—a situation I was growing accustomed to—and I was obviously not meant to live long enough to figure it out.

"Just tell us where he is, Inquisitor." Kay raised the sword and placed the sharp tip at the front of my neck. Behind me, the other man gripped my shoulder tighter.

"The prince is an idiot," said Kay. "And his days are numbered. You can be on the right side of things, or you can spend the rest of your life without ears."

"At least I wouldn't have to listen to idiots," I said.

Kay snarled. No sense of humor on that one. "It's your fingers after that. Then we'll march you back and set you on fire while Ulder watches."

"Garth's just a brat," said the soldier behind me. "Not worth dying for."

I had spent my time at Tomelac finding every reason to hate the prince. We all did. But I had also seen him risk his life to save someone. Even if he hadn't been smart enough to know it was a mistake, he'd shown the kind of goodness rarely found in kings. That, I suddenly decided, was worth protecting.

"Yes, he is," I said, feeling brave for the first time in my life. "I'm not going to tell you anything, Sir Kay, on my honor, you will never find—"

"Found him!" The guard behind me jutted his chin toward the shore. "He's getting' on a boat!"

Well, I tried.

Kay growled. "Go!" He pointed to the black vessel that Morrigin was unmooring. Garth was already on board.

The soldier let me go and ran to the beach. Morrigin finished untying the rope and jumped onto the boat, where she and Garth struggled with the sail. It caught wind in time to push them away from the pier, but just barely. There was obviously not an ounce of seamanship between the two of them.

Kay turned back to me and gave the sword a little twist. "It's over, inquisitor. I'm gonna get a medal for—"

"Hi, Erlin," came a casual voice from behind. It was Ywain, walking my way and talking with his mouth half full. "I found someone selling roasted nuts with hot oil, but they always let the oil get to the bottom. Don't you hate that?"

"Ywain," I said calmly, my eyes on Kay.

"What's even the point of oiling them if you're not going to do it right?" He kept walking my way, clearly oblivious to my peril.

"Ywain..."

"I have half a mind to go back there and—"

"Ywain!"

Ywain, who was now standing next to me, looked up from his bag of food and froze at the sight of the gigantic sword, finally realizing what he'd walked into.

Seizing an idea, I smacked the bottom of the bag and sent hot oil into Kay's face. It hit his eye with a sizzling hiss.

"Come on!" We ran past Kay, who had dropped his sword onto his own foot.

Morrigin hadn't been joking when she said she didn't understand boats. She and Garth were piloting the craft along the docks, barely avoiding a collision with several piers. We could hear Sir Kay charging after us, but we had a sizeable lead.

We trotted up a wooden pier just ahead of the black boat. It drew near, close enough for Ywain and me to clumsily step on board, but I couldn't help but notice our combined weight slowed the craft even more as we took our place on the unstable deck.

Sir Kay's voice burst from the shore as he screamed, "GET BACK HERE, SHE WOMAN!"

She woman? It was on odd thing to say, even for the dull-witted Sir Kay. I saw Morrigin blanch at the insult, but she quickly waved it off and returned to the matter at hand. The two of us grabbed the rudder control and pushed it left and right, but our speed was too slow for the rudder to save us.

Behind us, the other soldier had jumped into a rowboat and was quickly gaining on us. In about a dozen more strokes, his muscular arms would ram the rowboat into our vessel and probably knock our ship into pieces.

"It's hopeless," I said, watching Morrigin tug on one of the ropes attached to the sail. Whatever she was trying to do, it didn't seem to help. The smaller sail was folding over in a way that kept it from catching wind, and I tried in vain to push it into a better shape. I'd never felt so foolish. "We're doomed."

"Nonsense!" said Ywain. "We'll just spread out the ballast, point the beakhead port, and leverage the beam reach! I'll man the rudder. Morrigin, I hate to pry, but do you always let him fiddle with your backstay like that?"

CHAPTER FIFTY

WE SAILED QUICKLY under Ywain's guidance, easily leaving the rowboat behind.

The ship nearly turned over when Garth discovered that, while at sea, his belly, and his mind disagreed on which way was up. He would run to one side and lean over the rail, forcing Morrigin and I to dash to the opposite side to keep things upright while Garth emptied his stomach into the Sea of Glass.

It was during one of those moments, while I turned away from Garth, that I finally noticed the mist. Like it had a mind of its own, a white, cloud-like appendage reached for our vessel. Behind that slithering tendril rose a great wall of mist, high and thick, keeping us from seeing further out.

As if it saw me, the approaching sliver of mist slowed its approach, eventually grazing the hull. Ywain turned us away from it.

"Can we hide in the mist?" I asked. Sir Kay could certainly board a ship and might have already been following.

"Men get lost in there," he said, and Morrigin nodded in agreement. I could see why she had wanted to avoid making this trip without an expert seaman. "Don't ride into the mist," shouted Ywain, "is the only rule of boating out here."

"I've never seen it so thick," said Morrigin, looking at Ywain.

He shook his head slowly, like he was agreeing that every step of our journey was cursed.

We rode through the Sea of Glass, far enough out that we would be difficult to find, always moving westward while keeping the coastline in sight so we wouldn't get lost.

When night fell, Ywain pointed out a spot on the shore where the land curved inward, a natural cove just large enough to hide the boat. We silently moored the vessel by tying it to a tree that was growing out at an angle over the water.

As it became dark, I noticed this boat had been cleverly designed. The dark-colored wood blended in with the night, and when Ywain lowered the sails, we could hardly see it once we stepped away. The king's men wouldn't find us unless their own boat happened to crash into ours.

Of course, there was the question of why king's men were after us at all.

But what was more unusual was that Garth had taken this revelation in stride. Finding out that his father's men were trying to kill him should have wrecked his delicate mentality, but he'd already shrugged it off.

Morrigin and Ywain began clearing a space on the ground for a fire, and Garth and I headed into the forest to find kindling.

"Do you want to talk about what happened back there?" I asked.

"No. I never really liked boats. I apprenticed with the fishermen, and they called me mister gutsy because—"

"Not that," I said, stripping a few dead branches from a tree. "I'm talking about Kay trying to kill us. Don't you think that's surprising?"

Garth's hand went to his pocket, and I heard the crinkle of paper. "I guess nothing's gonna surprise me anymore."

He remained silent. I thought he wanted to say more, but then he turned away to pick up a stray branch.

###

We started a fire and kept it small. Morrigin slumped down, drawing up her knees as she stared vacantly into the flame. I was accustomed to seeing strength and confidence in her face, but now her features looked as tired as the rest of us felt. There was no hope of reaching Avalon without a guide. I understood that now. It may as well have really been a myth.

"You must remember *something* about how to get there," I ventured.

She shook her head slowly and gestured toward the Sea of Glass. "Out there. Somewhere. Takes half a day, I remember that. Only Gus knew the way."

Ywain, one hand in his rucksack, frowned. "No directions? Maybe if I knew where you were trying to go, I could see if it's on one of my maps."

I remembered his father was a duke who was also the guild master to a group of mapmakers. "Ywain, it would be remarkable if anyone made a map to Avalon."

His eyebrows rose in surprise. "Avalon? Not likely. I don't think it's real."

"Yes, it is!" blurted Garth. Looking embarrassed, he quickly shoved a piece of food in his mouth.

I studied him intently. "Garth...do you know something?" This was normally a question I didn't bother to ask.

He stared back, frozen like someone caught with their hand in a cookie jar. He shook his head. "May as well tell you. Mother taught me about Avalon."

"Bedtime story," I said. "Just a tale."

"Oh, no. Ma was always very serious about Avalon. Not a jokin' matter, she would say. Ma told me every king knew where to find the island, just in case they needed to go there. She taught it to Ulder when he became king, and later she taught me, but only when da wasn't around."

Garth obviously didn't want to dwell on the fact that Ulder had tried to keep him from learning about this place.

Ywain rummaged in his sack and pulled out a map. "Show me!" He unrolled it and held it toward Garth.

Garth initially puffed out his chest, but after one look at the big, unfurled map, he shook his head. "Do you have the kind of map we use in the capital?"

"Of course, an official state map." Ywain rolled the map and reached for another. "I have one. Not as accurate as most maps. It's more traditional."

Ywain had barely spread the map onto his lap when Garth pointed a stubby finger into the Sea of Glass. "There," he said.

Ywain squinted. "You'll have to be more specific."

"In the A." Garth leaned back again. "Specifically, in the little hole in the top of the A."

Next to me, Morrigin began breathing slowly and evenly to calm her nerves.

I scratched the back of my head and asked, "Garth, did the royal mother give you any other directions? Something with numbers?"

"Oh, sure. Something about temperature. I didn't understand it."

"Degrees," I said flatly. "That's how you travel by map. You must know the degrees."

"That's right. I told her that a map couldn't have a temperature, so she told me to remember it's in the middle of that A." He raised a finger. "The A in 'Sea.' Not the one in 'Glass.'"

Ywain frowned. "That's a bigger space than you realize...we could get lost. It's all mists out there anyway."

I looked to Morrigin. She stared back silently, knowing we were both thinking that when the sun rose, our hiding place would be easy for our enemies to find. We needed some place to go. Any place.

"We'll leave at first light," I decided. "Right now, Garth's directions are the best heading we've got. And if we're lost in the mists, then Kay can't find us."

We quietly set our minds to our food, each trying to hold a brave face.

"Let's get some rest," said Morrigin, after we'd eaten. "I'll take first watch." She dusted off her clothes and walked a little ways from the camp.

"First watch?" asked Garth. "Are we supposed to take turns?"

"I have no idea," I said. "Maybe she'll wake us up when she's tired."

The three of us curled up around the dying fire, pushing into its warmth. At sunrise we planned to get into the boat and let Ywain pilot us to Avalon, a place that, as far as I knew, was as real as the fairies who put sugar treats in your shoes during Yule.

It didn't take long for me to fall asleep, but I woke in the middle of the night as I rolled over and felt Morrigin's earring dig into my thigh.

I sat up, grabbed the earring from my pocket, and wondered if this was a good time to bring it to her, assuming she was still awake. Several hours had passed.

But when I sat up, I noticed Morrigin standing in the same place, casually watching the stars.

Shouldn't she be tired?

Like a pebble rolling down a mountain and turning in an avalanche, that one little thought was about to change my life.

CHAPTER FIFTY-ONE

I PUSHED MYSELF UP into a sitting position as a few thoughts circled one another in my addled brain. There hadn't been time for thinking lately, not with the running and climbing and jumping and trying not to die. But the few hours of sleep I'd just stolen had been enough to get my mind moving. My legs followed. I quietly rose, still not sure where my thoughts were leading me.

She woman. That insult from Kay had stuck with me, because it was such a strange thing to say.

At least twenty paces away, Morrigin stared out into the water. Moonlight reflected in the always-shifting mists, which seemed to grow as I stepped closer. It reminded me of the old stories of visiting lakes on full moon nights and hoping to find the—

Sídhe, I realized. Not a *She* woman, a *Sídhe* woman. The two words sounded exactly the same.

The Sídhe were magic people who lived in a mountain. Or near a lake. Or wherever your most superstitious aunt or uncle liked to keep them. Troublemakers, the lot of them, if half the stories were true.

These tales were as old as the hills, and only children believed in the Sídhe anymore.

But as I approached Morrigin, I finally put together the puzzle pieces.

I'd known something wasn't right the night Garth and I slept in her tent. If I'd been a little more clever, I would have spent more time wondering why her tent didn't have a place to sleep.

The same clue waved at me in passing when we dashed through the halls of Charyot Manor and found ourselves in Zephyr's personal chambers. His room, just like every other we'd passed in that hall, was missing a bed.

I clutched her earring. It dug into my palm as my grip tightened beyond the control of my shaking hand, and I remembered a certain story about the Sídhe getting their power from the stones of the earth.

I took a few more steps toward her and stopped, just an arm's length away.

Morrigin silently turned my way, her eyes large and knowing. She'd been awake for hours and didn't look tired at all, and the way I stared must have made it clear that I'd finally figured it out. Her eyes begged me not to speak the secret.

By the fire, Garth and Ywain sat up and watched quietly.

"It's you," I said, holding out the earring to Morrigin. "You're the Restless Ones."

CHAPTER FIFTY-TWO

SILENTLY, Morrigin motioned for us to sit around the fire, and then she began a tale I would never forget.

"Ages ago, the *Sídhe* took many shapes. Some looked like creatures of the water, and others like creatures of the earth. And some looked like nothing the world had ever made before.

"But some of us decided to look like humans.

"They call us 'The Fortunate Ones,' because we live in both worlds.

"And since the *Sídhe* cannot tolerate disorder, the Fortunate Ones were ordered to not only live alongside men, but to influence them toward better paths. My ancestors did this by forming an alliance with the Pendragon house, and we have spent generations advising them. It was our gift to Albion.

"During the good times, the kings of Tomelac, everyone in the line of Pendragon, have fared better than the neighboring kingdoms."

It was true. I'd often wondered why Tomelac had remained strong for centuries while other kingdoms rose and fell. At least, that's how things had been in the past. Even before Ulder's reign, Tomelac had begun to decline. Fortunately, Morrigin's story was about to clear that up.

"It was ten generations ago when King Alar asked my people for aid as he prepared to invade his enemy's castle.

"The Fortunate Ones promised to join him, magically sneaking him into the enemy's fortress and fighting alongside him.

"But the Fortunate Ones, like all the Sídhe, are a tricky people with no interest in war. When King Alar found himself in the enemy's fortress, he noticed the Fortunate Ones had not come with him. He and his knights were alone."

"I remember reading about him," I said, recalling a distant history lesson. "He died, but his knights managed to win the battle."

Morrigin went on, like I hadn't spoken. "King Alar's surviving sons traveled north, far north, in search of the Sídhe. After four years, they discovered the lake where the Sídhe can be found, a lake called Lyn Lydaw. On certain nights, their world and this one can meet in that magical place.

"They screamed at the waters. Alar's sons shouted that the Fortunate Ones were no longer friends of Tomelac.

"But the elders of the Sídhe were angry. Not at the Pendragons, but at the Fortunate Ones. For while the Sídhe are all tricky, we always honor our bargains.

"So, the Fortunate Ones were cursed."

At this point, Morrigin stopped talking and gave me an expectant look.

"You...don't sleep," I said. "You never sleep. None of you."

She went on. "But the Sídhe never gave up their side of the bargain. My people continued watching the kingdom, helping from the shadows. But because we had turned a blind eye to the king, we may never rest again.

"Even though we tried to maintain our vow, the royals easily noticed their halls were filled with nobles and knights who never slept. We could not hide our nature. Expelled from Tomelac, known suddenly as the 'Restless' and branded as unlucky, we fled the kingdom and never settled down. We called ourselves the Abrecans, kept to ourselves, and took up a nomadic life to hide our identity."

I finally understood how the Abrecans were always a step ahead of me. It was the same reason they were able to outperform and undersell any vendor in any town. Not sleeping meant they had several more hours a day to get ahead of the rest of us. But it must have been maddening for them.

"And this?" I held up the earring. "It's how you find us, isn't it? You left it for me to pick up in Tomelac."

"It's called Traveling," she said, speaking very heavily when she used the word. "We don't all have the same magics. When I was a little girl, I wanted to run away and suddenly found myself at Lyn Lydaw, a great distance from where I lived. The Sídhe found me by the lake, lost and confused.

"I'll never forget their ways. They some were green and moved through the trees in complete silence.

Others rose from the waters of the lake, blue and calm, with scales like a fish. Some flitted past on invisible wings.

"They told me I had found my power, or, rather, it had found me, and they gave me that pearl. It's a Traveling gem. I can send myself near it, no matter where it goes."

"And no one ever notices you just...poofing into existence?" I asked. Whenever Morrigin mysteriously showed up, it was like she'd always been there, barely out of sight, rather than appearing in a blaze of power like a wizard in a story.

She shrugged. "That's how Sídhe magic works. It's supposed to be used in subtle ways, so you never can tell if something has changed or if things were always that way. That's how you keep a secret. And when I saw you...staring at me in Ulder's court, I left this earring on the ground, hoping you would take it with you." She pointed at Garth. "That way, I could keep an eye on him when all of this started."

"How *did* all this start?" asked Garth.

"I don't really know." Morrigin let her shoulders slump. "One of the Moonriders heard that Escanor was having secret meetings with Ulder. That's all. But it was enough for me to be worried, so I went to Tomelac. I don't know why he's working with the King."

It made no sense to me, either. Garth was, in a strange way, Ulder's pride and joy. It was not unusual for the king to interrupt a conversation to tell us about his son, specifically about his conception.

King Cecil had been in charge of the kingdom before Ulder, and Garth's mother had loved him dearly—right up the day he died in battle. Ulder showed up the next week and reminded everyone he was Cecil's distant kin, which placed him next in line for the throne. Ulder married the queen and, to hear him tell it, bedded her just before she left Tomelac for a year of mourning over her dead husband. She returned with a child in her arms.

"Believe me, I don't understand why this is happening," Morrigin insisted. "I'm just trying to keep everyone safe."

I didn't believe her. Not entirely. But I finally realized that she was swept up in the same wave of events that had trapped me. Despite her confidence, Morrigin felt just as adrift as the rest of us.

"The Fortunate Ones still take the same oath to protect the king, even those of us who weren't yet born when the curse was cast," she said. "The Sídhe made us restless, unable to sleep, hoping that every long and sleepless night would remind us that our ancestors broke their oath. But I don't intend to break mine. I will protect the prince until I die."

"The prince?" Ywain looked at me.

I shook my head.

Ywain turned to Garth, who was balancing a beetle on his nose. "Oh."

###

You might think we'd have a difficult time sleeping after a conversation like that.

And you'd be right.

The three of us tossed and turned. We kept noticing Morrigin watching over us, trying to step quietly as she paced through the night.

We rose at the sight of morning's first orange light and returned to the ship. Ywain set a course for the island of Avalon, following a general heading he assumed from Garth's barely useful instructions. In the distance, we saw the mists rising to dance over the placid waters.

Ywain sat in the rear, holding the rudder control in one hand while gesturing with the other to give orders to Garth, who'd been wanting to learn how to pilot a ship.

Morrigin and I sat in the front, watching the approaching mist. We smiled at one another while the other two chattered about nautical things. Their voices faded into the background as her hand touched mine and a smile tugged at the corner of her lips.

CHAPTER FIFTY-THREE

"So, YOU DIDN'T just keep those cats around for fun," asked Garth, as he fiddled with the sail, "you actually *trained* them?"

"Of course." Ywain kept his young face pointed at the mist that gathered around the hull. He carefully pushed the control so we moved away from a growing cloud. "After a few training sessions with the right ingredients, my cats only attack when I tell them to. It all depends on the quality of the food and how smart they are, but it works."

Garth had been asking Ywain about his many hobbies for most of the trip, which I estimated had been at least six hours. Most of that time I'd been ignoring them, stealing glances at Morrigin while hoping to think of something to say. I needn't have worried. Keeping quiet worked just fine as we fell into silent companionship, amused by the conversation behind us and equally enchanted by the cunning mist.

"Ywain, you come from a truly unique family," said Morrigin pleasantly.

"My parents met when my mother needed a map of the outlying regions, looking for better food sources.

At the time, my dad just happened to be printing the very map she needed."

"How many cats do you have at home?" I ventured, uncertain if I really wanted to know.

"I'm not sure. The cats have got their own house. Dad's never been inside."

The hull groaned.

I relaxed again, listening to Ywain rattle off a few nautical terms while Garth pretended to understand. It was just the right amount of nonsense to be calming.

Until an arrow sailed overhead.

Morrigin and I watched it silently hit the water, making a tiny splash. After a moment of silent shock, we turned around. Behind us, on the other side of a misty plume, was the silhouette of another boat. Behind it, we could make out another.

The next arrow put a hole in the sail, causing Ywain to gasp. The arrow flew right through and left behind a sputtering flap of torn fabric.

"Open the sail!" Ywain shouted. "All the—"

The next arrow touched the top of his head as it flew over him. Had Ywain been wearing a hat, the arrow would have picked it up and carried it away.

"Hit the deck!" said Morrigin.

We crouched low. Ywain, in his seat by the rudder, wormed his way down as if he were melting onto the deck, keeping one hand on the control.

Another volley sent three arrows into the surrounding water. All three were further off the mark than the first volley, which seemed odd. Raising my eyebrows, I carefully glanced over the hull. A thick wall of mist had moved in between our boat and the others. "They can't see us. That's lucky."

"We won't see anything in a moment," said Morrigin, peering ahead where the white mist was rolling in thick plumes. "We'll get lost in there."

"Maybe..." Ywain bit his lip, thoughtfully. "Maybe we can skirt the edge."

"No." An idea struck me, and I looked him in the eye. "Steer us *into* it. The thickest part."

"Into it? I told you, people get lost in there and don't come back."

"Fine. *I'll* do it."

I scooted past Ywain. There wasn't time to analyze our options. Planning and thinking are my best qualities, but now there was only time to follow my instincts, and my instincts were telling me that the fog was less random that everyone thought. I internally reeled at the assumption, because it sounded like the sort of superstitious nonsense I'd spent my entire life looking down on.

Still, I reached for the control rod. The fog was building on our left, so I threw the rod in that direction.

Which apparently was wrong.

"No!" shouted Ywain, as the boat tilted away from the fog.

Not only had I forgotten the golden rule of the rudder (right goes left and left goes right) but I'd also pushed it about three times further than necessary, causing the boat to turn much faster than it should have.

Everyone screamed as the little boat tilted. We shifted our weight in the other direction but only slowed things down. The boat tilted further, slowly prepared to turn over and dump us into the sea.

Have I mentioned that I don't care for water? I've tried to trace this fear back to its source, to better understand my fears, and I believe it all started in my childhood when my father threw me out of a boat.

As I was trying to block out the dreadful memory, an arrow plunked into the hull right between Ywain and myself, hitting with just enough force that—combined with our efforts onboard—the ship righted itself.

"You turned it the wrong way," whispered Ywain.

"Thank you, captain!" I shouted. "Why don't you shut up and throw one of your cats at them!"

"Both of you shut up," yelled Morrigin. "Now, do it right!"

I reached up again and pushed the control rod to the *right*. Well, at first, I started to push it to the left again, because everything about boats was simply an affront to the ways of the universe as far as I was concerned, but Morrigin shouted a few harsh words before I could repeat my mistake.

I pushed the rod in the correct direction, and this time we turned softly toward the rising mists. The next arrow missed by nearly the entire length of the boat.

"Here's what we're going to do," I said. "You three take turns and peek out once in a while. Tell me where the mist is the *thickest,* and I'll turn toward those spots. Eventually they may get tired of looking for—"

"Bleed on that," said Garth rudely. Surprising all of us, he jumped into the narrow seat and grabbed the control rod. "Morrigin and Erlin, you two sit on either side to keep us balanced. Ywain, just work the sail and give me everything she's got. I'm going to see Avalon today."

Chapter Fifty-Four

THE PURSUING BOATS were lost in the fog after only a few minutes. We heard shouts from behind and a few more arrows plopped into the water, but before long, we were quietly cruising through the mist.

Garth continued to fearlessly steer into the thickest parts of the fog. The white clouds curled around us, creating a wall so thick we sometimes couldn't see the end of the prow as it disappeared into the haze.

When the fog was thick enough that I couldn't find my own hands, I was ready to ask Garth to turn us around, but just then the mist parted like a divine curtain.

The island was right in front of us.

We saw it just in time for Ywain to pull down the sails. The boat slowed while we got to our feet to take in the sight, Morrigin and I holding each other's hand for balance.

The small island was covered in trees that looked like they belonged in an orchard, but here they grew wild, creating a thick tangle of low-hanging branches.

"Are those..." Ywain squinted. "Apples!" He began rummaging around in his bag. "That's the only ingredient I couldn't find back in Kingsport."

I shook my head slowly. Morrigin elbowed me so I could see her silent laugh.

The boat settled easily into the soft shore. Her hand in mine, Morrigin and I made our way across the wet shore until we stood on dry land. Behind us, the mists swirled continuously, shielding us from the rest of the world.

"It's really here," I whispered. Then my sense of reason took hold of me. "Well, an island exists here. The legends of Avalon are still just legends. Could be hundreds of islands out here."

Morrigin let go of my hand. "The mists led us here."

"Atmospheric phenomenon," I said with a proud nod. I noticed I was suddenly unable to capture her hand again. "Doesn't mean we'll find..." Her gaze became cold, and I decided to stop talking. "You've been here before?"

"Once a year," she said, looking around. "It's not very large. Come on, I'll show you why we came."

"Why we came? I thought we were just hiding from Escanor." A new thought occurred to me. "Wait, if the kings know about Avalon, then Ulder knows where this place is. We're not safe at all!"

"We're not here to hide," said Garth, who stepped in between us. He walked on, intrepidly pushing aside branches as he entered the unknown.

It wasn't easy getting used to Garth knowing things that I didn't.

"Would you *look* at this!" exclaimed Ywain. He pulled the reddest apple I'd ever seen from the end of a dangling branch. "I've got to get more!"

"Careful," shouted Morrigin, "it's not safe…" She stopped, putting a hand over her mouth, and looked around. Obviously, she wanted to avoid attracting attention.

"What's so dangerous?" I asked.

Tree branches parted as Garth rushed back, crashing into both of us.

"Big…big…" He kept trying to say something while pointing behind him.

Morrigin raised her eyebrows at me and placed a finger over her lips, asking me to be quiet.

A lion stood ahead of us. Tail twitching.

It blinked.

Morrigin slowly blinked back.

The lion considered her and wandered off.

"What was that?" I asked.

She shrugged. "Sometimes it makes them trust you."

"Sometimes?"

"They're not exactly pets," she said. "Come on. We're headed for the middle."

###

As we pushed through the dense thickets of apple trees, I wondered if the lions were living off of the apples or on the unlucky sailors who happened upon the shores of Avalon. I wanted to ask Morrigin, but she wasn't in the mood for questions.

Now and then she would stop us with a quick gesture, and we would all hold still.

Then a lion might walk past or sniff in our direction before staring at Morrigin and then walking away.

"I assume your people come here often enough for them to know you?" I asked.

"Only a few of us are allowed." She slowed her walk, and Garth and I did the same. "The lions are...on edge today."

Ahead of us, a lion ran into a small clearing, threw its head back, and then ran off with a growl.

"I've never seen them this way," she said.

"If they're anything like a house cat," I guessed, "they're upset about something new being introduced into their environment. But they've seen people before, right? What's different about this time?"

Slowly, she turned to me. "Normally...only women are allowed."

"What about Gus?"

"Scared of the lions. Always stays on the boat."

But Morrigin didn't seem convinced that a few men had thrown the island into a state of anxiety. The birds made less noise as we traveled on, and soon we stopped seeing the lions completely.

Eventually, the trees thinned. I heard the sound of water coming from the center of the island just before Morrigin gasped.

A lion lay dead on the ground.

Its neck had been expertly slashed, and it was clear we had only barely missed the attack.

"Someone else is here," I whispered.

"Obviously," snorted Morrigin. It was the foulest mood I had seen her in. She led us around the body and further inland, silently staring through the trees like a predator.

I heard the soft noises of the lake just before I glimpsed it through a cluster of trees. I wasn't sure what was so important about a small lake in the middle of a small island, but it was apparently the reason we'd come to Avalon.

Morrigin held up a hand to stop us. We heard a noise—someone walking—and she stood behind a tree, hiding, and motioned for Garth and me to do the same. We quickly complied. Mind you, it's not easy to hide behind the thin trunk of an apple tree.

I peeked out and looked across the placid lake. There were barely any ripples on the smooth surface. Looking further, I finally noticed a stone column rising from the dark water in the very center of the lake.

And a woman stood atop it.

The lady at the lake wore an old dress the color of green leaves. Dark hair fell to her waist.

From my hiding place, I could see her bright blue eyes, which were violently fixed on something near to where I hid.

Someone else was there. I leaned out further to look.

A stone's throw from us, just at the edge of the lake, stood King Ulder.

CHAPTER FIFTY-FIVE

KING ULDER was in intimidating sight in his blood-red armor. It was decorated here and there with spikes, and I pondered adding those to my own outfits to teach a lesson to those pesky hugging types who avoid handshakes.

With one hand, Ulder carried a sword that looked large enough to cut a whale in half. It dripped with blood, and I remembered the dead lion we had passed.

"Give me the sword, you tart!" he screamed.

Atop the pedestal, the woman scrunched up her face, like he'd fed her a lemon. "Never."

"Sword?" I whispered.

Morrigin pointed at the lake.

Just in front of the column, I finally noticed a skeletal arm reaching out of the water. Its long-dead fingers held up a sword with a gilded pommel.

Ulder was asking for a boon from the Sídhe. Something to show that a higher power wanted him to rule, but I couldn't imagine why.

"He's already the king," I whispered. "Why is he—"

"This isn't the best time for an explanation," said Morrigin, "but, Garth...it's time to show Erlin what you learned."

Garth pursed his lips in thought, then nodded and reached into his pocket. He fished around and came up with the piece of paper Morrigin had given us at Charyot Manor.

I'd glanced at it before. Just a birth record. But I hadn't been able to read it in detail. While Ulder and the Sídhe women argued about the sword, I read the part of the document that listed the date of Garth's birth, and I finally understood.

###

Good King Cecil had ruled before Ulder. Those were better times. I didn't know Cecil, but everyone in the land remembered him as a fair ruler, which is saying quite a lot. Even the nice kings get selfish once they sit on the throne and realize how rich they can be if they keep everyone else poor.

When King Cecil died, news swept the kingdom that his cousin, Ulder, had stormed into Tomelac to take control. Cecil had no children, so Ulder bedded the queen upon his arrival, saying it was necessary to ensure the royal line above all else.

And it's common knowledge that the queen left for a year of mourning, as was customary, though it was widely joked (in quiet voices) that Ulder's bombastic arrival had not been good for her mood. She returned with young Garth in her arms, the product of Ulder's quick work.

Or...so we all thought.

The birth document said otherwise. Instead of a date in the late spring, as I would have expected, the certificate showed Garth's date of birth as "The First day of Yule in the year Good King Cecil died."

But King Cecil had died in late summer.

###

The island grew silent, distracting me from the birth record and from what it revealed.

I was vaguely aware Ulder had been yelling at the strange woman, demanding she give him a boon. And now she seemed to be considering it. She tapped a finger to her lips and then reached out, palms up, and slowly raised her hands.

In the center of the lake, I saw a rowboat rise to the surface, complete with a pair of oars.

The lady thrust her hands out, like she was shooing away flies, and the boat, all by itself, calmly glided toward Ulder.

"Come and get it," she challenged.

Chapter Fifty-Six

ULDER EYED THE BOAT, then the lady. She gestured downward, past her feet, to the gleaming sword.

With a curse, Ulder stabbed his sword into the ground and then, leaving the weapon behind, stepped into the boat.

That was as close as he got.

The boat rocked. Ulder leaned back to control his fall, but he lost his composure when a tentacle sprouted from the lake.

The tentacle was large enough to be a tree trunk, and I had the impression I was only seeing the tip of it. An ominous red orb, many feet wide, drew close to the surface, and my knees shook when I realized it was the creature's eye.

The tentacle swatted at Ulder, hitting him square in the breastplate with the sound of a spoon smacking a frying pan.

Ulder was thrown away from the lake. The little boat sunk, hiding under the water again. As he fell, Ulder's arms windmilled in hopeless circles as he flew, which would have been hilarious except that he landed right in front of me.

###

The king was on his feet in moments.

I, obviously lacking Ulder's adaptability to unique situations, was still mentally reeling from what I'd seen when he stepped around the tree and shoved me to the ground.

He looked around, taking stock of the situation, and then laughed. "You brought my son! This may be a good day after all."

"I'm not your son," said Garth.

Ulder crossed his arms. "Is that right?"

I pushed myself away from him and stood. Ulder grinned at Garth, sizing him up like prey. I looked to Morrigin and saw a hopeless look on her face as she realized we had worked so hard only to bring Garth directly to his murderous father.

"You're not the king," I said with a stutter.

"You've done me a mighty favor, inquisitor," bellowed Ulder. "I was worried I couldn't trust the Abrecans with my dirty work."

"Why?" I blurted, grasping for something to say, some way to start a conversation I could turn against him. Words were my usual weapon. "Why involve them at all?"

"It's not easy killing your heirs and getting away with it. Everyone suspects you. But the Restless? People will believe anything about them."

It was true. I'd built my career around the idea that you can blame anything on magic.

Morrigin lunged at him, holding a long branch she'd ripped from a tree, but the king heard her coming. He turned and grabbed the branch from her hands and shoved her back. Then he towered over her, brandishing the stick.

"Leave her alone," I said, realizing it was my turn to try something stupid. I approached him slowly, fists raised, wondering how fighting worked.

Ulder tossed the branch aside. "And here I thought I wouldn't accomplish anything today. I will soon see the end of the inquisitor and the end of my son."

"I'm *not* your son," Garth repeated.

I hadn't noticed, but while Morrigin and I were making fools of ourselves, Garth had picked up Ulder's sword. As he ran toward us, he swung the sword over his head with all of his might.

Ulder casually moved so his armor absorbed the blow. Metal rang upon metal, but Ulder didn't budge. The sword rattled in Garth's hands, and Ulder easily swatted it to the ground.

I heard the lady on the column make a series of unusual sounds, using a language I'd never heard, and then the frightening tentacle rose from the water. The appendage reached toward Ulder but fell short; he was too far from the lake.

"First, I'll kill your friends," boasted Ulder, looking at Garth. "The Sídhe woman and the smart man. Then I'll throw you in the lake because I know you can't swim."

Garth, Morrigin, and I glanced at one another. It was a grim moment. Ulder was a mountain as far as we were concerned, but it was obvious we all had the same idea: if we could budge him toward the lake, we might get him close to whatever creature lived down there.

But Ulder's laughter made me feel my own weakness and reminded me I still hadn't figured out whether I was supposed to move my feet during a fight. It was the sort of subject I felt deserved more scholarly attention, which would save many academics many embarrassing days in grade school.

Ulder pointed at me. "I've hated every single one of those stupid reports you make..."

He trailed off, looking over my shoulder. I only stood a few steps from him, so I didn't dare turn around.

Until I heard the roar.

You've heard of lion roars. And you probably think you know what it would be like to hear one. Let me assure you, you're not ready. Your bowels tremble as the low notes crash through your intestines, and your heart stops when the growling rambles through your ribs.

Eyes wide, I slowly turned around.

Standing some distance away stood an angry lion, its eyes fixed on Ulder.

And by its side, one hand on its thick mane, was Ywain.

Ywain pointed at Ulder and said, "Kill."

###

Ulder grabbed the sword in the blink of an eye and hurled it overhead. I gasped as it flew past me. The weapon spun over and over as it flew. The flat of the blade hit the lion's flank, making the big cat stumble in confusion.

Behind me, Ulder raced away, tearing through the trees like a madman. I saw him hit his forehead on several low-hanging apples, leaving them dangling in his wake. The lion rushed past me next, so close I felt the wind of its charge.

We caught our breath, only for a moment, and then chased after them.

Ulder only glanced behind him once as he ran, and it was enough for him to see the lion catching up. He tucked his head and pumped harder. My chest was burning and my legs were already weak when I saw Ulder reach the shore and run toward a small boat, obviously the vessel he'd used to get here.

Ulder jumped and landed hard enough to push his boat into the water. The lion stopped at the shore, roaring into the mists.

"You'll come back, boy!" shouted Ulder as he sat down and began rowing. "You'll renounce the throne."

"I'll never do that!" Garth yelled back.

Ulder laughed, loud as the lion's roar. "You'll do it, and you'll do it right in front of everyone, or in two weeks' time I'll kill your mother!"

Chapter Fifty-Seven

Ulder's little boat disappeared into the fog, pushed by his powerful strokes. He was gone in moments.

Dumbstruck, the rest of us filed back through the trees to the center of the island, where a very strange woman stood on a pillar in the center of a lake. My life had taken some odd turns.

When we got to the lake, I noticed the lady in the center was staring at us. But not all of us. After a moment, I realized her eyes were fixed on Morrigin. And she looked bitter.

"Nimway, stop it!" Morrigin cried.

The woman, Nimway, crossed her arms and squinted. "How's the city?"

"Nimway, I'm sorry. You know it's not my fault. This isn't fair."

"Do you meet men?"

"We don't have time for this," said Morrigin, hanging her head. "We're too busy right now for this conversation."

"You can't be *that* busy." Nimway pointed at me. "You met him."

"Doesn't she ever leave?" I whispered.

"No!" Nimway shouted from her perch. "I don't *get* to leave. Morrigin gets to Travel. Poof—I'm over here! Poof—now I'm here! Isn't magic fun!"

Morrigin could Travel. Escanor could...turn into a barrel. In the lottery of magical powers, it appeared Nimway had drawn one of the shorter straws.

"She just stays here?" I whispered. "And guards that sword?"

Morrigin gestured toward Nimway. "Garth. Erlin. Meet...my sister."

"Is something happening?" asked Nimway. "Something important? I had to find out from *Ulder*! I could have learned from my sister if she would visit me. On my island. On my column."

"Only Gus can get here. You know that, Nimway. We can't visit often or people will know."

"And you've brought *men*!" Nimway pointed at me. "That wormy one there, and..." she moved her outstretched finger toward Garth, and her bitter face softened with realization. "Oh."

Morrigin put her hands on her hips and gave her sister a very serious glare.

"Well." Nimway smoothed out her green dress. "That's different." She waved both hands upward and, once again, the little boat surfaced from under the water. It moved on its own to the water's edge, near us. "Get in."

"Get in?" Garth stepped back. "That thing will eat me!"

"Reginald won't hurt you," said Nimway, lifting her chin like a stubborn toddler. "Get in."

"Nimway," Morrigin growled. "Stop scaring them."

The sisters stared at one another while the island seemed to grow cold.

"It's all right," said Morrigin, touching my arm. "This is why I brought you. My people know that Nimway is the only person who can lead you to Old King Pendragon's sword. Garth, you just need to get in the boat—"

"No." I touched her arm.

Morrigin glared at me in surprise. She drew her arm away from me and I knew I had lost her trust, as completely as if I had stabbed her in the back. I immediately regretted not being more subtle, but it was too late.

"No," I repeated. "This is Garth's choice. I won't have him dangled around like the Abrecans' puppet. It's completely up to him." I turned to the prince. "You don't have to be king. You can save your mother by renouncing. There's no shame in that."

"Get in the boat," was all he said.

Garth and I walked over to the shore and stared at the rickety rowboat.

I may have mentioned that I am...uncomfortable in water. My lofty tower room in Tomelac actually has two windows. One overlooks the courtyard and eventually over the forests that surround the keep, but the other, which I keep shuttered, only shows me the ocean. The cliffs are a short walk from Tomelac, but I prefer imagining the sea doesn't exist.

So, my leg shook visibly while I put one foot in the little boat.

Garth studied the sword. "I heard Old King Pendragon had a special sword. It was bright, so bright it blinded people, and everyone knew he was the king because he had it."

Sounded familiar. But stories of old kings blended fact and fiction better than I did when trying to explain my job to anyone. But after what Morrigin had told me, I believed the first Pendragon could have carried around a boon like this sword to show people he was favored by some greater power.

And that Ulder might want one just like it if people were starting to doubt he belonged on the throne.

Garth settled in. I thought his trembling would upset the boat, but it stayed afloat. Morrigin and Ywain gave us a push. I sat in the middle and paddled with both oars, trying my best not to disturb the water, or the important moment I felt approaching.

Garth, in front of me, leaned over the side and gasped. I knew it was a mistake, but I followed his gaze and saw a tentacle sweeping by. Further below in the murky depths, I made out a gigantic red orb. The creature's eye.

Avalon was not a normal place, I realized. It shouldn't have been possible for anything to swim *under* an island.

I paddled on, and the boat nosed close to the pedestal. Slowing down, I could feel Nimway's narrow eyes bearing down on us as the sword drew near. The skeletal hand that rose from the water seemed to rotate toward us, beckoning Garth with the gleaming...

I stopped rowing. "Garth, I think you should wait."

But he didn't. Garth reached out just as Nimway started cackling. I heard a groan from Morrigin.

Up close, I finally noticed the sword in the lake was not kingly at all. Rust had eaten the edges, and the handle was rotted wood.

Garth put his hand on the pommel. Just then, the skeletal hand collapsed into dust. Garth lunged to grab the sword before it fell, and I reached for his belt to keep him from falling over.

The old sword hit the water with a *plop*.

Nimway snickered.

"Let it go, Garth!" I tugged on his belt as reached out, nearly upending the rickety craft. "That wasn't your sword."

"NIMWAY!" Morrigin screamed. "They're going to fall in!"

Nimway frowned. "You're no fun."

"It's just an old sword," I grunted. "She's playing a trick on you."

Frustrated, Garth fell back into the boat.

"Now help me down," said Nimway, "and I'll tell you where the real one is."

Chapter Fifty-Eight

It wasn't on the island. Not even close.

Nimway took us to a small encampment where she appeared to spend most of her time. Just a fire pit, a tent, and a well. She had been grabbing apples as she walked, and by the time we sat around the fire her arms were full of shiny, red fruit.

"This is the most people I've had at my place," she said, narrowing her eyes at Morrigin. "I don't have enough chairs."

"Nimway, I'm *sorry*!" Morrigin's arms flew through the air. "The Elders say you have to live here, not me! Do you want me to bring them here so you can complain?"

"No need." Nimway sat down, clutching her bundle of apples. Her eyes gleamed with cunning delight. "I'm leaving the island today!"

"You can't do that!" said Morrigin. "You're supposed to stay with the sword!"

"That's not true. The elders told me to wait here until a king asked for the sword. It's not the same thing."

"Well, you still have to give Garth the sword before you leave."

At this, Nimway pressed a hand to her chest in fake surprise. "Why, thank you, sister. I almost forgot! Where would I be without the great Morrigin to tell me how to do my job?"

"Just give us the sword."

"Not until we eat." She pointed at me. "That one's stomach keeps growling."

I looked down. It was true. Hoping to relax the mood, I asked, "What's for dinner?"

"What do you think?" She shoved an apple into my hand and then did the same for everyone else.

Just an apple? I turned it over in my hand, hoping she'd hidden a steak underneath.

"I love apples," said Garth. "We get 'em in big barrels at home and—" His eyes widened as he took a bite. Mouth full, he looked at Ywain and nodded toward Ywain's apple.

Ywain bit into his and then leaned back, his eyes rolling upward like a man in ecstasy. "It's incredible."

"It's just an apple," I muttered.

Nimway laughed at me. The wide sleeves of her dress were too long and her hands often disappeared into them. Her tiny fingers emerged from the cavernous sleeve, clutching an apple that she quickly devoured.

"Fine." I took a bite and swallowed quickly. "There. Just an..."

I put a hand to my belly, then turned to Morrigin. She smiled a little. I was full already, like I'd eaten at one of Ulder's feasts; the single bite had filled me up.

"How?" I was dumbstruck.

"It's..." Morrigin paused. "These apples have sustained us for a long time."

"Why don't you just tell him it's magic," asked Nimway.

"Because Erlin doesn't believe in magic."

"Oh, I see. We have to be sensitive." Nimway lowered her voice. "I would hate to upset his worldview."

Ywain inspected the place where he'd bitten into his apple. "It's potent. When I got here, I made a quick mix of my grandmother's recipe. I never saw a cat adapt to the training so quickly."

After nibbling our apples down to their cores, we tossed them behind us. I rubbed my hands and looked to Nimway. "So, where is that sword?"

She pointed.

I turned my head but saw only trees. The shoreline was in sight. "Is it...buried?"

Nimway shrugged. "I don't know."

Morrigin stood, and I saw one of her hands curl into a menacing fist. "Nimway..."

"I've never seen it."

"NEVER SEEN IT?" Morrigin's eyes shook so hard I thought I would have to reach out and catch them as they rolled out of their sockets.

Nimway threw her apple core at Morrigin's feet. "No one ever said the sword was on Avalon. You were just told to bring a king here if he needed a boon to prove he was *actually* the king. And my power is knowing where the boon is and who deserves it."

"You're supposed to *give* the king the sword! That's what you do!"

Nimway shook her head. "What did the elders tell you? When we were children?"

"That you would lead the king..." Morrigin fumed as she trailed off.

"It's my job to lead the king to the sword," said Nimway. "And that's why I'm leaving the island today!"

I stood still, hoping my next words wouldn't spark Morrigin's anger. "Nimway...do you know *exactly* where it is?"

"Yes." She pointed past me. "It's *exactly* that way."

"How far?"

She lowered her hand and cocked her head to the side. "I don't know."

A lot of yelling happened. Garth and Ywain kept their mouths shut, like boys who knew how to stay out of trouble at the family dinner table.

Occasionally the screaming was difficult to keep up with, but Morrigin had obviously expected Nimway to give us *something* that would help Garth look like a king. Here I'd thought she was taking us to Avalon to keep Garth safe on a magical, hidden island, but this was actually the linchpin to a larger plan. The Abrecans—the ones who didn't agree with Escanor—had decided it was time to come out of hiding and help Garth usurp his father. It was unfortunate that no one had told Nimway what was going on.

Sensing that Morrigin was about to stomp over to Nimway and deliver the sort of beating that is only lawful between siblings, I spoke up quickly with an idea. "Point to it again, Nimway."

She raised her arm, shaking the sleeve so her hand emerged, and pointed directly at the shore again. I guessed it was roughly in the direction we had come from.

I nudged her hand, so her finger pointed slightly more to the left. "That way?"

"No..." She made the slight adjustment. "There."

It felt like a lie. Something a traveling showman would do to pretend he knew magic. After what I'd seen that day, I really wanted to believe her, but I'd been a skeptic too long to accept magic so easily. Old habits die hard.

"We've only got two weeks," said Garth. "Can you tell us anything else?"

Nimway closed her eyes. "Yes. I can scry."

Chapter Fifty-Nine

I'VE SEEN SCRYING BEFORE.

To be more specific, I've seen people *claiming* to scry.

As you know, scryers are merely con artists who claim they can see things that are far away. (Sometimes they call it *auguring* if they want to sound educated.) It's an easy scam.

Years ago, Ulder called me to his hall and handed me a very sharp stick, telling me not to come back until I'd stuck it into a certain augurist who'd made quite a name for himself in the neighboring town of Loewe. "The bloodier, the better," Ulder told me, tapping the sharp stick.

I found the augurist in the middle of town, standing behind a pitiful table while a long line formed. *One answer for two coppers*, read his sign, and the locals clinked their coppers together as they waited their turn.

It was an old trick. I watched him for a bit, admiring his stagecraft. People would ask him where to find a lost trinket or a missing pet, and he would squint and rub his temples while pretending to conjure up an image of whatever they were looking for. Then he would provide them with an educated guess he attributed to mysticism. His bag of coins was bursting by the time I showed up.

Naturally, I set up a table exactly next to his. My sign read, *One answer for ONE copper.* He didn't like that. He also didn't like the fact that I answered everyone quickly rather than engaging in theatrics. His method was to close his eyes and grasp at empty air, making a show of it and taking several minutes to "see" anything.

But my customers didn't need to wait.

"I can't find my kitten," someone asked.

"It's hiding in your house," I guessed, taking their copper.

"My cow ran off," said one fellow.

"It's nearby—eating grass," I replied. "I'm sure of it."

"My brother stole my wife!"

"You can find another one in the next town."

"Could I make a living as a bard?"

"No one makes a living as a bard."

"Where can I find a husband?"

"Would you believe he's looking for you in the next town?"

I answered each question in rapid fire succession, and, as a result, my line moved twice as fast. After a few hours, the town scryer, having no more business, tore down his table and left on the next carriage.

When he was gone, I returned to Tomelac, leaving behind a long line of people who could have solved their own problems in the time it took to wait their turn. Remembering Ulder's command, I dabbed the end of the stick in a cup of red wine before returning it to him.

So, I was prepared for quite a show when Nimway announced she was going to do some scrying. She was, apparently, so in tune with the boon that she could see from its point of view, as if it had eyes.

"Please be quiet," announced Nimway.

I leaned back, wondering how long we would be waiting for her—

"There it is," she said.

"Already?"

"It's easy since it's the only thing I can scry," she said. "I see...a door."

"Well, we're practically there."

Morrigin elbowed me. "Keep going, sister."

"There's a lot of things in the way. I can't see much. But...I see those metal things..." Nimway, eyes closed, made useless gestures in the air. "They hold other metal things onto bigger things, so they don't fall down."

"Bolts?" I ventured.

Nimway shrugged. "They're holding the door to the wall."

"The door is metal?"

"Yes. Is that unusual?"

She really *didn't* get out much. Then again, iron doors were not common anywhere on the continent. The cost was excessive, and it wasn't easy to find that much iron. In fact, I'd only seen one iron door in my life.

I sighed. "Is anything written on the door?" I already knew the answer. I sketched a design on the ground. "Something like this?"

Nimway opened her eyes. "That's it!"

Garth's mouth fell open. "That's da's seagull."

"Sigil," I corrected.

"You know where it is?" said Morrigin.

"I do," said Garth. "That's the vault!"

Ulder's vault. There was only one key, and no one was allowed inside. Perfect.

"I think Ulder's been looking for this sword for a long time," I said, "but, if we're right, it's already in Tomelac. Why is he still looking for it?"

"Because it's clever," said Nimway.

"The...*sword* is clever?" I couldn't wrap my mind around it, but Morrigin nodded in agreement with her sister.

"It would just look normal to everyone." Nimway drew in the dirt, sketching out an ordinary sword. "Until Garth touches it."

My life began to feel very silly.

I'd treated Ulder's vault and his obsession with magical artifacts as a source of personal amusement, but Ulder was a cunning man. He'd been collecting magic items for years because he was hoping to find the sword of Pendragon.

And, apparently, he'd already succeeded.

"So, my Da has the sword, but doesn't *know* he has it?" asked Garth, making sure he wasn't falling behind. When everyone nodded, he said, "We have to get in that vault."

He wasn't wrong, but I had no interest in charging into Tomelac to break into Ulder's vault. None whatsoever.

Until a moment later, when I had a clever idea.

"This boon," I said to Nimway, "if Garth holds it, there will be no questioning who is the real king?"

She narrowed her eyes at me. "Yes. That's how it works. But I've never seen what happens when a real king holds Pendragon's sword." She pointed at Garth. "But if he's really the king, there will be no question. That is...if he's ready. The sword won't do anything if it thinks he's not going to be a good king."

"He is," I announced.

Garth didn't look so sure, but I didn't have time for his lack of confidence.

Morrigin glanced my way, looking amused because a smile was spreading across my face. My idea was turning into a plan.

I couldn't help it. These things just come to me. And something happens when you have a clever idea: it sticks in your head, even if it's foolish. You can't stop going over the details and riding the surge of excitement at imagining each angle of the plan work together. In a single moment, I worked out how to get into Ulder's vault and put the sword in Garth's hands, right in front of the entire court. Safe and easy.

"I know what to do," I said. To my surprise, everyone looked at me and waited to hear it.

But before I could explain, Garth touched my arm.

"Erlin," he whispered, "are you sure? I might not make a very good king. You...you and everyone else back home always say I'm—"

"Forget what I said. Forget what *everyone* said. Garth, I think most of Albion has forgotten there's such a thing as a good king, but I've seen enough to know that you're the best person to sit on that throne."

I meant every word of it.

###

There was only one key that could open Ulder's vault. Now some people would think that would be a limiting factor, but I always found constraints to be helpful guidelines when solving puzzles. It keeps you from looking in the wrong direction.

"Garth, I assume that vault can be opened from the inside without the key, right?"

"How did you know? There's a lever just inside the door. It's heavy, but I've..."

I took a moment to be silently amused that Garth had clearly locked himself in the vault more than once.

"In that case, we won't need a key," I said.

"That's a relief," said Garth. "Da keeps it on his belt unless he's asleep. But how will we get in?"

I held up Morrigin's earring. "With this."

I laid the plan out for them.

Ywain, who Ulder didn't know, would walk into the court with the earring, saying it was magical, that he'd heard of Ulder's collection, and wanted to bring it in for a reward. Ulder would throw it in his vault, like always. That's when Garth would return to court and tell everyone he had something important to say. At this point, Ulder would think the prince was about to publicly renounce the throne.

"We'll have to work fast," I said, "and Garth may have to do some stalling, but while everyone's gathering together for the announcement—"

"I'll Travel into the vault!" Morrigin realized.

"Exactly." We all grinned as the plan laid itself out for us. "It shouldn't be hard to get Nimway into the castle, and once you're inside, you can open the vault and let her in. Everyone will be paying attention to Garth."

"I'll find the sword in his vault," said Nimway. She turned to the prince as she worked it out. "And...then Morrigin and I will just...bring it to you."

"Right in front of Da!" exclaimed Garth.

I leaned back and watched their faces work through the whole idea. But before I let them get carried away with my plan, I needed to make sure everyone knew how stupid it was. "Garth, it's only a sword, you know. Ulder can still kill you and take the throne. Or maybe the crowd won't recognize the sword. We can still help you abdicate, give up the throne, and save your mother."

He frowned. "Mother would rather die. I know it."

Making decisions about someone else's life and death was certainly the domain of the king, and Garth was putting his foot down with as much confidence as any ruler who'd ever lived.

Ywain glanced over his map. "We'll need to hurry."

"Where did Dagonet say he was going?" I asked Morrigin.

"Troyes. We can get there in our boat. It's a coast town, just a bit north of where we shoved off."

So, it was decided. We would head back to Tomelac, pull the wool over Ulder's eyes, and place Garth on the throne. As I watched him and Ywain take turns blowing bubbles with their spit, I wondered what had become of my life.

I also wondered, once again, why the name "Troyes" seemed so familiar. It's a shame I didn't figure it out, because that would have saved me a lot of trouble.

CHAPTER SIXTY

YWAIN WAS CERTAIN the lion would fit in our boat.

The lion was skeptical.

Ywain nudged the beast across the muddy ground toward the *Sable*, valiantly trying to coax the big lion to climb aboard.

The lion had been loyal to Ywain. Couldn't deny that. It had slept with its colossal head resting on Ywain's scrawny chest and followed him around while he collected apples for breakfast. But the boat, which had held all four of us, looked tiny as the big cat hesitantly reached inside with a giant paw.

"Go on," Ywain said in uplifting tones. "You can do it."

The lion looked back at Ywain. Then it tried again, placing its heavy paw in the middle of the deck.

Ywain patted its side, then gently pushed on its rump. "Now, just..."

The boat slipped. The lion, already leaning forward, stumbled into the boat, face first. Its weight caused the boat to break loose from the muddy ground and drift out to sea.

For a few moments, the boat sailed on placid waters while Ywain's lion sat on its haunches in the middle seat. It stared back at us, quietly confused.

"We'll have to swim for it!" I realized.

We ran across the shore, struggling against the wet ground, until the water was deep enough to swim.

Of course, I took to the water like an anchor. My flailing hands kept me barely afloat and moving forward while I tried not to imagine the grotesque creatures that lived in the sea.

With a frustrated grunt, Ywain's lion, perturbed by the odd motion of the boat, leaped into the water and swam back to shore.

The lion and I crossed paths, sharing a silent, confused acknowledgement as we clumsily paddled by one another.

"It's just as well," said Ywain once we'd all climbed in. "He's a good lion, but I'm not entirely sure he was safe."

###

Ywain piloted the *Sable* to Troyes, where we paid a young man the docking fee and hoped our black-hulled ship wouldn't draw the wrong attention.

Morrigin and I headed into town, leaving the other three behind. It felt wrong to keep Nimway from seeing the city after her years of isolation, but we were in a terrible hurry. Between Nimway's curiosity and Garth's squirrel-like attention span, I didn't think the whole lot of us could walk across Troyes in less than a week.

Fortunately, I knew it would be easy to find Dagonet. He always placed his troupe where the fancy snobs couldn't ignore them.

As I walked the streets of Troyes, I had a strange feeling as I noticed the stocks casting a long shadow over the town square. I'd been here before, I just couldn't—

"They're staring," said Morrigin, sounding very anxious.

I winked at her. "Attractive women tend to draw the eye."

"That's true, but this time they're staring at *you*."

"Well," I straightened my shirt and stood up tall. "A few ladies have been known to—"

"That's not it."

I'd tried to ignore them, but Morrigin wasn't wrong. We couldn't walk a block without someone leering. But only one of the gawkers really concerned me.

A man stepped out from behind a column and leaned against it, looking past his long, curly hair while enjoying his pipe. He watched us with a casual smile as he crossed his arms. Unlike the rest of town, this curly-haired man acted like he was expecting us. The icy calm in his eyes made my spine shiver.

We heard applause from the far side of town.

"Matinee just ended," I said. "I know exactly where to find Dagonet."

The ale house closest to the stage was packed to the edges. Half of the drinking patrons were actually Dagonet's actors, while the other half had just seen his show and needed a drink to process it.

We pushed through until we found Dagonet at a table in the corner. He was flipping through a script and muttering about missed cues and someone wearing the wrong wig.

When a server dropped off a mug of ale, Dagonet looked up and finally noticed me. He froze. The foam at the top of the mug wobbled in his suddenly shaky grip. "What are you doing here, boy? Are you mad?"

Morrigin punched me in the arm.

"What are you talking about?" I put on a big smile. Sometimes when you pretend everything is fine then everyone else does too. And sometimes the universe even goes along with it.

His voice lowered. "Don't you know where you are?"

Before I could answer, someone tapped me on the shoulder.

I turned around to see a grizzled man staring at my face like it was a menu. The rest of the room held its breath, awaiting his appraisal.

My spirits sunk as his eyes widened. And just then I remembered exactly why I wasn't welcome in Troyes.

"He's come back!" he shouted, getting spit in my face. "It's Mirdal the Mad!"

Chapter Sixty-One

I suppose I haven't been entirely honest with you, so here's my secret:

In case you haven't figured it out, I didn't actually kill Mirdal the Mad.

I *was* Mirdal the Mad.

It was a lovely scam, and it's exactly the reason I ended up in Ulder's court.

We would start by putting the fear of Mirdal into a whole town. I would run around in a bright red robe, seeming to disappear at random, all while Dagonet spread dark rumors and made sure something was out of place everywhere we went.

In truth, my robe was red on one side and brown on the other. I simply turned it inside out and removed my false beard when no one was looking. Meanwhile, Dagonet would open cattle pens in the middle of the night and paint strange symbols on front doors. Mind you, we didn't cause any real trouble, but a little fear and a few tiny surprises are enough to work any town into a frenzy. Then Dagonet and I would stroll up to the town's mayor and promise we could get rid of this menace.

For a small fee, of course.

And it worked every time. After agreeing to hire us, Dagonet and I would perform a week-long magic ritual. For the sake of our own amusement, it usually involved asking the townsfolk to do something ridiculous. (We once got carried away and made all the landowners wear their pants backward the entire time.) Once our ritual was complete, Mirdal the Mad would never show up again.

It made us a lot of money, so, like fools, we took our act to Tomelac.

Why? It's the biggest city in Albion, and King Ulder had a reputation for hating magic and throwing money at anyone who could do something about it. Dagonet and I figured we could retire for a few years on Ulder's payment.

Scaring the people of Tomelac was great fun. Every time I stepped out from behind a tree, someone would faint into someone else's arms. But everything went downhill when I noticed my red robe was looking faded. We had to dye it every few weeks, because Mirdal's robe needed to be the brightest thing anyone ever saw in order to be memorable, and as Dagonet and I were planning our big reveal, we realized the costume had lost its luster. That wouldn't do.

Dyeing a robe means you need water, so we found a well in an empty alley and got work. I had gotten pretty good at dyeing the robe quickly while Dagonet stood guard, but I had just started applying the dye when he made a bird call to get my attention. Someone was coming. We could hear the footsteps of a guard patrol heading our way, and one glance down the alley might expose our fraud.

Lacking a better option, I bundled up the robes in my arms and we rushed through the nearest door.

Even though we'd been in town for a few days, neither of us had really mastered the city's layout. Specifically, we hadn't noticed that half the doors in the middle of Tomelac led into the sprawling castle keep, so we were very surprised to make our way through a kitchen only to hear Ulder's voice booming from somewhere nearby.

We walked blindly through a few hallways, trying to appear calm while hiding the incriminating robe I had wadded up in my arms, until we rounded a corner and found ourselves nearly face-to-face with a group of soldiers. They hadn't noticed me shoving the bottle of dye in my trouser pocket, but it wouldn't take them long to get close and realize I didn't belong in the keep.

I threw open the nearest door and rushed inside, then stopped in my tracks.

Men and women wearing their best finery stared at me from behind food-laden tables. All of them were still as statues, holding goblets or forks in the air. I had interrupted a feast. Fearing the worst, I turned to the far end of the room and saw King Ulder standing at the largest table.

I'd just invaded Ulder's dining hall, a place where people had been killed for eating with suspicious utensils. A few knights drew swords.

"Look!" cried a child next to the king. "He's killed Mirdal the Mad!"

I glanced down.

In my hands was the robe. Not only that, but my fingers were all red. The dye had only barely touched the robe; most of it was staining my fingers.

"He's got the blood of Mirdal on his hands!" someone cried.

The room was abuzz. I stood still, not wanting to disturb my luck. Meanwhile, Dagonet had simply kept walking. In fact, he kept walking until he was several towns away.

"That's...right." Drawing on all of my acting instincts, I turned to Ulder and unfurled the robe, showing off its dastardly runes. "I...just killed Mirdal the Mad. Yep. You're welcome."

What followed was a wonderful and believable story about Mirdal's defeat at my hand. The gathered crowd—appreciating a break from the court's usual tedium—listened closely to my harrowing tale, which ended with me stabbing Mirdal on his way to kill the king.

Naturally, the body had vanished like smoke. Which, I assured them, was what always happened when a warlock was killed. "Everyone knows that," I said, and I watched with satisfaction as most of the room quickly nodded along.

Thus ended my impersonation of Mirdal and began my new career as Tomelac's inquisitor. It wasn't the most noble of beginnings, but it could have been worse. Some layabouts got rich simply by outliving their parents. I felt noble by comparison.

While things had gone horribly right in Tomelac, there had been an earlier time when playing Mirdal the Mad had gone horribly wrong. As you can guess, it was the time we took our act to Troyes.

We only just began our work when we noticed the local reactions to Mirdal were far more violent than usual. It turned out this place had been telling stories of Mirdal the Mad for generations. Nothing unusual about that. After all, I didn't invent him. He was an old folk tale, which lent quite a bit of authority to our scam.

(I suppose I *could* have invented my own mystical persona instead of borrowing from a famous legend, but that would have been a lot more work. And when you rip off a classic story, you get to pass it off as an homage. Or so I've heard.)

We could have easily dealt with this town's frothing-at-the-mouth reaction to Mirdal if it were not for one little happenstance.

While changing out of my robe, I was startled to hear a growling noise just as a mangy dog grabbed my robe with its yellow teeth. The mutt dragged me for a few blocks while we fought bitterly, tugging back and forth and both trying to growl the loudest. I finally snatched the robe from its smelly mouth and started to put it on when I heard watery noises behind me.

I slowly turned to see an array of men laying in a pool. The dog had dragged me to the city bath.

There were splashing sounds as the men charged out of the water and descended upon me, and not a single one stopped to grab a towel.

And that's how I ended up being crammed into the stocks by a gang of un-toweled men, and how I first noticed that stocks tend to hold your face about waist high.

Dagonet's attention to detail meant that my false beard stubbornly clung to my face while I waited in the stocks. With my robe still half on, I looked the very image of a captured evil wizard.

During my second night of captivity, a young woman in the city guard let me out on the promise I would come back to kill her lover and his entire family, which numbered in the dozens. I agreed, promising I would one day return to Troyes with violence like the town had never seen.

It worked. But I didn't count on her telling anyone about my promise or on the city's long memory. As the tavern closed in on us, I realized the people of Troyes had spent years sharpening their knives in preparation for the return of Mirdal the Mad.

Chapter Sixty-Two

THE TAVERN ROOM was frozen still. Murder danced in the eyes of every patron, but none of them were completely sure who should stab me first.

The cook was in no hurry. Stepping away from the stove, he removed several knives from a block and carefully gauged each one.

Lucky for me, he was ignoring his cooking. While he tested the weight of a cleaver, his skillet of spicy potatoes hissed, reaching that point when food will no longer cook in a calm and orderly fashion.

I chose this moment to raise my hands dramatically.

Thanks to a breeze from an open window, smoke filled the room, and the patrons cowered at my "magic."

Covering my mouth with my sleeve, I grabbed Morrigin's arm and rushed her out the back. I heard Dagonet cough the word "bridge" under his breath as we scrambled past.

We ran by a few buildings and hid in a doorway, pressed against one another in the building's shadow. I could hear patrons stumbling out of the bar screaming about Mirdal the Mad between fits of coughs.

"I have to tell you something," I whispered.

"You dressed up as Mirdal to scam these people and now they want to kill you?"

I frowned. "It was a really good scam."

She looked toward the docks. "We'll have to get to the boat."

"No. I'm going to the bridge. That's where Dagonet parked. I'll get the red robe I used to wear and lead the rabble away from Garth. You get the others and bring them back to the caravan. Dagonet will take you the rest of the way. He acts cynical, but he'll do the right thing for Albion."

She turned to me, and even in the dark I could see the color of her widening eyes.

"Go," I said. "You don't need me for the rest of the plan. Just get Garth to Tomelac and put that sword in his hand."

It was difficult, but I pushed myself away, feeling cold the moment we were not longer touching.

In that moment, I wanted to know if she felt as cold and empty without me as I did without her. It was difficult to imagine a beautiful woman with magical powers longing for someone so ordinary as me, but her fingers still reached out, like she wanted to find one more moment together.

She opened her mouth to speak, but I turned away and dashed into a thicket of trees. If my mental map was correct, I could make a quick route around the town's edge and end up near the stone bridge leading out of town.

###

I emerged from the woods with a light covering of burs clinging to my clothes. Dagonet's caravans were gathered near a large bridge near the edge of town; they always tried to park where they could make a quick getaway.

I knew which wagon held costumes. The back doors had been left open. I climbed up and searched the clothing racks until I spied a bright crimson cloth. The robe of Mirdal still held every bit of its charm. I jerked it from the hanger and balled it up.

"What do you think you're doing with that, boy?" said Dagonet, who stood at the entrance to the caravan.

"Get out of the way." I pushed past him and hopped down to the ground. "They need Mirdal and Wart needs to get to Tomelac. The mob won't notice you taking him away if they're chasing me."

"Wrong," came Morrigin's voice. She was suddenly behind me. I'd forgotten about the earring. I could see Nimway, Garth, and Ywain heading our way along the road, far behind. She had gathered them up, and then Traveled to get to me first.

I thought this might be because she did, indeed, miss me. But before I could ask, Morrigin's fist landed in my jaw. I fell to the ground and then felt the robe being pulled from my hands.

"You're braver than you let on." She donned the cloak, which billowed effortlessly over her shoulders.

She whispered, "but Garth needs you more than he needs me."

Morrigin pulled the hood up and tucked her hair in. She ran back toward the town, into the bright afternoon sunlight, where the maddened crowd would surely take one glance at her embroidered red robes and give chase.

I wanted to run after her.

After a moment, Dagonet slapped me on the back of the head. "Get in, you dope!" he shouted as he ran for the driver's seat.

We all piled into the back of the caravan. I was the last one, and I was barely on board when the whip cracked and the big wheels carried us away. I held the back doors together with my hands, not ready to latch them in place.

"Don't you think you should close that?" asked Ywain.

I couldn't help it. Morrigin was running for her life out there. I peaked out through the space between the doors, but only saw an empty road behind us.

Nimway screamed.

I spun around and saw a man emerge from behind a rack of clothing.

I'd seen him before.

It was the creepy man from the square, the curly-haired watcher who had given me chills. He raised a knife and silently walked toward Garth.

Naturally, I threw Ywain at him.

The caravan was moving entirely too fast and crashed through a series of potholes. We all grabbed onto the nearest wall for balance just as Ywain slammed into the assailant. The two of them teetered around trying to keep their balance.

This certainly was a well-informed assassin. I couldn't fathom how he'd gotten here.

The curly-haired man, deciding I was a threat, shoved Ywain aside and stumbled toward me, knife in hand.

Of course, he hadn't spent much time in over-sized carriages. He didn't know how to predict when the horses were slowing down to take a corner, for example, so he wasn't prepared when the caravan turned sharply.

But I was.

I threw open the door and stepped aside, offering a polite salute as he tumbled away. I shut both doors and latched them in place this time, but not before stealing a glance at the road behind us. Nothing out there.

"He'll be back," said Nimway.

"Not anytime soon."

"Yes, he *will*! My sister thinks she's so special. Lots of Abrecans can Travel."

My mind went to the pearl in my pocket. If he was a Traveler, it explained how he'd shown up in the caravan.

Nimway pointed at my waist. "Get rid of it!"

"Get rid of what?"

"The Traveling gem. I can *sense* it. Throw it out, or he'll keep coming back!"

I dug into my pocket and held out the pearl for a moment. If I got rid of it, Morrigin wouldn't be able to catch up with us and we wouldn't be able to sneak her into Ulder's vault. Our entire plan was shot.

Muttering every impolite work I knew, I hurled the earring through a back window. It touched down in the middle of the road and then bounced to the side. I watched it gleam as it tumbled down the hill towards the sea and crashed into the busy docks, where fishermen were pulling up nets.

I had no idea where the earring ended up or where Morrigin would be if she tried Traveling to it. Maybe she'd find herself standing on a dock. Or underwater. I wasn't sure what I had done.

"Now what?" asked Garth. "Without Morrigin, we can't get into the vault."

"It has a key, doesn't it?" I snapped, louder than I intended. "Any door can be opened."

Everyone fell silent. We'd just left Avalon, and my brilliant plan was already broken.

The caravan rocked and we all reached out for something to hold on to. Dagonet was pushing the horses and carriage to their limit before anyone from town could catch up, which would work as long as our vehicle held itself together. I'd never heard so many groans from so many beams and axles.

"But how can we do it without Morrigin?" asked Garth.

I felt like jumping out of the back door of the caravan, but then I remembered something Morrigin had told me. "Garth, back in Tomelac, did you ever notice the garden on top of the small building near the stables?"

He shook his head.

I'd almost forgotten about it myself. If it weren't for my high-rise window, I might never have noticed the cozy collection of plants gathered on the little rooftop. "Morrigin told me those gardens are kept by Abrecans, and they meet in those gardens on full moons. That means we have an ally in Tomelac, someone Morrigin would trust. Someone who can help us. There's a full moon in two days, and we're going to see who's up there."

Chapter Sixty-Three

It was Petunia.

We made our way to Tomelac just in time for night to fall under a full moon. The wagons were breaking apart, but still working. I'm pretty sure everyone in the city could hear the joints squeaking as we rolled up.

The moon garden grew on an empty roof just inside the city wall, and as Dagonet and I approached, we could see someone sitting in the moonlight, surrounded by plants that preferred to bloom at night. Noticing a ladder, we climbed our way to the top, but my feeling of accomplishment sank when I saw Petunia's cunning face outlined in silver light. There was a time—a simpler time—when this petty gardener had been my only nemesis.

Occupying the only chair, she quietly watched Dagonet and me find places to sit on the ground. After deciding on a spot mostly bereft of dirt, I settled in on the hard roof. Riding at breakneck speed had left my body aching in places I had never considered.

Petunia sipped her tea and waited.

"Morrigin said we could trust you," I said.

She shrugged. "I brought her here, didn't I? That day you stepped in horse manure? Was a Moonrider myself when I was young."

"I didn't realize horses had been around that long."

Our old feud slipped around me like a robe.

"You sure warm up when I mention Morrigin," she said, stirring her tea. "Maybe I'll tell her about the time the outhouse walls collapsed while you were inside."

Petunia's practical joking had been especially precise that day. And the walls had fallen just as the king walked by leading a parade.

"Where is Morrigin?" she asked.

I told Petunia everything. Her mask of indifference fell as I explained our tribulations, and her eyes took on a shrewd protectiveness when I spoke of Garth.

"And now we need a way into the vault," I said, concluding my tale.

"Use the key."

"Excellent idea, as always, Petunia. The key. The key that Ulder keeps on his belt. The key that no one but Ulder is allowed to touch on punishment of torture. That key?"

She nodded. "That's the one."

"I guess I'll have to lift it."

Dagonet snorted. "Lift it? Boy, we tried that scheme in seven cities and you never so much as pinched a coin from a corpse."

"If you have a better idea, I'm all ears." Truth be told, I *wasn't* much of a pickpocket, but I understood the basics. Distract the target, move fast, then distract the target again. It always *sounded* easy.

"You'll need a diversion." Dagonet tapped at his chin. "Nothing's more distracting than art. Let us set up our stage."

"Might work," said Petunia. "It's a feast day tomorrow. Ulder will take lunch in the courtyard."

Petunia and I rolled our eyes at the same time at the idea of another feast. There was almost always a feast happening in Tomelac. Ulder didn't like to go a whole day without eating in front of someone.

"What is it this time?" I asked.

"The feast of *candles*," she said. "Ulder made it up last night and then asked for a hundred boars, so the royal hunters are in the woods now hoping they bring back enough to avoid going to jail if they only find ninety-nine."

I really hated that man.

Dagonet and I began scheming. I could get near Ulder by dressing as a servant, and Dag could easily orchestrate a few distractions while I pilfered the key. It was starting to sound fun.

"But will Ulder let us set up the stage?" I asked. "He's not a fan of theater when clothing is involved."

Petunia smiled, and I grew worried.

"He will," she said. "I have the authority to bring in entertainment." She patiently drank more of her tea, waiting for me to say something.

"But...you want something in return...oh, no."

She winked. "Oh, and don't forget about all those big, strong guards Ulder keeps around. I know how to deal with them, too. It'll just cost you..."

I shook my head. "Forget it." I knew Petunia's price, and it was too high for me. "You can't ask for that."

"Boy?" Dagonet touched my arm. "I think the kingdom's at stake here."

My head fell. After years of being at one another's throat, Petunia had won our feud. "Fine. You can have my quarters in the tower."

Petunia clapped.

Her celebration was interrupted by a voice from below.

"What!"

Dagonet and I lowered our heads, hoping we couldn't be seen.

"What's that old codger doing here?" I asked.

"What! What!" shouted the unmistakable voice of King Pellinore. His words came with a metallic echo as they moved through his steel helmet. "Who goes there?"

We heard a sharp scrape as a sword left its sheath. A very sharp sword. I remembered that Pellinore, while he seemed harmless, had once been the oldest man to win a tournament.

"What do you want?" Petunia shouted down.

"Thought I heard scallywags up there! Madam, do you need saving?"

"You need to clean out your ears!"

"What!"

"Exactly."

"Why, the insolence! I'm a king! Of The Manly Isles!"

"You should go back. Maybe they still remember you."

It was fun being on Petunia's good side.

We heard Pellinore stomp off. The squeaks from his armor's metal joints echoed long into the night.

"He's hunting a creature," said Petunia. "At least, that's what he says. I think he's just bored."

Dagonet and I went back to our scheming. It was going to be a long night, but the planning is the best part.

Chapter Sixty-Four

The next day, as one hundred slain boars were laid on the outdoor banquet tables (with apples crammed into their yawning mouths) we rolled through the city gates.

True to her word, Petunia escorted the caravans into the courtyard, assuring everyone we were the day's entertainment. The guards believed her, but they insisted on searching everything.

Simple disguises were all we needed. I kept juggling so my face was hard to see. You might think Garth would be simple to spot since his face was so well known in Tomelac, but wearing a bird costume and holding up a script was all it took for him to go unnoticed.

We drove into the courtyard and saw a meager crowd gather as we pushed the caravans together. It was always a spectacle to behold, the way the huge wagons could park next to one another and create a wide stage. And while that was going on, Garth and Nimway slipped away and hid in my tower chambers.

Mind you, it wasn't my room anymore. By that morning, Petunia had already moved in and placed my belongings outside the door.

Getting Garth and Nimway to the tower without being seen was obviously critical to the plan. Garth removed his bird costume (without Wendy's help, we were forced to cut him out of it) and then dressed as an old, blind nobleman. Nimway would play the part of his servant and guide him around the keep.

To me, this was the riskiest part of our plan. Only one person needed to recognize Garth for things to go awry, but no one gets what they really want out of life without a few big gambles along the way.

Since Garth hadn't had time to hone his acting ability, we wrapped a blindfold around his eyes so he wouldn't have to pretend he couldn't see. I had barely finished tying the knot on the blindfold when Garth took a step into a clothing rack and got his arms tangled in a moth costume.

"Why don't you just kill him?" asked Nimway.

I pointed to Garth. "Him?"

"No, the king."

"Oh."

"If you can get close enough to steal Ulder's key, then why don't you just *stab* him while you're there? That's what I would do."

I dragged Garth away from the clothes and untangled him. "Because, Nimway, it would be nice if a kingdom changed who was in charge without anyone being killed."

History books are kind to those plucky warlords who lead rebellions. We like to imagine them as dashing leaders, full of morals and responsibility. According to popular songs, they're always carefree mavericks who govern with ease. But, truthfully, it's notoriously expensive to raise an army and take over a kingdom, and once that's done you have to keep paying all those well-armed soldiers who got you the job, which means raising taxes until every potato in your kingdom costs as much as the farm. And once you've squeezed every coin from your own people, you'll have to go to war and take your enemy's money if you want to have enough to pay your own blood-thirsty army. And once you've exhausted both the greedy and violent options, you're stuck with patriotism as your last resort to maintain their loyalty. But since patriotism never paid any bills, it doesn't take long for your underpaid, overtaxed populace to find a new, more popular warlord who's willing to string you up on your own gallows and settle into your throne, only to be yoked with the same burdens you weren't sorry to leave behind.

I thought it would be nice if—just this once—a kingdom could change management without anyone dying.

In my defense, I tried.

###

Nimway and Garth stumbled away while I whispered a prayer, begging anyone who could hear me to get those two into my quarters without incident. My stomach did not settle until I looked up to the tower window and saw Nimway glance out with a wave. With the prince safely in place, I could focus on my part in the scheme.

I donned a thick pair of glasses and used Dagonet's vast costume collection to dress as a servant. Pickpocketing the key would be a cinch; all I had to do was wander near Ulder and then signal the actors for a diversion. A little handiwork and the key would be mine.

Checking my apron ties, I turned to the actors. "You know what to do?"

With stern faces, they all nodded.

"I'll keep them in line," Ywain promised, tapping a rolled-up parchment. "That's why Dagonet gave me the script."

Actually, after forgetting his lines several times, Dagonet had bestowed upon him the great honor of "script supervisor."

We were geared up like a well-oiled clock. Sure, maybe it was the sort of clock from which grotesque animal carvings emerge to a nonsensical tune, but a clock no less.

I left the caravan and stood in a corner of the courtyard, holding a tray and a pitcher of water. Someone always did that at banquets. A pair of servants hauled out an ornate chair and placed it in front of Ulder's table. He wouldn't be far behind.

Chapter Sixty-Five

I QUICKLY LEARNED that a pitcher full of water is heavy, far too heavy to hold up on a tray for any amount of time, so I poured it out onto a plant when no one was looking and told anyone who asked that I was carrying the royal spittoon.

Ulder arrived late, with his entourage in tow. He strolled past the tables, laughing at one of his own jokes as he grabbed an apple from the mouth of a boar and took a loud bite. Behind him, Sir Kay led the rest of the knights. His face still bore an ugly burn mark from the oil I had thrown on him in Kingsport.

Ulder towered over the table and used both hands to tear into the boar. I spied the key dangling from his belt, tied by simple twine.

Knowing this would be our best shot, I tapped my nose several times. On stage, a few actors tapped their noses in return. Everyone was ready.

With my stomach in a knot, I walked along the nearest wall, inching toward Ulder's position, and squeezed the small knife I held under the tray. It was just sharp enough to cut the twine.

An actor took center stage and grabbed everyone's attention by doffing a colorful hat and taking a deep bow. "For you, our most prestigious audience, it is our *honor* to present our most famous play!"

People clapped. The rich and famous enjoy being told how important they are.

The actor continued. "We are proud to perform..." He lowered his voice like he was telling a secret. "...the play with no name!"

There were whispers of approval throughout the crowd.

I knew it had taken a lot of effort for Dagonet to resist using one of his offensive plays. This one wouldn't upset anyone.

It began with a few pantomime mules wandering into one another before giving birth to nobles with two faces. (Some of the symbolism was lost on me.) After some mesmerizing dances, planned silences, and backward conversations, it eventually ended with a parade of Dagonet's best acrobats wearing his strangest costumes, all of them running through their most complicated maneuvers at the same time.

This might sound ridiculous, but it was one of the most famous plays in Albion. Dagonet refused to tell anyone what the act was about, even refused to name it, which, naturally, created an irresistible urge amongst intelligent people, who rushed to promote their own interpretations of the nameless play. Like cats to catnip, the learned population of Albion could never resist slapping their point of view onto anything incomprehensible. It might have been an exploration of the human condition. Or a meditation on the nature of suffering. A vocal minority believed the play with no name demonstrated how pointless it was to search for any meaning at all.

They were close, because this routine of Dagonet's actually had no inner meaning. No deep thoughts dwelled beneath the performance, and no interpretation was necessary. This play was nothing but random stage pieces and endless dancing, but Dagonet would never admit that as long as it made him famous.

I smiled as the first two-faced politician emerged from the back end of a mule costume and crawled blindly around the stage. But as more actors gathered to add to the spectacle, I heard a groaning noise. A creaking moan shot through the courtyard.

I recognized it. I'd heard that sound a dozen times on our way here. The sound came from one of the caravans, tired and weary from being driven too hard and holding up too many dancers.

Before either pantomime mule could give birth again, one of the caravans broke in half and spilled actors onto the grass. The mules were separated; each half scrambled apart as an avalanche of bright costumes tumbled from backstage and flitted through the courtyard like the ghosts of a circus.

With a sharp crack, the other caravan fell in half as the stage took its final bow.

The courtyard was still. Had I made it all the way to Ulder, I would have tried to get the key right then and there, but I was still two steps away and everyone would notice if I took those last steps in a hurry.

At first, there was no sound. Even the birds fell quiet. But the emptiness was soon filled by Ulder's laughter. The lords and ladies began laughing along, which was always wise. The troupe, scattered and confused, looked around with no idea what to do next.

Ignoring them, Ulder turned his attention to his meal, and I suddenly felt exposed. I couldn't get close without being noticed, but it was too late to turn back. Unfortunately, Ulder had lost all interest in the play, which meant the actors weren't going to be any help.

Or so I thought.

Just then, an actor strolled forward, stepping past the wreckage and right up to Ulder's table.

Ulder slowly stopped pulling apart one of the boar's front legs. His quick temper was famous, but few knew that when the king's blood *really* boiled it slowly built up like a silent volcano.

Before him stood Ywain, who had quickly dressed up like the King, wearing the costume we used for *The Calamities of King Ulder.*

Courage takes different forms. Sometimes it looks like a desperate soldier rushing into a hopeless battle, or maybe a child who stands up to the school bully.

But other times courage looks like a frightened actor who's finally remembered his line.

CHAPTER SIXTY-SIX

"IT'S A GOOD DAY FOR BATHING IN COW URINE!" shouted Ywain.

Ulder fumed.

Apparently, the king *had* heard of my magnum opus. Judging by the way his face turned red, he was well aware that country people enjoyed a play where he was the butt of every joke. I was flattered.

No one heard exactly what Ulder said next.

Mind you, everyone *heard* it. Ulder stood and screamed some guttural, indistinct syllables, the specifics of which did not matter. It was surely a variant of "GET HIM!" or "KILL HIM!" or "WHY ARE HIS EYEBALLS STILL IN HIS HEAD?" Something like that.

Ywain staggered in place, trying to hold their attention in order to create the distraction I needed.

Sir Kay rose first and drew his sword. Now, just about any sword is capable of killing someone. Even those scrawny-looking swords can tear you open before you can make fun of the other guy for having a scrawny-looking sword. Fancy swords, everyone knows, are impractical and just for show. But knights weren't known for being practical and Kay wasn't known for being intelligent, so the sword he drew was large enough to skewer six men at once. You know, just in case you need to stab an entire tenor section.

Kay leaped onto the table, making a great show of himself, and pointed his absurd weapon toward the trembling Ywain.

"You heard what tha' king said!" shouted Kay, who had most certainly not heard what the king said. "Let's..."

I assumed Sir Kay paused for dramatic effect, but I was mistaken. I heard someone snicker from behind a growth of snapdragons and realized this was another one of Petunia's contributions.

The big sword wavered and wobbled like Kay was conducting a very slow opera. Then his eyes rolled up and he lost his grip. The weapon knocked over several goblets and plates when it slammed onto the table, and then Sir Kay knocked over the rest when he fell face-first onto the nearest boar. Grappling and confused, he and the boar rolled off the table like a pair of lovers.

The rest of the knights had also risen to their feet, but the act of standing quickly made them keenly aware of their own stomachs and, more importantly, the extra ingredients in their food. Soon, every knight of Tomelac lay writhing on the ground.

The knights, of course, ate from a different, special part of the kitchen, making it all too easy for Petunia to target them with her poisons.

The actors, including Ywain, ran for it. Badly. It staggers the mind to see how a group of talented dancers capable of twirling on point or flipping over one another could completely fail to jog across a yard without looking like idiots who had never used their legs before, but their misguided and frightened efforts were enough to escape the knights who crawled over the grass in slow pursuit.

It was a perfect distraction. With one swift motion, I cut the key from Ulder's belt.

The knife dropped back into my sleeve, into a small leather hilt I'd sewn in there, and then I crept away. I walked over to the stone wall and stood under the tower window. My old room was up there, a few stories high, and I knew Garth and Nimway were waiting for the key.

I also knew they had lowered a string all the way down to the courtyard.

No one had noticed the long thread dangling from my window. I tied the end to Ulder's key and gave it a tug, and then I watched the key skitter up the wall. I looked around to see if anyone noticed, but the courtyard was filled with clumsy actors pursued by angry, crawling soldiers. Not a soul was looking my way.

I glanced up and saw the key disappear over the windowsill. Nimway and Garth would take it to the vault and find the sword inside. All I had to do was join them. It was a shame Morrigin wasn't here to see our plan working.

Entering the keep was my next step, but as I looked around the courtyard, I noticed the doors were blocked, all but the entry to the kitchen. Ulder had tightened his security. Lifting my empty tray, I headed for the only open door and pushed through a hectic room of ovens and chopping boards until I emerged in a long hallway. Most doors were shut and guarded, so I kept walking.

At each intersection I pointed my feet in the general direction of the great hall and quickly found myself in a large storeroom. Along each wall stood barrels and crates filled to the top with food, supplies for Ulder's feast.

The sound of armored footsteps stopped me in my tracks. They were coming from the next room and headed my way.

Thinking fast, I sat on a barrel and grabbed a potato from a nearby box. Letting the knife drop from my sleeve, I began peeling. I had never done it before. By the time the first soldier passed by, I'd peeled off a few pieces of the smaller end, which I thought wasn't bad for my first try.

The patrol marched through the room and out the side door without even glancing at me. I breathed a sigh of relief and wondered if I should save any of these potatoes for Garth's next collection.

Just then, something moved underneath me, and I realized my mistake.

THE ONCE AND FUTURE IDIOT

I was sitting on a *barrel*.

Chapter Sixty-Seven

The barrel grew arms before I could get away.

An inexplicable hand reached out, coming from somewhere under me. I fell and landed just beyond its grasp.

I pushed away and got to my feet, mostly stunned by watching Escanor transform. I knew I needed to escape, but the sight of a barrel turning into a man was something I couldn't turn away from.

While dispensing homespun wisdom, my father once told me I could win a fight by doing something the other person didn't have the will to do. Most tough guys would actually hesitate before biting an ear or sticking their finger in someone's eye, he told me. That was supposed to be comforting.

Unfortunately, Escanor, who now stood before me, cracking his knuckles and flexing his arms, didn't look like he was facing an ethical dilemma. He straightened one end of his mustache while sizing me up. Apparently concluding I was about as threatening as a beached starfish, he took a step in my direction.

That's when I played my only card. I let the little knife slip from its hidden place in my sleeve and lashed out.

You know, it always seems like really muscular guys will move slowly, so I was surprised to see the burly Escanor take a graceful step back and elude my clever attack.

I had missed. But it got worse. Escanor reached out and grab the knife from my hand, easily as you pick a flower. He laughed at my frightened face and threw the knife aside.

At that moment, I finally realized what Escanor wouldn't do. Sure, he was exactly the sort of person who would bite an ear or poke an eye. But do you know what was below him?

Running away.

I bolted.

But I only took half a step before he shoved me in the back. Off balance, I spun stupidly while my arms flailed like a bird who's just realized it isn't the sort who can fly. Before my feet could settle down, he backed me into a wall and pinned me with a hand around my throat. The worst part was looking into his laughing face. He'd defeated me easier than if he'd stepped on a bug.

He was the shorter man, but that didn't stop him from squeezing my neck and dangling me like a rag doll.

"King Ulder told me to sit here and watch for the inquisitor, but I never dreamed you'd make it *that* easy."

I pulled at his arms and punched at his face, all the things that are supposed to work when you're being overpowered, but it was like hitting a mountain.

A door opened on the far side of the room.

I struggled to breathe while a suit of armor clanked through the doorway in slow, rusty movements.

"What!" cried the newcomer.

Escanor turned around. "Get out of here, old man."

The armored figure drew its sword. "Nonsense! Just hold that vagabond still!"

I kicked at Escanor, but he didn't notice.

"An enemy of the state! What!" Pellinore's razor-sharp sword waved in the air. "I'll run that miscreant through!"

His ancient greaves clanged like pots and pans against the stone ground. While I struggled, Escanor kept his eyes on me and ignored Pellinore, which is what most people did.

The suit of armor was nearly there. "Time to gut that scalawag like a fish!"

Nearly out of breath, I looked over Escanor's shoulder and said, "Would you please hurry up?"

I have to give Escanor credit. Before it was too late, he realized what was going on. For the briefest moment, his eyes showed that surprised look that happens when someone's figured out they're being fooled. And right after that, his eyes showed the sort of surprise that happens when someone's being stabbed in the back.

Pellinore's sword poked right through Escanor and all the way through his stomach. The very tip reached my shirt and pulled off one of my buttons. "Could you be a little more careful?"

The visor flipped up, revealing Dagonet's face inside the old helm. "Well, pardon me, your majesty."

The night before, we'd decided it would be useful to have someone in the keep, so Dagonet snuck inside and stole Pellinore's armor. No one heard anything on account of the snoring. If I was right, Pellinore wouldn't call for help, since it wouldn't do for a king to admit he'd lost his sword and armor. Dagonet's easy impression of Pellinore's voice completed the illusion.

"Well done, friend." I leaned against his armor to catch my breath. With a series of squeaks, he used one gauntleted hand to pat my back.

"All in a day's work, old chum. That's what friends are..." His eyes took in the sight of Escanor's fallen, bloody body. "What have I done!"

"What do you mean?"

He held up the sword and grimaced at the bloody tip. "Oooh!" He dropped it with a clang. "I've...I've *killed* him!"

"Well, yes, that's what generally happens when you put a sword in someone. He had it coming, Dagonet. I'm sorry, but you had to do it."

"He's *dead*!" Dagonet was quite good at acting, but never had the stomach for the real world.

"He was a mustache-twirling villain, just like in one of your plays. Get over it. Besides, no one *forced* you to kill him."

He pulled off one of his gauntlets. "By my own hand...this man..."

"Dag, you're not fooling anyone. You're just being dramatic, and I certainly don't have time for the entire routine."

He reached upward. "What have I done!"

"If you're going to run through your whole regret monologue, then I'm leaving."

After grasping at the sky, the next move was usually falling to his knees and screaming, but the rusty hinges on his greaves refused to budge, so he bent over at the waist and yelled at the ground.

Chapter Sixty-Eight

Leaving Dagonet only halfway through his grieving process, I ran for the vault.

I was thankful to find the door open, meaning Garth and Nimway had gotten there already.

Outside stood the statue of old king Pendragon, reaching for his belt as he rushed into battle. A hopeless battle, if the stories were true. I made eye contact with him and felt as if we understood one another.

"How about this?" came Garth's voice. "It looks like a sword!"

"That's an umbrella!" shouted Nimway.

The conversation was not promising.

"What's going on?" I said, stepping inside.

But as soon as I entered, I immediately realized the problem.

The vault was larger than we had imagined. Like an unending hallway to hell, it led down, down, down, along an unending wooden staircase into darkness, both sides flanked by shelves that were stuffed, end to end, top to bottom, with weapons, clothing, and shiny trinkets. All items Ulder had assumed *might* be magical. And there must have been a thousand swords.

"I didn't bring him this much," I said.

"He got things from everywhere," said Garth. "People brought him stuff all the time."

"Fine," I said, looking at Nimway. "Just find the sword."

"It's not that easy!" she screamed.

"Focus, Nimway. Isn't this what you do? Use your power."

"I can't! Don't you understand? I can't!" A tear formed in her eye. "It's been...tricky ever since we got to this city. I *feel* it, but I can't tell if we're near it. Everything feels the same!"

Nimway, I realized, had never been near the sword. It had always been far away, and she'd never had to use her power to find it when it was close by. Apparently, it was like finding a single blade of grass in a meadow. She knew it was nearby, but that was all.

"I don't know how far down this hallway goes," said Garth, desperately. "I've grabbed a few things, but nothing happened."

"How will we know if we find it?" I asked Nimway.

"It is supposed to...act different when he's around. As long as he's ready." She closed her eyes. "The elders told me the sword would...show itself to the king, but nothing's happening!"

"I'm the problem. As always." Garth looked down, ready to sink to the ground. "I'm not ready. That's the only explanation. The sword is in here, but it knows I'm just a stupid prince who doesn't deserve it."

"You don't know that." Actually, his thesis seemed very possible, but I wasn't ready to quit. "Listen, Garth, this is a puzzle, and I was *made* for puzzles. We're going to use our brains. Do you understand me? Any puzzle can be solved."

He nodded sternly.

"We'll organize every sword by its age. That should narrow it down. Nimway, get a torch from the hallway."

"I can't," she said.

"Why not?" I turned around and immediately understood.

Above us, at the top of the stairs, Ulder's silhouette darkened the vault doorway. "Someone stole my key," he rumbled.

Any puzzle can be solved, but the key ingredient is time, and we were completely out of that.

"Your mother's in a cell," bellowed Ulder, glaring at Garth. "So, you're about to step into the courtyard and tell everyone you're renouncing your claim, because if you don't, she's gonna be dragged out of that cell and marched to the gallows."

Garth balled up his fists, preparing for one more fight. I put my hands softly on his shoulders and whispered, "Do as he says."

My heart nearly broke when he turned to look at me with the face of a man who's been stabbed in the back. But it was time to quit. We were outplayed, beaten in every way, and the only remaining path was to tuck tail and run for the hills.

"It's over, Garth." I patted him on the back. "Just go with him and do as he says. We tried."

Garth hung his head as he walked up the stairs. Then he lunged.

"Don't!" I shouted, but it was too late.

Garth jumped at Ulder, but the king was too strong. Garth's fist landed in the middle of Ulder's massive breastplate. The king grabbed his wrist and turned it so hard I heard bones crack, and then he threw Garth to the ground.

Garth landed at the foot of the statue. Old king Pendragon even wobbled a little, and I held some hope that the statue would topple and land on Ulder, but it found its balance and returned to its previous stance.

Garth shot me another look of anger. Clearly, he had expected me to back him up, but I knew it would be useless. And since Ulder needed Garth alive in order to make his renunciation in public, I knew the boy was in no danger. Not yet, anyway.

"Tomelac deserves a better king than you," said Garth, rubbing his wrist. "Just because you're big doesn't mean you're right."

Ulder ignored him and looked down the stairwell, his hand on the vault door. "I hope you two like my collection. This door won't open once I bar it from the outside. I'll wait a good month before coming back, and by then you'll—"

He was interrupted by a blinding flash of light.

Even though the light was bursting from behind him, it was bright enough to stun Ulder.

I couldn't see much. There was a series of loud clanging noises while Ulder staggered in place. The sounds got worse, and I realized I was actually hearing metal being torn apart.

When the light dimmed, we saw Ulder stumble away from the vault entrance like a confused drunk. Behind him stood Garth.

And the boy was holding a sword that glowed like a candle.

Garth swung again. Ulder's armor cracked. Another blow and the breastplate fell in half, the top still dangling from its buckles. The next strike knocked Ulder to the ground.

Nimway and I slowly made our way out of the vault and stood at the entrance, stunned by the sight of Ulder lying on the ground, turning back and forth in pain. His armor hung in tatters, which I honestly didn't know armor could do.

"Garth," I whispered, pointing to the sword. "Where did you get that?"

Garth pointed at the statue. "He gave it to me."

I finally noticed.

The statue was different. Nothing lay in the stone scabbard. Instead of reaching for his sword, old king Pendragon's marble hand reached out, empty, and a subtle smile split his stone face.

In retrospect, our timing was incredible.

Garth must have walked past that statue a million times in his life without Pendragon so much as raising an eyebrow. But Garth had been different back then.

Sure, he'd been the castle brat when we left for Hanbury, but our journey had taken him to parts of the kingdom that most royalty never see. The prince had faced real magic and shown real bravery, and he knew exactly how tough life could be for people outside the castle walls. Garth barely resembled the boy I had known before.

So, as he lay on the ground and complained that kings should be fair, I suppose old King Pendragon noticed Garth had done a lot of growing up and decided it was finally time to pass along that sword.

My sense of wonder was shattered as Sir Kay and a handful of knights stomped into the hall. They stopped as soon as they entered, halted at the sight of the glowing sword.

"This isn't over!" Ulder got to his feet, keeping his distance from the sword. "I'll burn you *and your mother!*"

Normally, Ulder's words made everyone scared, but this time every eye was on Garth, specifically on the sword.

Ulder stood face to face with Sir Kay and pointed back at Garth. "Kill him!"

Slack jawed, Sir Kay stammered for a moment before quietly saying, "No."

Ulder furrowed his brow.

"He's...the king," said Sir Kay, like he didn't believe it.

Watching Kay's face, I finally understood the power of the old stories. I was a relative newcomer to Tomelac, but the families who made up the kingdom all knew about the king who once wielded a magic weapon from the Sídhe, a sign that he was chosen to govern with fairness and justice.

So even a chunkheaded sycophant like Kay immediately knew what it meant when a royal lad in Tomelac held a glowing sword handed to him by an old statue.

But Ulder wasn't ready to give up.

CHAPTER SIXTY-NINE

MOVING QUICKLY, Ulder scooped up Nimway before I could react and fled the hall while she screamed over his shoulder. He was out of sight before any of us could register what had happened.

"After him!" shouted Garth, pointing with the glowing sword.

Without questioning him, we ran after Ulder, following the path of stunned onlookers he'd left in his wake.

After leaving the keep, running through the courtyard, and following his trail around the city walls and up the hill toward the cliffs, I realized what he was up to.

"He's going to throw her into the sea!" I said to Garth. I noticed the prince was, for once, not having any trouble keeping up with me, and his wrist seemed fine.

"Why's he doing that?" he asked.

There wasn't time to explain. We reached the tall cliffs, where the sea crashed into the land far below, and saw Ulder holding Nimway like she was a squirming puppy.

"Surrender!" he bellowed.

Garth held up the sword. A sizeable crowd had gathered by now, and they gasped at the sight of the glowing blade.

"Put her down, d—" Garth shut his mouth just before calling him "Da." Habits are hard to break. He tried again. "Put her down, traitor."

This time, Ulder spoke quieter, so only a few of us could hear. "Give me the sword, or everyone will watch me throw her over the cliff."

It was a devil's bargain. Garth was about to lose all credibility with the people of Tomelac if he let Ulder toss Nimway into the sea. Ulder was so close to the edge, he could fall if he took one more step backward. I imagined running up and pushing him the rest of the way, but I couldn't figure a way to do it without pushing Nimway along with him.

Oddly enough, Nimway had stopped struggling. Her eyes rolled back in her head, and she muttered something under hear breath.

"That's long enough!" yelled Ulder. "If you were half the man you think you are, you'd have given up the sword by now. So much for the justice of the Pendragons!"

"Wait!" said Garth. He held out the sword in both hands.

Ulder smiled.

I gripped Garth's wrist and whispered, "Don't." I had an idea.

"He's going to kill her!"

"Garth, just...trust me. Don't give in to bullies. Not this time, anyway."

Resuming his more confident stance, Garth once again pointed his sword at Ulder. "This sword belongs to *me*. The Sídhe want *me* to have it, not you. Because you're not my father."

Loud whispers filled the air as the people of Tomelac began their rumors. Frankly, the notion that Ulder was not related to Garth was a very easy one to accept.

Ulder hefted Nimway in his arms. "Why should the Sídhe decide which family rules?"

"I...I'm not sure," said Garth. "I think they don't like you because you're mean."

With that, Ulder turned away from us and threw Nimway off the cliff. She disappeared over the edge without making a sound.

Behind me, I could sense the stillness of the crowd, their distrust in Garth already growing. Ulder had just sown a seed of discord that Garth might never live down throughout his reign. This was bad.

Garth glanced at me with a brief look of confusion while the crowd murmured.

"You see!" roared Ulder. "The Pendragons are *nothing*! He let a woman die just to keep a sword! I won't let the Sídhe decide...decide who..."

He stopped talking as a gigantic tentacle appeared over him. Ulder looked up, swore softly at the unexpected appendage, and turned around in time to see more tentacles reach over the cliff.

The next thing we saw was Nimway rising in the air, sitting cross-legged on something large and rubbery. Underneath her rose the head of the creature I had seen swimming in the pool at Avalon. At that time, I only saw its enormous eyeball, and I remember trying not to extrapolate the creature's size. It had risen far enough now that its enormous dark eyes were staring just over the cliff's edge.

The creature reached a tentacle around Ulder and easily lifted him into the air. At the same time, it politely laid out another tentacle in front of Nimway. She stepped onto it, and the beast delicately lowered her to the ground, near me.

"Thank you, Reginald." She patted the tentacle.

Hanging upside down, Ulder struggled with the creature, but he was no match for it. The creature continued its rise from the waters until we could see its mouth, which was shaped like a large beak with a strange, forked tongue flicking just inside.

Nimway turned to me and said, "Do you want to watch Reginald eat that man?"

Truthfully, I did.

The beast dangled Ulder over its sharp beak and glanced toward Nimway like it was asking for permission.

"Don't!" Garth shouted. "The Pendragons *are* merciful!"

Nimway frowned.

"Tell him to stop," insisted Garth. "Tell Reginald...to show mercy. To let Ulder live."

Garth's words must have been lucky, because despite the high winds, the crashing waves, and the general confusion, I believe everyone in Tomelac could hear him begging for Ulder's life. While we were certainly impressed with Garth's morals, we were also a little disappointed; none of us had ever watched a man get eaten by a sea monster.

Garth stood before the gathered crowd and held his sword high. The light was bright enough to even distract them from Nimway's creature.

"We're different in Tomelac," said Garth. "I've been traveling with my friend Erlin, and if there's one thing he taught me, it's that everyone deserves to be treated fairly. No matter what."

I felt a swell of pride.

"Even Ulder," said Garth. "And that's why we're going to bring him back to Tomelac for a fair trial."

There was a crunching sound. I looked at Nimway, who nervously bit her lip.

"Here in Tomelac," Garth continued, "Ulder's trial will be the first sign of our return to the days of justice..."

More crunching noises followed. I closed my eyes tight.

"Justice, mercy, and kindness will...will be the new...Erlin, what's that noise?"

Grimacing, I turned toward the creature just in time to see it shoving the last of Ulder in its beak. It chewed greedily, then, with an agitated expression, spit something out.

Garth jumped back as Ulder's mangled armor landed at his feet.

I later learned that, among the creatures of the sea, the word "mercy" simply does not translate.

CHAPTER SEVENTY

IT WAS A WEEK LATER when Garth sent for me so we could discuss my job.

We'd been meeting all week, mind you, Garth, myself, and anyone else in Tomelac who knew anything about anything. Garth needed all the help in the world getting things done, and he knew it. But he had long ago gotten comfortable asking for help, and after a few days the entire keep was hopping with orders from our new king.

But this time was different. I entered his chambers and noticed I was alone with him. Garth looked out of a window and didn't speak for a few minutes while I waited.

"Erlin...how long have you worked here?"

"Four years, your majesty."

"And, in that time, you've...kept us safe? From magic?"

I wasn't sure how to answer. "The kingdom seems to be in good shape."

He nodded solemnly, and then finally turned my way. "All those stories. Burning warlocks and eating bats. Remember the time you trapped that coven in their own cave?"

I rubbed my chin. "Maybe."

"It's just all so...violent, don't you think? I mean...magic *helped* us. And I'm not even sure why we were afraid of it in the first place. Sometimes I think Ulder just didn't want me to meet the Sídhe and find out I was king."

That made me smile. Given enough time, Garth could figure things out.

He let out a worried breath. "I have to give you an order, and I don't want you to be upset with me. I realize you only killed those people because my father wanted you to."

I held up a finger. "Your majesty, there's something you should—"

"And I know you would have found another way if it weren't for your orders."

"Well, maybe it's time I let you in on a little—"

"Would you stop? This is very hard for me!"

I made a show of shutting my mouth and gestured for him to go on.

Garth had gotten flustered. "Erlin, I don't want you to kill people anymore. It's not right! From now on, you have to do your job...nicely. Instead of killing people, just make sure no one's getting hurt. Can you do that? Stop killing people?"

I bowed deeply. "It would be my pleasure, your majesty."

Some will tell you I wiped a tear from my eye, but I maintain that the room had not been properly dusted.

A loud noise got our attention.

"It's here!" shouted Garth.

He ran out of his chambers, down the stairs, and into the meeting hall.

This was the big room where Ulder yelled at us. Similar to the grand hall, which was the big room where Ulder yelled at us in front of company. I couldn't help but notice that every table and chair had been removed. Only the royal throne remained, pushed into a corner.

"Here it comes!" said Garth.

Some men were wrestling...something through the door. It took me a moment to figure it out, but I soon realized they were rolling a gigantic circular table on its side. It was tall enough that in nearly reached the stone ceiling, and it had to be tilted precariously on its edge to roll through the double doors.

"Wendy gave it to me!" said Garth. "She once told me her father owned this huge wooden table, so on my first day as king, I sent her a letter and asked if Tomelac could have it. Isn't it great?"

The table was set in the center of the room, and a series of tall chairs were brought in and placed around it.

"What's it for?" I asked.

Garth slapped me on the back. "You." He walked to one side of the table and put his hands on it. "You'll sit here. And Ywain, here. Even Sir Kay."

"All of us?"

"Do you remember that time you, Ywain, and Morrigin all sat around that tree stump with me and helped me understand what was going on? Well, I thought to myself, what if that tree stump was big enough to hold *all* of my smart friends? Just like that tree stump, at my roundish table you can all speak freely and tell me things I don't know. I'll be the smartest king ever if I just listen to you and the others. And Da...Ulder used to say he sat at the head of the table because he was most important, but at a round table, *everyone's* important!"

I touched the edge of the table and pondered the possibilities. Garth would never be the smartest person in any room, and he would probably never develop any particular skill, but he was genuinely a good person, and I realized I had been waiting all of my life to find a king who was also a good man. I never thought it would be Ulder's boy, but life has a way of surprising you.

I was shaken from my thoughts by a screeching noise.

Behind me, Garth was loudly dragging the throne across the room. He shoved it against the table, where it towered over the other chairs.

Garth wiped his hands. "That's so people know who's in charge."

CHAPTER SEVENTY-ONE

YOU SHOULD HAVE SEEN HIM.

At the first meeting of the roundish table, every seat was filled with someone from Tomelac who knew something the others didn't. Ywain spread out his maps next to me and pointed to every location that was mentioned. Nimway sat on my other side and—when she wasn't under the table arguing with a beetle—explained magic to the rest of us. Sir Kay surprised everyone by being the most committed member of the knights of Tomelac. He apologized for our past squabbles and set himself to obeying King Garth's every command. I still found him to be a detestable bore, but no one could outmatch his devotion.

Even Pellinore was there, as an advisor. He didn't like one bit of Garth's decision making. I asked Garth later why he'd bothered to invite old Pelly since the two never agreed on anything, and he explained that the room would be empty if he only gathered advisors he agreed with.

"When I was traveling with Erlin, I noticed potatoes were more expensive here than in smaller towns," said Garth.

"Taxes," someone told him. "Last year we noticed our banners are falling apart, and someone has to pay for them."

"Why do we need banners?" asked Garth, full of childish innocence.

"Why? What!" Pellinore nearly jumped from his seat. "How will anyone know where they are without the banners of the kingdom flying majestically overhead?"

Garth pondered. "Well...if anyone is lost, I'll be glad to tell them what city they're in." He nodded with satisfaction. "So, no more banner taxes on potatoes?"

No one in the room could come up with an argument.

That first meeting ended as the sun was setting. I walked over to a window to watch it set, squinting into the distance. Maybe I hoped to see a dark-haired woman riding our way.

"Erlin, can you help me with something?" asked Garth.

"Of course, your majesty." I was tired, but a lot of work needed to be done if Tomelac was going to find itself again.

"It's about...Wendy."

"Oh? Is she coming to visit?"

"No." His face fell. "Her father wants to negotiate her marriage. I don't understand it."

"Lots of money is involved in a marriage like this, Garth. I'm sure Wendy wants to be here as much as you do. I remember how she used to look at you, and that was *before* she knew you were the king."

His face lit up, and I realized he hadn't thought of it that way before.

"Can you help me?" Garth was not a king at this moment. He was a boy begging for help. "I mean, I don't understand anything about negotiating. Or about getting married. Do you?"

"I can help you with the negotiations," I assured him.

"I'm worried she won't want to marry a king. Or maybe she doesn't...feel the same anymore. Do you understand any of those things?"

"Garth, the things I don't understand about women could fill a book."

CHAPTER SEVENTY-TWO

TWENTY DAYS PASSED before I saw her again.

The bells rang from a lookout tower to signify visitors. I ran from my new ground floor dwelling and dashed up the stairs.

I had told myself to stop doing that. It made no sense to rush out like a child every time a visitor was announced.

I reached the top of the wall and saw them riding across the countryside. Women on horseback, carrying the flag of the Moonriders. Morrigin rode at the front.

Later on, I found out what happened to her after we fled from Troyes. The earring, it turned out, had bounced its way down to the docks and into a fisherman's net just as he was pulling it from the water. A small thing, it landed unnoticed among the flopping fish.

But after a few minutes, in what would be dubbed "The Miracle of the Mackerels," a curly-haired man appeared in the nets, swearing he'd expected to find a costume rack.

The fisherman, concluding that such a miracle was sure to repeat itself, left his fish and nets untouched and began charging admission. The story spread, and in about an hour an eager crowd had gathered.

By then, Morrigin had led the people of Troyes on a merry chase, making sure never to let them see her face under the red hood. When the mob grew too close for comfort, she Traveled to the earring, believing I still held it, leaving the red robe behind when she disappeared.

Of course, she wound up in the same net, completely buried by fish. She dug her way up and out of the mackerels, digging a fish from her bodice, and emerged to the confusing sight of an applauding crowd.

After that, Morrigin had been forced to hike and hitchhike back to Kingsport, where she reunited with the Moonriders.

I stood in the courtyard as the portcullis raised and the Moonriders galloped through. She dismounted, handed the reins to an attendant, and stomped straight toward me. I couldn't read her impassive face.

"We had no choice!" I said as she approached. "Don't be mad! That man was going to kill Garth, so I had to throw your earring away!" She was only a few steps away now. "You know, it was really Nimway's idea—"

Our lips touched.

Her hands held me close, and we suddenly found that our bodies could not bear to be apart while our mouths spoke secrets to one another.

And, once again, I was not quite sure what to do with my hands.

HISTORICAL NOTE

As you know, this book is dedicated to my friend and mentor, Jeremy duQuesnay Adams, who left us in 2016 after a beautiful life of laughter and learning.

While attending grad school and working at a university for ten years, you could say I met a lot of smart people. And you might think it would be difficult to choose which of them was the smartest—but there was no contest. Everyone who met Jeremy knew he was a cut above the rest of us.

Professors from every department would drop by Jeremy's office to get his opinion. Can you translate this word the anthropology department has never seen? How long did it take to build a Viking ship? When were cats domesticated? The questions came from every corner of human experience, but Jeremy never flinched. He cheerfully answered each query in his basso profundo that rattled with joy, invoking several linguistic oddities and a few humorous asides along the way.

His brain was like nothing I'd ever encountered. He could recall nearly everything he'd ever read, which I didn't believe was possible before meeting him. At the mention of Sophocles, I once tried to impress him with an obscure line from Antigone; he grinned and recited the next line...in ancient Greek. I hung my head in defeat.

His mind shone especially bright in the arena of linguistics. There didn't seem to be a European language he hadn't mastered, which meant he often forgot which language he was supposed to be using. A sentence scrawled on the blackboard might be born in Latin, meander through Catalan, and then finish off in Old English. In these moments, my notetaking was reduced to a series of hopeless question marks.

Upon realizing he had—once again—written out the assignment in ancient Greek (his favorite), he would remind us that several campus buildings were adorned with Greek lettering, which meant we should be able to muddle through.

On a visit to Spain, I noticed his accent changing with each conversation. When I brought it up, he didn't seem to have noticed he'd been adding a lisp or elongating certain syllables—like an international spy—to match the dialect of every cab driver and tour guide we met.

To a simpleton like me, his brain was downright intimidating.

I'm the sort of student with a flair for research and writing but absolutely no ability to memorize facts. Jeremy was a kind soul, but he was truly baffled that the rest of us couldn't remember things like the coronation date for King John or the name of Livy's horse.

It was all written down in his brain, easily accessible—even after several glasses of wine.

Despite being so different, Jeremy and I got along perfectly, partly because we shared a strong desire to laugh. Nothing made him happier than a good joke, which set him apart from the stuffy scholars swarming the school who—as far as I could tell—had vowed to never employ a sense of humor. Sadly, that stereotype about academics is often very true.

But while Jeremy didn't take himself very seriously, he was serious about his work. At conferences, no one was better dressed. He stood with an air of confidence and authority when he spoke, and he never failed to hush the room. His renown was such that crowds followed wherever we walked, begging for a word or a moment of his time. It reminded me of stories from people who had traveled with the Beatles. (Close enough. He was the real-life inspiration for a character in their trippy submarine cartoon, after all.)

Despite my great respect for Jeremy, I did once laugh at him. And I'll never forgive myself.

It was during a lecture on King Arthur. He got my attention when he announced that, after doubting for many years, he'd come around to the idea that King Arthur had been a real person.

I scoffed.

Out loud.

And Jeremy glanced at me, raising one bushy, caterpillar eyebrow.

At the time, I was going through a phase. Grad school had shown me—through a series of embarrassing conversations—that some of my favorite history moments never actually happened. To get my act together, I tried to always be the most skeptical person in the classroom, believing this would keep me from being tricked by any more rumors or folk tales. A childish approach. I had yet to understand that certainty is the enemy of learning.

Besides, why was I so sure King Arthur was a myth? I'd never studied him for a moment in my life. Who was I to say?

After thinking over Jeremy's words, King Arthur's legacy started to remind me of the legend of Pythagoras. He's a household name and stars in dozens of stories (which are much older than Arthur's), but we don't have primary or even secondary records to prove he existed. Even worse, the stories about Pythagoras don't match and often came about centuries after he died.

But historians almost always believe Pythagoras was real. His fingerprint on history is just too strong to dismiss him outright. Something started that legend, even if that something was only one percent of the final myth.

So, what about Arthur?

Picture this. There was a time when England didn't have one king but instead had several at once, all competing for power. Like middle managers. And everyone expected these kings to be petty, annoying tyrants. (Like middle managers.)

Now you can imagine how exciting it would be if your local king turned out to be a good person for a change. It would shock the countryside if one of them didn't try to exploit you, and maybe even fought for you. That's the sort of leader you would tell stories about.

So, just like Jeremy, I eventually came around.

I don't know how the legends of Camelot started, but it's easy to believe that a benevolent king once sparked England's imagination by living out the important truth that still guides every story of King Arthur: might doesn't make right.

Whatever it was that kicked off the legend, we're still talking about it. And I think we always will be.

Adam D. Jones is writer from Paris, Texas. Most of his time is spent planning novels, studying history, and bravely wrestling his cat.

To find more of his books, visit *AuthorAdamJones.com*

Milton Keynes UK
Ingram Content Group UK Ltd.
UKHW040834141024
449705UK00006B/224